**In Lonnie's Shadow**

Chrissie Michaels is a tree-changer who has happily settled into a country lifestyle. Her favourite pastimes are growing enough vegies for family and friends to share, and going for long strolls on the nearby beaches. She spends the rest of her time as a freelance writer, as well as teaching part-time at the local secondary school.

Born in Lancashire, England, she arrived in Australia aged six and grew up in Melbourne's eastern suburbs. Her published work includes short stories, poetry, children's fiction and educational texts.

*In Lonnie's Shadow* is her first young adult novel.

*For*

*M,*

*R, E, S, D, M*

*JB and Ladybird*

# IN LONNIE'S SHADOW

Chrissie Michaels



FORD ST

First published by Ford Street Publishing, an imprint of
Hybrid Publishers, PO Box 52, Ormond VIC 3204

Melbourne Victoria Australia


2 4 6 8 10 9 7 5 3 1



First published 2010

National Library of Australia Cataloguing-in-Publication entry:
Author: Michaels, Chrissie
Title: In Lonnie's Shadow
ISBN: 9781876462918
Dewey Number: A823.3

Cover design: © Michael Hardman at Gittus Graphics Pty Ltd
In-house editor: Saralinda Turner

Printed in Australia by McPherson's Printing Group

Spur
'Squatters and other wealthy men sometimes raced fine horses recklessly through the streets of Melbourne, especially after the hotels closed. Perhaps this is a relic? 27/22/49'

Little Lon Collection
Museum Victoria
http://museumvictoria.com.au/littlelons/selobj.html

*C'est double plaisir de tromper le trompeur.*
It is double pleasure to trick the trickster.

Jean de la Fontaine
17th century

# PUBLIC EXHIBITION

Long after Lonnie, Daisy and Pearl departed this world, after the bitumen sealed in the mysteries of Casselden Place, after the pollies turned a sod or hammered a commemorative plaque onto the likes of Miss Selina's Home for the Wayward & Fallen, and shortly before the asphalt was ripped up to be replaced with a towering office block – someone came up with the idea of an archaeological dig.

Casselden Place was one of a cluster of lanes branching off a mean backstreet in the Melbourne grid. A block known as Little Lon that over the years became marked as a slum; the people living there thought of as one long dirty tapeworm, all packed together as murderers and thieves and lodged in its innards.

Until the time team came along. Using diggers, shovels and brushes, they tore up the tar, dug back to the cobbles and bluestone foundations, swept and scraped and sorted through the history. A retrieval of memories overlaid by time. And when they'd dug enough from the cesspits and spoil heaps, they placed some of those unearthed secrets, eight thousand or so of the squealing bits and pieces – the shoes and the buckles; oddments of flannel and wool; a shirt and a cap; buttons of wood, white glass, shell and bone; the pots and coins and bottles and ironwork – into the museum for public display.

Sometimes you have to strain your eyes, look under the scum on the surface, to see what really goes on …

# INVENTORY

*As requested from main location site – Casselden Place, for public exhibition.*

| | |
|---|---|
| Bottle for medicine or poison | Item No. 4261 |
| Shard of amber glass | Item No. 135 |
| Pickaxe handle | Item No. 4929 |
| Alabaster figurine | Item No. 47 |
| Shoulder protector | Item No. 5111 |
| Pearl button | Item No. 2856 |
| Leather strap | Item No. 130 |
| Horseshoe pin | Item No. 6248 |
| Oak stave | Item No. 4321 |
| Coins and a token | Item Nos. 647, 648, 649 & 650 |
| Three empty French wine bottles | Item Nos. 31, 32 & 33 |
| Oyster shell | Item No. 27 |
| Hoop handle from a trapdoor | Item No. 2018 |
| Work boot | Item No. 19 |
| Skull | Item No. 1834 |
| Broken hinge | Item No. 654 |
| Empty flagon | Item No. 641 |
| Perfume bottle | Item No. 4 |
| Jingle from a tambourine | Item No. 7332 |
| Cracked saucer | Item No. 1198 |

| | |
|---|---|
| Horse brass | Item No. 5439 |
| Padlock | Item No. 7765 |
| Epaulette | Item No. 1841 |
| Piece of bent wire | Item No. 1035 |
| Sewing bobbin | Item No. 1446 |
| Bottle | Item No. 23 |
| Fragment of washbowl | Item No. 6531 |
| Golden guinea | Item No. 772 |
| Hairpin | Item No. 6551 |
| Hard rubber pipe | Item No. 455 |
| Iron filigree | Item No. 3080 |
| Dark lantern | Item No. 903 |
| Brown paper | Item No. 4642 |
| Frazer's Sulphur Powders' box | Item No. 368 |
| Timber pole | Item No. 221 |
| Slate pencil | Item No. 3577 |
| Piece of string | Item No. 7543 |
| White glove | Item No. 906 |
| Woollen sock | Item No. 333 |
| Frozen Charlotte doll | Item No. 6150 |
| Doorknob | Item No. 718 |
| Tattered piece of paper | Item No. 3947 |
| Eiderdown | Item No. 445 |
| Velvet drape | Item No. 749 |
| Leather shoe | Item No. 5117 |
| Red band | Item No. 4 |
| Mug | Item No. 558 |
| Scrap of hessian sack | Item No. 5786 |
| Blade | Item No. 1338 |

| | |
|---|---|
| Riding whip | Item No. 956 |
| Hobble | Item No. 1616 |
| Flat iron | Item No. 21 |
| Velvet coverlet | Item No. 6772 |
| Heavy leather belt | Item No. 4273 |
| Jar lid | Item No. 955 |
| Billiard ball | Item No. 4169 |
| Small ingot of gold | Item No. 3524 |
| Wall hanging | Item No. 727 |
| Trophy | Item No. 3769 |
| Brass knuckle | Item No. 3965 |
| Iron grid | Item No. 732 |
| Racing silks | Item No. 5127 |
| Framed newsprint cutting | Item No. 1791 |

# BOTTLE FOR MEDICINE OR POISON

## Item No. 4261

*Brown glass bottle with stopper.*
*Contained medicinal compound.*
*Exact contents not known.*
*Found in cesspit.*

Pearl clapped a hand on one ear and rolled over on the iron bedstead. Cruel enough trying to grab some shut-eye with all these nitties chomping ferociously at her crevices and her having to scratch and flick them on their way, now she had to battle with the wails from the room below. Stabbing her ears out they were. Poor girl sounded like a banshee. Pearl buried her head into the muddle of greasy rags which served as a pillow, their stink of unwashed sleep so strong she could scarcely breathe, and gave a silent curse at being stuck here in this dirt-swallow mess of an attic.

But there was something spellbindingly ill-fated about that noise. It made her ears prickle, sent the shivers running into her back. She climbed out of bed with a grim inclination to see the goings-on for herself.

Slight as a kitten, Pearl padded down the stairwell and shrank into the dark space of the landing. A sour vapour drifted across, bringing a whiff of musk and carbolic acid. Better not let on she was spying, or else Annie Walker would wipe the floor with her.

A smudge of gaslight revealed the gloomy room beyond. The walls were mildewed from the damp and in need of a good scrub down. There was the same impassable gash of a window, planked up on the outside, as the one upstairs. No shimmering lace curtain blown by a sweet breeze here; only a bed as sorrowful as all the others where the girls were made to spend their working days and flea-bitten nights.

Pearl could see Biddy lying on her back, her hair spread damp and defiantly loose by her side. She had dirty skinny ankles. Her knees were bent and her stomach wobbled like sloppy blancmange. Slasher Jack, a man they all despised, pinned Biddy down roughly by the shoulders, while Annie Walker leaned against the end of the bed. Her blood-smeared hands were meddling with the creases between the girl's legs.

Biddy let out a violent wail.

With a swift wrench of her arm, Annie pulled up by the neck what looked like a pale, palm-sized doll.

Although Pearl's past four years had stamped a permanent print of this dirty life, she was shocked to the innards at the sight of these crooked leeches doing their unholy business on poor Biddy. This was the first time she had ever witnessed the horrid and joyless event with her own eyes. And though she knew she should be turning away, she stood gawping, her eyes refusing even to blink; the lids could have been stuck open with hat pins.

Annie flashed Slasher a pitiless glance as she thrust the silent, milky-white piece of flesh towards him. 'One less for the baby farmer.' That woman may have been no bigger than a small barrel but she was as acrid inside as pickling vinegar.

A fit of grief seized Biddy; sobs wrenching out like cramps from her belly. Perhaps at the unfairness of this baby's life – a misery in the making and its gruesome, forced end. Perhaps just for her own terrible existence.

Annie gave the girl a sound slap across the jaw. 'Stop whimpering before yer wake the dead. Yer not the first to spit out a lump of lard before its time.' As if struck by a sudden forlorn thought she put an apologetic hand on the girl. Her voice came out sharp and strange. 'Pull yerself together. It's all done with. Put it behind.'

Through vacant eyes, Biddy nodded dumbly.

Right there and then, Pearl made up her mind that (supposing she was up the duff, which she wasn't, but if and when the time came) there was no way she would be fed any strange concoction from a medicine bottle to help a poor girl out of a slip-up. No way that any babby of hers would be torn out early by the hands of those filthy maulers. She blessed herself in the name of good sweet Jesus (wouldn't her friend Daisy be relieved to think she was calling on the Almighty) and swore on her mother's grave (although she wasn't really sure if her ma was indeed dead) that she would never again do for another man in Annie Walker's name. Not ever. And to be doubly sure, she blessed herself again.

That same night, as Pearl plotted to leave one Little Lon madam to go under the protection of another, a wild and unnatural storm hit the streets. The spouting rains tumbled from the heavens and a deathly wind swept through the town's very centre. Water ran so fiercely it surprised like an avalanche. The overflow raced in torrents along the channels by the roadsides, churning up stones and muck. And reek it did, like diluted diarrhoea, of blood and pig gut from the slaughter yard, dung from the stables, malt and barley from the brewers. A rush of unwelcome sludge slid around every corner and filled every hollow, flooded over doorsteps and swamped the cellars. Barrows and billboards and anything else not fast tight went with it; the whole stinking mess racing to a finishing line at the river.

Three deaths were reported. Forked lightning

took careful aim at a horseman riding at full gallop, killing him instantly in a blue flash. A hansom cab overturned, the driver jumping to safety but the lone traveller inside killed. The last casualty of the night was the lifeless body of a part-formed infant, wrapped in calico and day-old *Argus* newsprint; the bundle sliding and slopping its way along the gutter of Spring Street before becoming lodged against the wheel of a dray outside the very gateway of Miss Selina's Home for the Wayward & Fallen.

Afterwards, Daisy told Pearl how the dead miniature babby looked perfectly all right except for a look of sheer horror on its dear seraph's face. That the Sally's Drum Major called it a precious little martyr, and how it drifted to Miss Selina's by divine intention; God flushing it in baptismal waters and delivering the little angel to a safe resting place away from evil, where it would bask in eternal light. Hallelujah!

But Pearl, who knew the bitter sin of the entire sorry episode, having witnessed with her own horrified eyes how Biddy's babe was torn out early, and knowing full well that the babby was never christened by holy water so would float forever in a state of damnation without ever seeing Heaven, stared down at the ground and kept the truth of the unhallowed birthing quiet as death.

# SHARD OF AMBER GLASS

## Item No. 135

*Shattered fragment of amber glass*
*with curved edge, probably from a fanlight.*
*Found on site of 6 Casselden Place.*
*Believed foreign to this location.*
*More commonly used in neighbouring,*
*more affluent suburbs, such as Carlton.*

Keeping low, the youth crept through the shadows of the nightcart lane. The afternoon was already curtaining into early darkness. He turned up his collar against the drizzling rain and came to a standstill. All in all he couldn't have chosen a better hour to do his business.

Only a dozen paces across a bluestone yard kept Lonnie McGuinness from the door he planned to force. He fought the temptation to tear across. *Hold on, mate,* he steadied himself, *don't be too foolhardy*. Once he made a move, there'd be no turning back.

From his vantage point the line of houses had a forlorn look, not too different from where he lived across the gardens. But their plain rear walls were a lie. Odds on they'd be much grander inside than he'd ever seen. Of course, he had only ever been in one big house. Mrs B's. All red velvet and golden drapery and set up solely for comings and goings, you might say. Not that he had ever frequented the Big House for its real purpose, only sneaked in with Pearl to have a squiz at the high jinks. He shook his head. All those fathers and sons, uncles and nephews, never reckoning on Mrs B penning each and every name into a ledger alongside a list of their antics. Lordy, if he'd been a bit of a dodger he could have bled a fortune to set aside for his old age. No doubt Mrs B already had this in mind. As if she'd never know an opportunity when it smacked her in the face.

With a last glance around, Lonnie pulled down his cap and hightailed it to the murky recess of the doorway. No backing out. Didn't have no choice. He made his way quick as a tack over the cobbles. A neighbouring dog barked at the tip-tap of his leather boots. Once across he wedged himself safely into the corner.

The barking grew to a volley of snarls. Lucky for him the dog was behind a high gate. He could hear the scratching of the animal's paws as it pushed against the palings. Its ears would be quivering, its muscles taut, ready to spring. Lonnie licked a line around his dry mouth and wished the mutt would shut it. He plastered his back hard against the stone wall like a gargoyle and waited.

When he felt safe enough, he pulled out a curved

iron bar from its hiding place in his jacket. A jemmy. The housebreaker's tool of trade. Skilfully, swiftly, he prised the back door latch. As the iron claw splintered the jamb, his thoughts moved to his da. He could almost feel him breathing down his neck from above, for the woodwork skills he had taught Lonnie were never meant to be used in this way. *Sorry Da*, he mouthed silently towards the heavens, *but I think you'll understand*.

The door sprang open. He slipped inside, feeling his way forward with one hand. His fingers seemed to disappear into the dark world. Ever so slowly he edged along a hallway. His steps felt heavier, more clumsy than usual for the weight of his small frame. Each footfall was a trespass. Lonnie was only a shrimp of a lad after all, but every noise, even the wooden floor itself, seemed to cry out a warning that an intruder was here.

Barely able to see, he entered the parlour towards the front of the house. Why hadn't he thought to bring a dark lantern? What a mug. He could just make out a fireplace. He touched the blackened chimney stone. Cold. There was a heavy staleness in the room and an odour of musty linen. A kind of certainty fell over him about what lay ahead.

Unexpectedly, a yellow circle of light flooded in through the open curtains. A sudden fear of being caught ripped through his body. He sprang back and jerked his head towards the source, fully expecting to see the owner returning to the house, or worse, a white-helmeted constable ready to march him off. Outside, a street lamp fizzed up in fury at the rain. Lonnie followed the tapping of the pole as the lamplighter made his way through the winter evening towards the next lamp. He should have known, for it was as common a sound as a blind man's cane. There was nothing untoward to worry him after all.

Lonnie stared out at the evening streetscape and cursed himself for being so jittery. A yellowish haze now embraced the double-storey terraces. With the rain and the shadowy reflections from the leadlight panels, their iron lacework dripped like chains of coloured gems – amber, green, red. Jewels. The thought of treasure nudged Lonnie back to why he was here. He forced himself to breathe more evenly. *Sharpen your wits, mate. All's well.*

The circle of light was both a blessing and a curse as he edged away from the window. At least up until now the house seemed to be unoccupied. Even so, he knew no good would come from prancing and bounding around like a larrikin on a street corner. The lamplighter might not be the only witness around, innocent or otherwise.

All about him strange shapes covered in pale dustsheets formed into outlines of ghostly grey. The room was filled with household goods; more furniture and belongings than would fit into the entire row of houses in Casselden Place. They were arranged higgledy-piggledy, as though someone had been moving house, stacked them all together, then been interrupted. He could only guess where the rest had come from. No mercy for even the poorest of the poor.

One by one he picked out the items. A high-backed chair. Bedstead. A table with drop down sides whose cloth reminded him of a shroud on an undertaker's slab. Lonnie flung away the cover. From underneath he picked out several forks, one silver-plated; a sharp, bone hatpin; a blue cup patterned with a boy fishing. He flicked through a wad of pawn tickets. Odds and sods, all pouring out their story at the same time.

Another dustsheet he pulled aside laid bare a timber and glass cabinet. Imprisoned behind the panelled glass was a stash of jewellery – lockets, studs, bracelets, necklets, rings, pins, gents' and ladies' watches. At the sight of all the simple wedding rings he thought his guts would turn over. Payne had no common decency. Wouldn't that be the last thing to demand, payment owing or not? How could anyone ever believe he was a gentleman? When Lonnie studied all the personal belongings stashed here – all the life treasures, all the heartbreak involved – he wished he could give everything back to everyone. If only he had the power to fix things.

He tore a strip from the dustsheet, wrapping it around and around his right hand like a boxer bandaging for a bout. Clenching his fist, he smashed through the brittle pane and cursed as the broken edges of the glass tore into his unprotected forearm. He drew slivers of glass from the gash, flinching as he did so. Quickly, he unwrapped the material, tied it around the wound to stem the flow of blood and reached back inside the cabinet. From the rear he took a horseshoe pin, flecked with gold from the diggings, which he slipped inside his jacket pocket. He nodded to himself. Satisfied. A job well done. Give or take a drop of blood. Time to move.

But a feeling deep in his belly prevented him from leaving. Later he tried to explain the feeling. How a sense of foreboding crept up on him there and then. Whispering in his head: *Not yet, mate, reach back inside.* How all he needed to do was open his eyes and snatch the pocket watch. He knew the inscription well enough before he'd even flipped open the spring lid. But it cut him sharp as a blade to see the watch physically in his hand, here in this house owned by Henry Payne. He snapped the cover shut, hurriedly shoved the watch into his pocket and stormed wild as a young bull out of the house, back the way he had come.

Auntie Tilly's horseshoe pin was one thing, but he had found more than he had bargained for. He swore out loud. How could he not have figured out what had become of the watch?

There is an indifference which comes with anger. It was here with him now, sitting like a spiteful imp on his shoulder. Lonnie stormed to the back lane, searching for bluestone and large chunks of it. Like the Push, he knew exactly how to put it to good use. He picked out a fist-sized chip and hurled it smack at a window, wounding the glass good and proper. So what if the sound of the smashing glass was heard by dogs, lamplighters or neighbours' ears? His makeshift bandage was sopping from the blood and the rain, his arm ached, but he'd be damned if he was going to be silent or try to curb his temper. Payne deserved a good beating and his house would do for a start.

It didn't take long before the mongrel dog was going berserk, barking for blood. *Run*! – a cautionary voice yelled in his head. Rage, however, had taken control. Armed with more bluestone, he shot back into the house and pounded the hallway fanlight, then the leadlight border of the front parlour window. A shower of amber, green and red fragments arced out onto the street, smashing to smithereens. Recklessly, he picked up a shard of glass, waving it around like a dagger, promising himself that if Payne should come along right now he would slash his throat and delight in it. Back in the yard. Breathless from his own fury. Taking aim at a narrow window. Flinging the bluestone. Watching it fly through the air and bang the glass hard. Served Payne right if he brought down the whole house.

Timber creaked and groaned as the frenzied dog pushed against the gate. The cautionary voice warned Lonnie once more. *Run*!

'Wait till I get hold of you.' The bellow from a neighbouring window finally shook Lonnie out of his dark, destructive mood.

He realised with a jolt what damage he had done. It hadn't been his intention. He had only come for the horseshoe pin. Still, it served Payne right.

'I'll break your neck, you snivelling larrikin,' the neighbour threatened again.

Why do they always do it, Lonnie thought, call out to you first about how they're going to get you? Didn't they ever reckon it would give you a head start? He was glad he was only sixteen and still thinking at times like a tacker. *Catch me if you can, you and your flea-bitten mongrel. But I reckon you're too slow.*

Tucking the jemmy under his good arm and with his bounty stashed in his pocket, Lonnie backtracked and tore off down the nightcart lane.

# PICKAXE HANDLE

## Item No. 4929

*Hickory shaft from a cutting tool*
*with a heavy double-pointed head.*
*Used to break rock or hard surfaces.*
*Imported from Europe.*

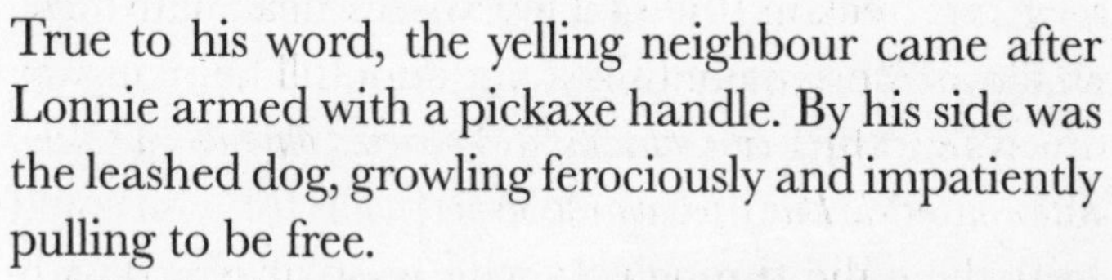

True to his word, the yelling neighbour came after Lonnie armed with a pickaxe handle. By his side was the leashed dog, growling ferociously and impatiently pulling to be free.

The warning had given Lonnie valuable time. He sprinted onto the wider street where the flaming gas lamps spread their light more evenly. A stolen look behind told him the man was powerfully built and well up for the chase.

Lonnie shot into the shadows. As long as he kept out of sight he knew he had a good chance of escape. No way was he going to be caught. If Payne found out what he'd done, leastways he'd be beaten up, left black-eyed and bruised.

Lonnie was intending to head straight back to Casselden Place, when a worry about his mam crossed his mind. If he turned up home in a sorry condition, there'd be a lot of explaining to do. His eyes darkened at the thought of the watch; some explaining from both sides. By now that slavering mongrel would have picked up his scent. A dog's sense of smell was many hundreds times more sensitive than that of a human's. This beast would arrive only seconds behind. No, it wasn't safe to go home.

He had to throw the mutt off his trail. What he needed fast was some water. Too bad the rain had eased. There was the river, but he'd never make it that far. Not that he fancied wading through those shallows. Too many things underfoot. The river was always spewing out muck, and worse, drowned souls, all bloated and stiff with holes as big as fists you could hear the wind through. Lonnie wasn't going to risk the winter river. Besides he couldn't swim too well.

But the grand exhibition building and the city gardens across the road were giving him the nod. It was a colossal building, a great hall that dominated the landscape, with its ornamental towers and pavilions and portal entries built to show off the wonders of the industrial world. As the moon broke out from behind the clouds, the roof's silver-slate dome seemed to fill the sky like a guiding beacon, offering the escape route he was looking for – the stone fountain in the courtyard filled with water. Say he paddled around the edge then made a quick retreat? Could give him a fair chance of distracting the dog. With this in mind, he turned sharply and made a beeline for the gardens.

The clatter of a bell made him spin around. For an instant Lonnie thought he was done for. Seated high on the hansom cab, it took all of the driver's strength and horsemanship to wrestle the shying horse away from the lad who had stumbled and fallen in their path.

'You nearly killed me, mister,' Lonnie bawled at the cabbie, as he hauled himself to his feet. His chest was heaving, his heart nearly jumping out.

The driver cussed at him. 'Yer dolt, leaping out like that. Watch yer step or yer'll end face up on a slab.'

The threat was more real than the cabbie knew. Lonnie's pursuer was gaining ground, his dog thirsty for blood.

Lonnie quick-footed off. As he shot around the corner of the great building, the fountain in his sights, he heard a wild shout from the cabbie. 'Keep yer mongrel away!'

The dog was following his scent all right, snarling and snapping too close to the horse, which shied and kicked out. Lonnie heard the crack of the driver's whip. Ordinarily the sound would make him cringe, but right now it was fine by him if the men squabbled. The few extra moments would put more precious ground between him and them.

He'd only been a tacker when the throng of

people pushed their way through the great hall to see all the new inventions – the hydraulic lift, the mechanical motor for cutting the grass, the typewriter and calculating machines. He could have done with the likes of that crowd here and now to hide amongst.

He reached the fountain to find the water shut off for the night, although there was still enough of a lake to wade through. A sudden flaw in his plan struck him. The dog would simply run around the fountain until it found his scent on the other side. He shuddered at the thought of what would happen if the mutt caught up, imagining the pain of those jaws locking around his leg, the gnawing and crunch of those teeth. That mutt would feast on him like a marrow bone from the butcher's.

The only certainty was that he needed a lot more water. He wished the heavens would open and create deep puddles for him to splash his way through. Of course! The roadside gutters of Spring Street were already swollen with winter rain. They should be running like a river. Now he was thinking.

He sprinted over the empty flowerbeds, spread for replanting with black soil and looking like a row of newly turned graves. An avenue of elms, laid bare by the season, led through the lawns. Still running hard, he began ripping the bloodstained bandage from his arm and threw it high into the nearest tree. Maybe the heavy scent of blood would fool the dog. A dog barking up the wrong tree! He managed a half smile at his own joke. Every second gained was a bonus.

One more road to cross and only a few strides left to cover before he reached the wide stormwater-filled drains. This time he was more alert to the passing traffic and easily dodged a drayman rumbling along with his barrels of grog.

True to form the gutters were flooded. The risk of typhoid was ever present; it was a dirty disease, as he and his mam knew sadly enough. He plunged knee-deep into the filth, splashing and slopping through the sickly mess with his mouth clamped shut, his only other choice being whacked bloody-eyed with a pickaxe handle or savaged by a mad dog.

A young girl stood by the wall of the Governor Burke Hotel, idly plucking at loose threads on her garishly patterned dress. As he ploughed through the water almost upon her, she looked up and chuckled. 'Hey Lonnie, what's the rush?' The sight of his bloodstained sleeve quickly wiped the laughter from her face. 'You're hurt.'

Lonnie pulled up short and tried to drag in breath. He was stinking like a dead horse. 'I'm in deep trouble, Pearl.'

'Up to your knees in it from where I'm standing.'

He glanced back towards the gardens and made out the silhouette of the dog clawing at the tree trunk. 'There's my trouble,' he puffed out. 'If they see me, I'm dead.'

'Too late, yer chump, they already have.' Pearl pointed down the street. 'Head for the Wesley. Leave them mugs to me.'

With the chase on again Lonnie blindly obeyed her directions. He swung around the corner, the spire of the Wesley Church in his sight. Avoiding his own home, he shot past the hotels, shop fronts and tenements that jostled each other for room on the crowded street. A high brick wall surrounded the back of the churchyard. He followed the unflinching line – no curves, no bends, no corners.

Catching sight of the mob of men by the rear gates immediately reminded him of what Pearl had obviously not forgotten. His spirits lifted. She was a cracker, quick thinking enough to remember that the ordinary, working class men of Little Lon were holding a meeting in the church hall. About now he bet she would be stepping out in front of that mad man, ignoring the snarls of the vicious mutt, as she tried to delay him with an offer. Anyone could easily be misled by her milky, china doll face to think that Pearl was washed out and too delicate; when like the rest of them in Little Lon she had the guile to take care of more than herself.

Lonnie nearly collided with a freshly-painted banner, on which the words *Work not Charity* were daubed in red. The men gathered here were in the thick of the struggle for a living wage. Come the next day, they were planning to march to the steps of

Parliament House and make their demands in a loud but peaceable protest.

'Quick, hide me,' he gasped, gulping in the life-sustaining oxygen. One hand clutched the jemmy as though it were a weapon. His other pressed the place in his side that hurt so much, his fingers searching for the knife he felt must be embedded between his ribs – so much pain it couldn't be only a stitch.

On recognising Lonnie, several of the tough faces softened, not immune to the humorous side of the young lad seemingly running for dear life, almost too out of breath to speak. Their mood twisted bitter when they spotted who was after him.

The mob closed ranks. A murmur passed along like a Chinese whisper. 'Payne's man.' Lonnie was shuffled through the gates and hidden like a wild card in a deck. Many of the men were Payne's tenants, their own belongings stashed inside the Carlton house as payment for arrears. They stood shoulder to shoulder, a column of centurions holding out their placards like shields, forcing the man and dog to a sudden halt.

Payne's man glared at them. 'Tell that ruffian you're hiding away – and I reckon from his flamin' crop it's that lad McGuinness from Casselden Place – if I ever can prove what he's done tonight he'll be locked up quicker than he can say his worthless name.'

'You're mistaken, my good man,' came a voice,

''tis not young Lonnie you chased. He's here amongst us and has been for over an hour.'

A second voice chipped in, 'Did you ever see the face of the poor soul you turned that beast on?'

The man's eye twitched uneasily. 'No, I didn't. He hid in the shadows away from the light, the way all common thieves do.'

'We know well enough who the thief is around here and it's not McGuinness.' The speaker turned to the crowd. 'Did ya know this dimwit of Payne's been chasing Lonnie's shadow halfway across town?'

There was a loud roar of laughter. The man's face pinched over. Baring its teeth, the dog let out a slow growl. But the mob wasn't finished. 'We've had all the threats we're going to take from the likes of you. Get lost while you're still in one piece. Before we lose our tempers, and you and your mongrel dog find yourselves cooling off in the Yarra.'

Lonnie had disappeared behind the mob and dropped to his knees while he listened to the goings-on. Thankfully because of this army of friends, not even the dog would be able to locate his scent mixed in with theirs. He double-checked the contents of his jacket pocket, relieved his treasures had not fallen out during the chase. His thumb traced over the horseshoe pin, but it was the gent's watch that troubled him the most. Wondering what he should do next, he flipped it over and over with uncertainty.

# ALABASTER FIGURINE

## Item No. 47

*Victorian replica.*
*Grecian style alabaster figurine (white lady).*
*Located at a site known to have*
*operated as a backstreet brothel*
*in the late nineteenth century.*

Madam Buckingham, who fancied herself as the queen bee of Little Lon and had crammed her overblown figure into an amber- and black-striped dress for such an occasion, was not taking too kindly to anyone trying to muscle in on her territory. It was as if all her body parts were wriggling and buzzing on the verge of temper, the seams of her dress pulling like lurid lightning strikes across her cleavage with each heaving threat.

'Pearl's with me, where she wants to be. So stay off my patch.'

She squared herself up for another slanderous scrap with the punch-fisted woman who was glaring dirty daggers at her.

Lonnie shook his head at the antics of Mrs B as she took on Annie Walker. Lordy, he was in no mood for any more confrontations. After leaving the Wesley, still checking guardedly over his shoulder, he had dashed past the furniture mart in the direction of Casselden Place where a burst of oriental firecrackers had nearly made him drop dead. The stink of the slaughter yard hadn't exactly steadied his nerves either. Now, two doors away from home, when he thought he was safe, who'd he come across but this pair screeching blue murder at one another. Guessing he could be stuck for a while, he slipped into the doorway of number four.

The two harridans remained oblivious to the fact Lonnie had approached them through the darkness.

'Says who? You don't make the rules.'

'I'm the law around here, you old scrag. There's friends of mine in both parties.' Madam Buckingham gestured towards Parliament House, whose roofline loomed over the rows of topsy-turvy terraces like a Grecian colossus. 'I've spent years building up my reputation. You and your filthy girls ain't going to drag it down.'

'Drag it down?' Annie blustered. 'Drag it down? You weren't the only one to entertain the Duke.'

'Long time's passed since you were able to shilly-shally around town with anyone on your arm. Who'd pay you, I wonder?' Mrs B tapped her chin and threw a peevish look down at Annie's squat figure. 'The slaughtermen? The muckrakers? Nah! Too good for the likes of you.'

Annie Walker returned with a mouthful of her own. 'I well remember the time yer sold yer wares for a copper a go. If yer think my girls are so scabby, why're yer trying to steal 'em? I want Pearl back, yer filcher. She owes me. Otherwise I'll set Jack on the lot of yer.'

Slasher Jack. That was a low-life of a name. He was a mover in the night, a mauler, who thought nothing of throttling a girl until she was senseless. He had been known to slice a gash from ear to ear with one cut of his blade.

Not that Mrs B was afraid of anyone. She drew a hatpin from her bonnet, causing strands of mouse-coloured hair to fly out in all directions, and prodded with it at Annie's chest. 'You just watch who you're threatening or I'll pinprick those balloons of yours till they pop and then pick out your eyes! See if I don't.'

The door behind Lonnie slipped open. Someone tugged on his injured arm and he flinched. A hushed voice breathed from behind. 'Don't rat on me to Annie.'

Pearl, the reason for the argument between the two madams, drew him hastily into the front room of number four. Lonnie breathed in the smell of shellfish and his stomach growled, a grim reminder he hadn't eaten all day. He looked hopefully through to the scullery, but a clutter of empty oyster shells told him there was little hope of a feed here. Looked like he'd have to hold on a while longer for a bite. Pearl most frequently ate from the oyster bar around the corner or brought home hot currant cakes from the bakehouse. Not like two doors down, where his mam would keep her big iron pot filled with a beef broth that warmed him through to the very bones.

'That's twice in one day you've rescued me, you cracker,' he said. 'Don't know which is the worst to take on, the maniac with the dog or those two outside.'

'Couldn't stop the wild beast. Used all my charms as well.'

Lonnie raised an eyebrow. 'The man or the mutt?'

'Well, glad to see you haven't lost your sense of humour,' Pearl said. 'Ain't you going to tell me what you been up to then?'

Lonnie stood by the mantle. The hearth was cold. He contemplated the lack of comfort in the tiny front room. There was nothing truly cherished here. Everything spoke of trade rather than enjoyment. A figurine, the statue of a woman in flowing robes, was chipped. The wine glass next to it stood half-emptied and scummy. The velvet *chaise longue* dragged from Mrs B's Big House was worn pink in patches, no longer fine enough for the pollies and the toffs who went there for their bit of skylarking. Lonnie answered with a sense of deep shame on Pearl's behalf, 'You know me. Trouble seems to follow.'

'Let me at least clean you up.' She reached over. 'Can't let your mam see you looking like something the dog dragged in, or smelling like one, either.'

He drew away his arm. 'Stop fussing. I'll just hang around until those turkeys quieten down. Sounds like Mrs B's about to kill her.'

'Stop arguing, yer soft chump.' Pearl fetched her washbowl. 'Sit down now and let me see those wounds.' She led him to the tattered French lovers' chair, inched off his jacket and tended to the cuts on his arm. 'Anyways, you may have quite a wait. They'll scratch and tear at each other, but it'll stop short of murder. Annie's no real match for Madam. Although I'll sleep better when this business is over and done with.'

Lonnie could see she was putting on a brave face. 'She has to tire of coming after you, sooner or later,' he said, knowing full well about the threats Annie Walker had been making of late. Pearl's safety depended upon her working off an unreasonable debt of twenty-two pounds, two shillings. An amount Annie Walker decided had been lost to her business when Pearl crossed over to Mrs B, and which she was now claiming, in order to force Pearl back into her employ.

'Annie may be no match for Madam, but you don't know what she's like with us girls.'

The shouts of the two women silenced Pearl. She

hoped Madam was indeed the stronger of the two, for her choice to come under Big House protection had been a deliberate way of ensuring her own survival. She wouldn't go back. Never. Not after what she had seen Annie do on the night of the wild storm. Pearl couldn't even utter the words out loud; Biddy's precious babby wrapped in newspaper and tossed out like a clot of muck; left to wash along the street in the stormwater. There were things you dared not reveal. Vile and heartless things. And all she'd done was stand there gawping. She should have done more. Maybe if she had, Biddy would have carried the little mite a full term. Although the truth of it was, and didn't she know it, things would have all ended up the same way.

Lonnie interrupted her thoughts. 'You should've walked out on Annie a long time ago.'

'Don't you think I've told myself that already? The only way to get her off me back once and for all is to pay up. By the time Madam creams off her percentage, there's not much left over.'

'If I had some spare coppers I'd willingly hand them over. As it is I'm giving Carlo a hand for the extra. It's been tight since Da.' He stopped, knowing they sounded like feeble excuses.

A dark frown creased Pearl's forehead. 'I don't expect nobody to fix things. Needless to say I'm on me own with this one.'

The fiery argument between the two women was

still going strong. Annie's voice rose harsh and shrill. 'I'll stay out of yer rotten streets for now. But I want me girl back, or I'll have her fixed good and proper.'

'And I'm telling you, Annie Walker, you're not the only one with brawn behind you. My Burke'll take anyone on blindfolded, with one hand bound behind his back. It'll be over my dead body before I ever answer to the likes of you.' Suddenly her tone changed. 'But think for a minute, woman. What good will it do either of us if we let Burke and Jack kill each other?'

'I'm wise to them two madams,' whispered Pearl, as she listened in. 'Annie will never see reason, while Madam Buckingham is apt to think things through. But I'm banking on Annie not being game enough to let Slasher nab me because she won't go an all out war with Madam Buckingham. Still, no one with a sound mind messes with Slasher. He scares me to death. Not as if I can hide from him anyways.'

'If he tries anything. If he comes anywhere near ...' Lonnie broke off, feeling an immense surge of pity for his friend. He couldn't deny Annie's man was a menacing brute whose main business was to keep the working girls in line, but he hoped Pearl had guessed right. He hurried to reassure her. 'Don't forget you're Mrs B's latest girl. She won't let anything happen to you.'

'Where've you been? Don't tell me you missed Miss-Ruby-Come-Lately parading up and down town with a white feather stuck in her bonnet. I'll just have to watch my own back. Anyways, I've done it for long enough.'

True. Pearl had only been a very young girl when sent to work on the streets with her own white feather for sale to the highest bidder. Maiden virtue came at a good price; it enabled her mother and father to take off without so much as a see you later. For the first year she had half expected her parents to come back and claim her, waited for something to happen that would explain her abandonment, but in the end she thought less and less about them.

As she drew out the last splinter of glass, she shook her head at him. 'Looks like you took on the whole Glass and Bottle Gang.'

She was speaking about one of the most notorious mobs of larrikins, who roamed the neighbourhood armed with broken bottles. Their leader, Billy Bottle, as he liked to be known – although his real name was Francis Todd – had always been a mean, foul-mouthed lad who trained in the art of nastiness from the moment he could spit out a curse. Billy's principal amusement as a child had been to rip the wings off blowflies and toss stones at birds. Not much had changed. Fully grown, he'd become an unsettling hood, with eyes and hands that were everywhere and a brain like a brick wall.

Lonnie had never liked him and didn't Billy Bottle know it. So these days Lonnie tried to steer clear, more at ease in the company of the other main mob, the Push, led by George Swiggins. In reality he did not want to mix with either gang. His slight preference for the Push was only a matter of survival. He was neither a Bottle nor a Push. Lonnie liked to tickle the nose hairs by saying he was a Bush or a Pottle.

When he remarked as such, Pearl chuckled. 'So Mr Bush or Mr Pottle, which one of you wants flirting with?' She didn't wait for an answer. 'Well, I daresay you'll live. If you don't poison yerself first.' She passed him his jacket. 'This smells like a horse's backside. Still rolling in the muck at Golden Acres, I'll bet. I don't know how you can stand all the stink around there.'

He gave it a quick sniff. 'Too true,' he agreed, pleased her mood had brightened. 'I'm doing a bit of track work on the sly as well.'

'So, have you caught up with Daisy lately?'

'Not since last week.'

'She's been having those nightmares again.'

The shouting between the two madams ceased. Heavy footsteps stomped off in opposite directions.

Pearl shrugged. 'All clear. And just in time I reckon. We're expecting a party of la-di-dahs at the Big House. Better you leave this way.' She ushered him towards the back door. 'A drop of French wine, a bit of hoity-toitying, lots of tweaking and pulling of beards, even if some of them lads have barely a whisker.' She pinched her fingers together, playfully prodding Lonnie's chin, moving along his shoulder and chest, down to his waist. There her fingers paused. 'Shame poor Ruby, the little chump, can't have a turn all by herself. Let's hope Madam gets a good price for her white feather, then she may go a little easier on me.'

A great desire to sleep came washing over Lonnie. He handed over the two heirlooms from the Carlton house. 'Will you hang on to these, please?'

Pearl scrutinised the horseshoe pin, then flicked open the watch and read the inscription. She stared understandingly at Lonnie. 'So that's what you've been up to. I should have known.'

'Only for a few days,' he pressed.

Pearl answered by slipping them down her front. 'This'll keep'em safe.' She pulled his hand so it brushed against her bodice and winked mischievously. 'No better hiding spot.'

'Easy does it.' Lonnie turned scarlet. For all that Pearl was younger by a few months, she was much too knowing for the likes of him.

'You get along home,' she said, with a swift turnaround, acting more like his mam. 'Tuck yourself into bed and get a good night's sleep.'

As he left he heard her sigh. 'Huh, all right for some.'

# SHOULDER PROTECTOR

## Item No. 5111

*Padding made from hide. Used to protect a nightcart man's shoulder from the weight of the soil can.*

Lonnie, who blotched up crimson at the drop of a hat, was still flushed as he left Pearl's. She was a fast girl, there was no doubting it, and much too flirty. Pearl had been right about one thing, his mam would have a fit if she saw him in this state, but with a smidgeon of luck she would be fast asleep.

As he opened his own backyard gate only two doors down, he heard the snarl of a dog. This was his only warning. A hand grabbed the back of his coat and pulled it roughly over his head. The sickening thud across his skull sent him crashing to the ground.

*And left his body lying …*

Lonnie came around panting for air, but only managed to gulp in a foul stench. He found himself lying face down by the old cesspit. The winter rains had caused it to ooze out its history, straight up his nose and into his open mouth.

His mam spoke of the smell as a curse. When Lonnie was younger he imagined it steaming like a spectre from the cesspit, a decaying corpse floating in the air. This ghost place still gave him the shivers.

A dark shadow loomed from above. It reached out and wrenched him to his feet. Instantly, Lonnie was a ten-year-old, circling around the edges of the old cesspit with Daisy and Pearl. He could almost hear their chanting whispers, *Around the rick, around the rick,* and the old bottles clinking together as they beat time. *And there I found my Uncle Dick. I screwed his neck. I sucked his blood …*

They never succeeded in conjuring up the broken bodies they believed had been tossed into the cesspit. But that same feeling, those sneaking, creeping insects crawling along his spine up towards his neck were suddenly back with him all these years later.

It took him a few moments to realise this was not one of the dead creatures rising with the foul air from his childhood memories, but the nightcart man on his nightly run up and down the lane, clanking full cans of night soil from yard to wagon.

The broad accented voice was full of concern. 'What's ailing thee?'

Lonnie's jacket pockets had been turned inside out. The only money he had, tuppence, was gone from them. He said shakily, 'I've been bashed and robbed.'

The nightcart man shook his head. 'Who'd rob

thee? Everyone around here knows tha's got nowt.' He gave Lonnie a sly grin. 'Tha's not been messing with someone's girl?'

Lonnie rubbed the back of his head. 'No. And I don't reckon this bump was from anyone around here.'

He now knew what it felt like to be belted with a pickaxe handle. Still, a battering and bruising from one of Payne's men was luckier than a mongrel dog being set on him. He was still alive. Relieved too, that he'd left the horseshoe pin and watch in safekeeping. They were out of harm's way and that's what mattered most of all.

# PEARL BUTTON

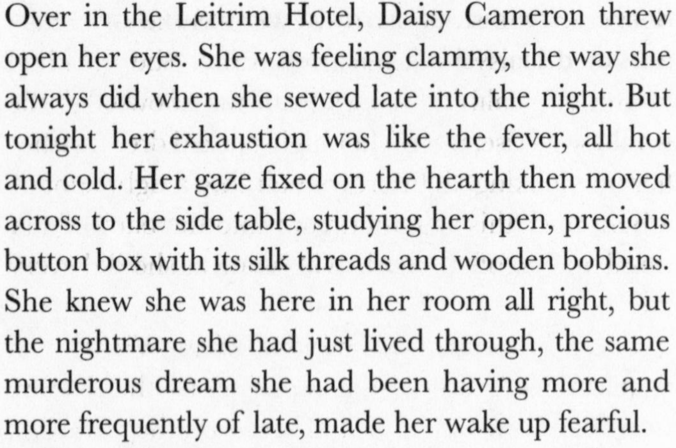

## Item No. 2856

*Decorative pearl bead*
*used for buttoning gloves.*
*One of six matching found.*

Over in the Leitrim Hotel, Daisy Cameron threw open her eyes. She was feeling clammy, the way she always did when she sewed late into the night. But tonight her exhaustion was like the fever, all hot and cold. Her gaze fixed on the hearth then moved across to the side table, studying her open, precious button box with its silk threads and wooden bobbins. She knew she was here in her room all right, but the nightmare she had just lived through, the same murderous dream she had been having more and more frequently of late, made her wake up fearful.

The nightmare always went the same. First a sharp, hot pain. Then the swishing sound of a hard strap. A feeling like she was leaping out of her skin. Hands tossing her into the air. Reeling off in the direction of the sky. In front of her very eyes the skull-faced clouds rearranging into a high, stone staircase. And there she was in her own skin again, sliding across the floor, falling, tumbling downwards, down those bone-crunching steps. A crumpled body lying motionless. Not her body, but a man's, his head smashed against the bull-nosed bottom step, glassy-eyed, staring into nothingness, blood dribbling from the corner of his mouth. Then the scene vanished and all Daisy was left with was a sensation of being carried away, shaking all over and a mind numb with dread.

The noises outside – the creak-creak of the nightman's cart and the clapping of the horse's hooves on the stone roadway behind the Leitrim – informed Daisy it was nearly sunrise. She breathed in and out, calming herself with the knowledge she would soon rise, put on her high-necked dress, gather her fine-looking, light brown hair into a tight knot of a bun, push this spiteful dream into the back of her mind and go off to work. The same as she did every day.

She was determined not to falter. Virtue and respectability came from working at the factory twelve hours a weekday and seven on the Saturday. The hours were tiring but they were honest, a characteristic on which Daisy prided herself and which gave her the will to carry on. If the Lord meant her to sit in an airless room, along with fifty other girls, and sew shirts with six studs and day dresses with twelve buttons down the bodice – not to mention the private trade in attire for the Big House she did of a night – well, she had no choice but to do her duty. Nightmare or not.

With a sigh she yanked the cover over her shoulders up to her neck, awaiting the knock of the window tapper who would soon sound his wake-up call and herald in the comforting light of the day.

# LEATHER STRAP

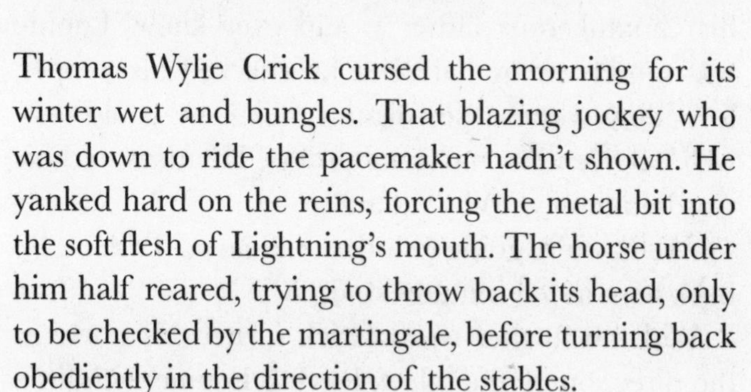

## Item No. 130

*Fragment of a bridle strap used for securing the bit.*

Thomas Wylie Crick cursed the morning for its winter wet and bungles. That blazing jockey who was down to ride the pacemaker hadn't shown. He yanked hard on the reins, forcing the metal bit into the soft flesh of Lightning's mouth. The horse under him half reared, trying to throw back its head, only to be checked by the martingale, before turning back obediently in the direction of the stables.

'McGuinness, what're you doing?'

The short-tempered question startled Lonnie, whose mind was with the two-year-old horse he was about to mount and exercise. Even though a few days had passed, he still sported a lump on the back of his skull the size of a marble, his cuts were still sore and he was in no mood to be polite, even to the boss's son. 'I'm doing what yourself asked me to do only yesterday, walking and exercising the horse.'

Lonnie's gruff swipe went by seemingly ignored.

After all, Thomas Crick was not one to pay much heed to a stable hand, even one following his own orders. 'Have you ever galloped a horse at full speed, boy?'

At the word 'boy' Lonnie clamped his own whippet tongue tight, forcing himself to stop saying what he would really like to, which was, 'Of course, I have, you thick-brained mushroom.' Because he had, many of them – Crick's precious horses, here in the dark at breakneck speed. Not that Crick or his cantankerous father would ever know. Lonnie was too clever by half. But he checked his temper, for riding without permission meant he could very well be given his marching orders. He measured his words carefully. 'Why's that?'

'Well, you're going to today. Saddle up Trident. Be back here in ten minutes sharp.'

With no further word Crick turned his horse in the direction of the office, leaving Lonnie with little choice but to lead the bay over to the stables, where he unsaddled. He stroked the horse affectionately. 'I'll see you a bit later.'

The nervous chestnut stallion he brought over as pacemaker was sixteen hands high and a beauty. All around said that if only Trident could race as well as he looked he would be unbeatable, but the horse was already marked as a bit of a loafer, shy and stubborn. Lonnie spent several minutes whispering encouragement and stroking his mane. 'Go easy, you beaut, remember I always ride you well. There's no need to fear me, no need at all.'

Meanwhile Crick had hitched up Lightning outside the Golden Acres office. He threw open the door and bawled across to the head foreman who was warming himself by the potbelly stove, which, stoked with red gum, spat and spluttered its heat through the building. 'That bloody jockey of yours hasn't turned up again. I'm getting McGuinness to ride this morning.'

'That's a bit impulsive, Mr Thomas,' the foreman replied.

Crick brushed off the hint of rebuke. 'Every stableboy wants to do track work, try his hand at being a jockey. McGuinness is no different.'

'What if he falls? He's only ever exercised horses, never ridden one at full pace. Don't you go forgetting that death we had. You'll put out your father's temper if anything goes amiss again.'

'If anything happens I'll just replace him. My father wouldn't recognise one ginger-haired nut from another.'

The foreman, who'd been employed there before Thomas had even been born, and was known to be a hard man himself, looked shocked at the callous indifference of the comment.

'You know what I mean,' Crick said dismissively.

'And as for the horse, no harm will come to it either. Even if it did we both know it wouldn't be such a great loss. It's not as if Trident is set for future glory. And I don't expect my father to hear anything about this. Understand?' At eighteen, Thomas wasn't quite man enough to face his father. And he certainly wasn't going to risk being disinherited. He grabbed a brace of whips from the rack and strode out.

Lonnie mounted Trident and arrived at the practice track only seconds before Crick came riding hard towards him. He thrust a whip at Lonnie who looked back at him with a slap-down question written all over his face.

Crick eyed him like he was a moron. 'Take the whip. You do know what it's for?'

'We don't need 'em in work out.'

'Says who? I don't want any slacking. I want Lightning to see you on his tail. He won't race properly unless he's pressured. Use the whip. Follow my lead. Do as I do. Canter most of the way around the track. On my signal, gallop hard for the last quarter. Try to keep up. Don't fall off! And whip the horse hard if you have to, do you hear?'

As Crick rode off ahead, Lonnie muttered under his breath, 'I hear you well and good, you oafish mullock.'

# HORSESHOE PIN

## Item No. 6248

*Gold pin fashioned in the shape of a horseshoe.*
*Elaborately decorated with jewels*
*set in flecks of gold from the diggings.*

After the track work, still fuming over Crick's constant talking down, Lonnie dropped by number four, set on picking up the watch and pin he had left with Pearl for safekeeping.

As she handed them over, he told her all his woes; how he had been hit on the back of the head and then been saved by a ghost from Uncle Dick's cesspit, who turned out to be the nightcart man. But she was far less sympathetic about his bumps and bruises than he'd hoped for, brushing off his injuries. 'Yer soft chump, you'll live.'

She seemed much more interested in his grumbles about Thomas Crick. 'Funny you should mention the right honourable. Wait till you hear what I found out.' The tittle-tattle started pouring out of her mouth by the barrow load. 'While I was at the Big House the other night, I came across him. And wasn't he all hot and bothered about an upcoming horse race through the streets of Melbourne, blathering on no end about some gents who are wagering a lot of money on the outcome. He let slip that Lightning is running, but he ain't going to win.'

'Everyone knows Lightning's never been beaten,' Lonnie said, as he took in what Pearl was telling him. An illegal race through the streets held after the hotels closed was not so unusual. They'd even been known to race pigs once or twice. But Lightning set to lose meant someone was up to mischief. A race fix. So who was going to win? He quizzed Pearl further. 'Know any more?'

She shrugged. 'Only that it's late one Saturday night. Starts at the Exhibition Building, past Parliament, down Bourke Street and up Swanston, turning and ending back at the fountain. That's all I know. You should be able to find out more, considering you work for the Cricks. It would be good if you discover who's going to win, then I could have a bet myself.'

Lonnie knew Pearl needed a break. Finding some money quick smart would see her free of her debt. And she had given him something to think about, what with Lightning being involved, although he hadn't heard a breath about this at Golden Acres. 'I'll keep an ear open.' He brushed off any more conversation, agreeing to meet Pearl later that evening on the promise of hot, battered oysters.

For the time being he had some unfinished business. First up the horseshoe pin, which thanks to his good sense was back safe and sound in his pocket.

Auntie Tilly lived within cooee in a nearby laneway called Cumberland Place. Her house had wooden shutters the colour of dark chocolate on each side of the front window, and would have been a canopy of gloom without the glass shone daily to a mirror and a central window box spilling out peppermint daisies and the promise of lilac remembrance.

Her welcoming door always stood open. Like all the unruly doors of Little Lon, over the years its scarred timber had twisted so the door never properly closed. It took a kind-hearted woman like Tilly Palmer to turn this weakness into a neighbourly welcome.

Fresh cooking smells of hot jam and buttered dough greeted Lonnie as he came in. He was one of many in the neighbourhood who had spent their childhood wandering in and out of Tilly's home. No matter what time of day, there was always a bite to eat laid out on the snowy tablecloth. Piping hot plates of currant pastries. Freshly baked oatmeal rounds made with a teaspoon of honey and a dollop of laughter. It gave Tilly great joy to feed the children of Little Lon. Not that she didn't expect good manners. 'What do you say?' she would ask if Lonnie forgot his, stretching out her hand and clipping him across the earhole with a sting that made him hear bells ring.

He took the few short paces into the simple kitchen of gully trap, table and netted cupboard strung up high to deter the rats. With her back to him, Tilly was not aware of his arrival, or so she made out. Trying not to let on, he crept up and tied her apron strings to the leg of the table. Sometimes unknowingly she had walked off dragging a piece of furniture behind her. It usually put a smile on her face. This time she must have felt the slightest tug. She raised her head in surprise. 'Lonnie duck, I'm not in the mood. Untie me now.'

'What's up, Auntie?'

She smoothed down her apron with indignant strokes.

Lonnie held out a closed hand. 'This'll cheer you up.'

'You better not have another one of those spiders or cockroaches in there,' Tilly warned, 'or I'll tan your hide, as big as you are.'

'I haven't, I promise.' He opened his hand, revealing the horseshoe pin. 'Reckon this is yours,' he said brightly.

'Ducky, for the life of me, what you gone'n' done?'

His mind flicked back to the house in Carlton with its booty of other people's belongings. Instinctively, a hand moved to the watch still hidden in his pocket.

'Better you don't ask.'

She shook her head. 'Time you stopped your tomfoolery.'

'Serves Payne right,' he said, in his own defence. 'It's not as if he's been fair.'

'Fairness has nothing to do with it. If you don't pay your rent, a landlord has the right to chuck you out. People like Henry Payne may be criminals in our eyes, but the law is on their side and that's all that counts.'

'You can't let people walk all over you,' Lonnie said. 'Payne should let you be, not threaten to come in with the bailiffs and take all your belongings.'

'What's done is done,' Tilly said sadly, 'it's too late to change anything.'

'What d'ya mean?'

Lonnie soon realised. She was to be evicted from Cumberland Place. Payne had flatly refused to let her stay, sending word he didn't run a charity. Wouldn't even face her in person. The sum of her possessions collected over twenty years – the plump well-worn armchair and twist-legged table, the brass bed, the side dresser dusted down with loving care and waxed to a shine, plates and spoons and English teacups, the copper her dearly departed had installed in the rear yard with firewood stacked ready to boil enough water for a weekly sponge all over – were to disappear with the bailiffs. By the end of the week Auntie Tilly would have nothing left to call her own.

'But you know ducky, life knocks unexpectedly at your front door. Alfred, my widower cousin down in Blackburn, the one with the parcel of land and a well-fitted house close by the lake – I know we haven't always seen eye to eye – but I've agreed to help out with domestic duties in exchange for a bed.'

'You're not serious? You can't go maryanning.' In Lonnie's view, poor Auntie Tilly was far too long in the tooth to scrub floors and do the laundry for an ungrateful relative. She deserved better than scouring until she became bedridden, or even worse, dropped dead.

It was a crying shame that all the women Lonnie knew would be well worn out before their time. Why, even at sixteen, Daisy was already squinting something shocking from too many hours doing close needle and point work. Pearl, with her hard-handled body and she only sixteen as well. His own mam, scrubbing for the toffs for a living. All these hard workers had something in common. They didn't know an easy life, but they wouldn't settle for charity, either.

'I've lived here far too long to ever think of leaving willingly,' continued Tilly. 'Over the years everyone around here has been so kind. No one ever made me afraid before. But it's a cruel world when a man can blacken us good folks' character by saying we're all bludgers who waste money and won't pay our rent. What does he know about hardship?'

Lonnie had never seen Tilly in such a sorrowful state before. She was plumb true when she spoke about Little Lon, no matter what outsiders believed. He knew how he would feel being forced out. Why, he was even named after the place, dropped there by his mam and proud of it, too, although in true Irish spirit his grandad always reckoned it was in honour of Londonderry and wouldn't hear any different. If Payne thought Lonnie was going to stand by and let this happen, the man had better think twice.

Already with an inkling of a plan, he patted Tilly's shoulder consolingly. 'You can't keep your house, but we'll make sure we pack away your belongings before those scoundrels have a chance to steal them. What d'ya reckon about this? By midnight tonight we get your stuff out of here. I know a good bloke who'll take you safely on to Blackburn.'

Tilly greeted this moonlight flit idea with some serious doubt, never in her life having done anything dishonest. Lonnie saw she would need some coaxing. 'Don't you worry, this mate owes me one. Start packing now. Then take a night bag straight to my mam's and wait there. If anyone turns up in the meantime tell them you've called in the rat catchers. I guarantee you'll never have to set eyes on Payne again. Consider what we're doing the spirit of the law,' he urged, 'not the letter. The laws were never made to evict people in hard times like these.'

After lengthy consideration, Tilly clasped his hand

and agreed to the offer. 'I suppose it has come to this,' she said sadly. 'You're a thoughtful boy. But watch out, ducky, your good heart will cause you big trouble one day, especially if you cross men like Henry Payne too often.'

Lonnie grinned. 'Don't go worrying about me. I can take good care of myself.'

The only thing left to do was for Lonnie to tee up the move. Heartened by his own good intentions, in fact warmed down to the very toenail poking through his work boot, he stepped lightly over the doorstep into the Cumberland lane. For not only was the horseshoe pin an unexpected gift returned to its rightful owner, at last he could finally repay Tilly for her kindness to him over the years.

# OAK STAVE

## Item No. 4321

*From a broken barrel.*
*Adapted as a spoke for a cart wheel.*

Ever since Lonnie was knee high he had loved the smells and sounds and colours of Cumberland Place. Next door to Auntie Tilly lived Moon, the Syrian hawker who worked at the Eastern Market selling sweets and spun sugar on a stick. The whole street knew when he was cooking in the backyard copper, the syrupy scent perfuming the air as it drifted over the rooftops. Two doors down were Mamma and Poppa Benetti. Alongside their clutch of sons and daughters, they raised a succession of potted tomatoes and green vegetables in all shapes and sizes, sharing the pickings with the many aunties and cousins who came to visit and stayed on. Here the Benettis crammed noisily and happily into a double-storey terrace painted a vivid maroon and royal blue. If fate had made Lonnie an orphan he would have singled out this lively and emotional Italian family, with their larger-than-life smiles, as his next of kin. It was not surprising when the Benettis' eldest son, Carlo, quickly became his best mate.

The Benettis owned two horse-drawn wagons. One was run by Poppa, the other entrusted to Carlo, who had been tinkering with it since he was twelve. For what better thing could a father do than promote his eldest son. Let him move up from barrow boy to his first man job as an owner-driver. Let him stay close, happy with his lot, working hard. No son of his would ever need to run away to the goldfields in the west, steal off to the bush as an overlander, or be lost to the clippers as a deckhand.

These days Carlo's main trade was fruit and vegetables in the wintertime and green ice-cream in the summer. Poppa had brought over from Italy the delights of ice-cream making, set up a small ice works in the back of the house and fitted out the barrows so they could be packed with salt. But Carlo had already set his sights on a factory of his own. Bigger and with the latest patent machinery. No more cranking by hand. His ices would be tangy fruit rainbows that no other ice-cream maker could match.

Three of the littlies now ran the barrows, their signs announcing 'Benetti and Sons, Fresh Produce'. The bright colours, which matched the lavish house front, brightened up the lane no end. At the end of the workday the place was so cluttered that Lonnie or any other passing pedestrian had to turn sideways to squeeze past.

Lonnie found Carlo's wagon parked in the usual place with the wheel off.

Carlo grinned. ''Bout time you arrived to give me a hand, mate.' He passed over a mallet, picking up where he'd left off, attaching a spoke he'd made from an oak stave cadged from the barrel maker.

Francesco and Antonio, miniature doubles of their elder brother, with hair and eyes dark as pitch and skin the rich colour of olive oil, were perched up on the front seat pretending to drive. There was no horse to guide; Bella being rested in the stableyard around the corner.

The boys were two of the littlies, a name Lonnie had given to Carlo's brothers and sisters, born one after the other in quick order. Carlo and Lonnie often spent their early friendship plotting ways of avoiding the interruptions of Maria, Sophia, Antonio, Giuseppe, Francesco, Pasquale, Bruno, and Mario Benetti, who took it in turns to get under their feet, bringing countless messages from Mamma, then hanging around and pestering them relentlessly, only to disappear when the older boys hoodwinked them with hoaxes and impossible-to-keep promises. If that didn't work, Lonnie and Carlo would set the littlies up on sentinel duty while they made their escape. As a last resort, a good fright would always send them mewling to Mamma like a litter of puppies.

'Hope ya don't mind,' Lonnie said, 'I've booked ya for tonight.'

'Doing what?'

Lonnie motioned towards the two littlies.

'Frank, Tony, get lost.' Carlo clicked his fingers at the pair who these days were more easily dispatched.

When they were out of earshot, Lonnie explained. 'Tilly's in deep. The bailiffs are after her.'

'What're we gonna do?'

'A moonlight.'

'Where to?'

'Blackburn. All's fine, mate. I only need a bit of muscle from you to help load up. I'm calling in a favour from another mate to do the driving.'

Without hesitation, Carlo agreed. 'No worries. Tilly's a good soul. I just gotta finish this wheel first.' He beamed fondly. 'Word's around you been in a bit of mischief. Gonna show me the scars?'

Lonnie displayed the gashes on his arm and indicated the lump on his head. 'Can't keep anything a secret around here for long.' Still, he was grateful for a bit of sympathy at last.

'Nasty. But I'm glad you did what you did. Someone's gotta do something about those mongrels. So, any news to top that?'

'Pearl's onto a race fix.' Lonnie retold the story. 'Lightning's just about unbeatable. Someone knows something we don't. What I wanna know is which horses are running against him.'

'How do you expect to find that out? If it's illegal, they're not gonna publish the info in the *Argus*.'

'Bookie Win will be running a book.'

Carlo stood back for a few seconds admiring his

wheel-fixing skills. 'Well, mate, I reckon we should pay him a visit. I'm done here.' He offered Lonnie a note of caution. 'D'ya reckon you should take Pearl's word? She twitters on a bit. You know as well as me what happens when she starts on one of her schemes. Spells trouble with a capital P.' He counted them off on his fingers, 'Punch-ups, pranks, pain, past experience …' He rubbed his behind. 'Never harmless, mate. I'll remember that blooming goldfish till the day I die. My arse was so sore I couldn't sit down for a week.'

Lonnie realised too late he had stepped right into a retelling of what had become known to them all as the Blooming Goldfish story. Carlo could never quite forgive Pearl for the times he'd been given a hiding over one of her hare-brained schemes. All the aggravation came about when Pearl convinced Carlo they should get one of the goldfish on offer from the rag-and-bone man, who was trading fish for rags or scrap metal.

'Only I got nothing to trade.'

Those appealing puppy eyes of Pearl's, the undoing of many a lad, fired up. 'Bet you have Carlo. Things your mamma won't miss. Or are you gonna be a scaredy-dare?'

Before Carlo had cottoned on about life, the threat to his manhood always seemed to work in Pearl's favour. Having been so cunningly and willingly in this case, tricked, he could only find an old woollen coat of his poppa's. One with torn elbows and frayed cuffs that smelt of olives and tobacco. A coat the littlies loved to bury their heads in.

'Poppa never wears it anymore,' Carlo said uncertainly, for didn't Mamma always get round to cutting old clothes down a size or two and passing them on?

Pearl grabbed the coat, ordered him to find a jam jar, bounded outside and swapped Poppa's jacket for a goldfish before Carlo had a chance to change his mind.

He had to admit he admired the trade. That is until Poppa Benetti came across them. 'What's that you gotta there?'

'A goldfish we've just traded,' Pearl said. 'Isn't it a beauty?'

'So you make a trade?' Poppa Benetti was amiable enough at first, noting his eldest son's business prowess. 'What you trade?'

Pearl burst in. 'Only an old brown coat.'

Carlo gave her a swift kick in the shin to shut her up. She shot him a glare. The exchange didn't go unnoticed by his poppa who eyed them suspiciously. 'From where you getta the coat?'

'We swapped the old one you never wear anymore.'

Carlo knew Pearl's loose tongue had landed him in trouble big time. He gave her another kick. 'We need to find a bigger jar, Poppa, this one's too small.'

Mr Benetti was no fool. 'Never mind look for big

jar, swappa the fish back for my coat.'

'But you never wear it, Poppa.'

'Now!'

Carlo dragged Pearl off, the order sounding alarm bells in his ears. But Pearl was set on keeping the goldfish. 'Let's pretend we dropped it and it died. Can't swap it back then, can we?' Pearl had already made up her mind. All they had to do was stay out of sight for a short while, then return with their story. Surely Poppa would understand how this unfortunate accident had left them with no chance of retrieving the coat.

Her entreaties gave Carlo no choice but to let Pearl take home the fish and lie to his poppa. Pearl hadn't reckoned on Carlo finishing up with a belt across his rear end; Poppa explaining he wasn't thrashing his son over the loss of the coat, but over the lie. Unfortunately for Carlo, Poppa had watched the rag-and-bone man leave in one direction, while Pearl went the opposite way carefully carrying the fish.

Poppa Benetti was not a hard man. But he was a good Catholic and just to prove it, he tied saintly leather scapulars around each family member's neck at birth as a badge of their devotion, made them recite the rosary together every evening – ten Hail Marys being the solution to all life's problems – and would not tolerate, above all things, falsehoods or heathens. The exception was their Syrian neighbour, Moon, who he conceded was kind-hearted by nature and thus was excused; although Mamma prayed late into the night that Moon would one day convert. Faith, like prayer and punishment, was a potent tonic.

So Carlo received a hiding. Within a week, as a kind of divine retribution, conclusively proving Poppa Benetti's point, the goldfish died.

Carlo could have cited a dozen more mad notions with a capital P as to why he vowed never to be caught up with Pearl's schemes again. Like the time she persuaded them to stow away on a ship heading to Williamstown, but in the nick of time they overheard the bosun say the ship was heading out over the Tasman and on to the old country. But he rested his case on the Blooming Goldfish story, finishing off with, 'Don't say I didn't warn you.'

Lonnie had no comeback. He could only laugh. ''Bout time you let bygones be bygones, mate.'

# COINS AND A TOKEN

## Item Nos. 647, 648, 649 & 650

*Various coins.*
*A shilling, a threepenny piece,*
*a Chinese coin most likely used*
*as a gaming chip, and a token halfpenny*
*from Professor Holloways' ointments*
*and pill company, dated 1860.*

After a speedy detour to set up Auntie Tilly's moonlight flit with their driver mate, the two lads were soon strolling through the back lanes towards Bookie Win's. The narrow stretch in Little Bourke Street, known as Chinatown, was crammed with furniture marts that were stacked to the ceiling with assorted bamboo baskets and wholesale grocers selling dried bird carcasses, pungent spices and incense. Behind these facades, hidden in a maze of rooms, were the private clubhouses, temples and homes of the local Chinese people.

The boys stopped briefly at a shopfront loaded with crates of swollen, spiky fruit. They picked out a penn'orth, peeled them down to the size of a grape and enjoyed the burst of milky liquid from each bite.

'Can't resist 'em, mate,' Lonnie said appreciatively.

At the doorway of a cabinetmaker's they grinned down at some young children who were crouched like small Buddhas on the front step and yammering ten to the dozen in their singsong language. They passed through the joinery with all its dark lacquered furniture, down a back hallway lined with paper lanterns and into Bookie Win's betting shop.

Like most of the locals, his family had come out to the gold diggings. More lately they'd been running an enterprising business of wholesale and supply, with gambling on the side. Bookie's real name of Li Ha Win had been put out of use by this current trade.

Lonnie tipped his cap at a group of men who were drawing cards and flourishing counters. These men, dressed in long blue smocks and wearing hats like upturned bowls over their pigtails, didn't seem to be feeling the pinch of hard times. As they jigged their heads back in friendly greeting, they continued piling up the ante, throwing threepences, sixpences and even shillings into the centre of the table.

Bookie Win bowed. 'You want make bet today, Lonnee?'

'Only information, Bookie.' He lowered his voice. 'In private, if you don't mind.'

Bookie led them to a secluded room where the

tables were shut down for the day. 'Business slow,' he said with a shrug.

As Lonnie expected, Bookie was well aware of the illegal race.

'How you find out?' he asked. After all, it was supposed to be a secret. The fewer in, the easier to safeguard them all. 'Don't want make trouble.'

Lonnie reassured him. 'Nor do we, mate.'

Bookie knew the boys well enough to take them at their word. He listened intently as Lonnie broke the rumour about the jockey on the favourite, Lightning, deliberately set to lose the race.

As the bookmaker for the event, Bookie showed great concern. Depending on the amount of money wagered, he could lose heavily. There were too many signs the Melbourne slump would not turn around for a long time. Look at his betting shop, affected already. Further problems could spell the end of his business. 'Maybe we help each other,' he suggested.

Bookie told them what he knew. No jockey had yet been named to ride Lightning and money had been mysteriously staked on another horse in the race: Trident. 'Put on by Crick men. You hear anything from Golden Acre?'

Lonnie shook his head. He tried to make sense of the facts so far. The Cricks were running two of their horses in the race, both Lightning and Trident. If Lightning was the favourite, why wasn't Thomas Crick down to ride him the way he always did? He had definitely heard Pearl right when she told him Lightning was going to lose. Now here was Bookie telling him Trident was being backed to win. He bet his life the Cricks were behind this fix.

'At least we know which horse to back,' Carlo said. 'My money's on Trident.'

'But it isn't right,' said Lonnie. 'What about all those not in the know?'

It seemed clear enough to Carlo. 'They lose their money. Simple as that.'

'Nah, it ain't fair.' Lonnie thought back to his conversation with Auntie Tilly. Fairness had nothing to do with it.

As they left Chinatown, Lonnie knew he would have to do some more investigation at Golden Acres. Chances were he could pick up some clues, although he already had a good idea what the Cricks were up to.

The day just kept getting busier for Lonnie. His head was throbbing, the night was quickly folding in, he'd promised to meet Pearl at the oyster bar and he still had to honour his promise to Auntie Tilly. He reached into his pocket where the watch lay waiting. Lordy, here was more unfinished business, undoubtedly the most unsettling of all.

# THREE EMPTY FRENCH WINE BOTTLES

## Item Nos. 31, 32 & 33

*Found in cesspit.*
*Thought to have been from one of the more upmarket brothels around Little Lon.*

Pearl stood shivering at the corner by the Governor Hotel. It was a grim night, the wind taking bites out of her skin and blowing hints of grubby slum houses through the laneways. She cursed Madam's choice of dress for her; a lickety-split of such frivolous green material that would surely have floated away with the wind if not for the satin band which pinned down the folds at her waist and refused to let go. She pulled a woollen shawl around her shoulders, cursing that muck-snipe Ruby who was at this very minute working in the warmth and luxury of the Big House, her sacred white feather having well and truly been plucked, while Pearl was left stuck out here in the cold.

She heard her own name being called from inside the Governor. 'Get yerself in here, Pearl. Come kick up yer heels!' The shrieks and beer swilling made her feel sick. Only one more customer, she pledged, and then she'd slip away to meet Lonnie at the oyster bar.

Served Madam right if she scarpered for a while. Mind you, she'd be getting more than a belt across the earhole if she were found out. All because Annie had turned Madam's mood so sour. (Not to mention that mooching Ruby with her whimpering ways, plotting to put Pearl on this miserable street corner instead of up at the Big House or at number four, where at least she would be keeping out of the bitter night.) So what if she took some time off? She deserved it. The thought of those hot steaming oysters made her want to devour them in one, solid, tongue-licking swallow.

Back at Casselden Place she had secretly stored some bottles of choice champagne. Didn't see why the toffs or the pollies should have all the fun, when it was her legs going blue with the cold. She had mastered a trick of leaving half a glass in the bottom of each bottle, especially as the night grew older and the clients grew drunker. She would quickly whisk the open bottle away out of sight and return with a full one. Pearl learned quickly that a client always knew if he had ordered three or four bottles. There was never any problem, as long as his bill had the correct number. By the end of a good night, she was able to fill two or three bottles with the leftovers. Mixers, she called them.

Of course, mincing Miss-Ruby-Come-Lately had

already stuck her nose into the affair and caught her out. Pearl had threatened her – if she ever spouted off to Madam about the little trick, then wouldn't she know a proper what for. She'd think twice about messing with the likes of Pearl ever again.

If Lonnie was game, Pearl planned to take him back to number four to sample her latest blend. (And that was only for starters.) The other night when she had cleaned Lonnie's wounds, she had sensed with a twinkling certainty that manly thoughts about her had crossed his mind. Anyways it was about time he grew up, instead of blushing to the roots whenever she teased him. She knew what men wanted. Only one thing after all. He wouldn't be any different. She made up her mind to give Lonnie a coming-of-age for which he would be eternally grateful. She really wanted him to like her. And she was as good as anyone to be his first. Anyways, he needed cheering up after that bump on the head. It was a wonder he hadn't lost his senses altogether.

She hoped Lonnie had been thinking more about the horse race. The right bet with good odds would see her debt fixed up. She worked out the sums. Win more and she could walk right out of the game, have enough to set herself up in St Kilda, with tramcars running past her door and the seaside across the road.

Her mind flitted to her other friend. Pearl loved Daisy Cameron dearly. Together with Lonnie, the three of them were inseparable, even though Carlo always tagged along and put a damper on everything. Daisy was all sweetness and kindliness, especially now she had found the Sally Army. Sometimes Pearl wished she could be more like her.

Strange how fortune played out. Daisy would have been lost to the streets as well, but for some perverse act of kindness from Madam Buckingham. No one had ever fully understood why she took a shine to Daisy, settling her in a room at the Leitrim and then enabling her to make a respectable living as a seamstress. If Madam Buckingham could help Daisy, maybe she would treat Pearl kindly. This had been in the back of her mind, the reasoning behind her move from Annie to the safety of the Big House. (Not that she'd seen any kindness so far.)

She was deciding which to do first, pop in for a quick chinwag with Daisy or drop in at the oyster bar, when a man sidled through the shadows. *There's me answer*, she thought, giving a sigh and striking a dramatic pose. (*But he's my last for the night and then I'm knocking off.*)

A rough hand grabbed her by the throat. She gave a strangled cry. Only a whiff of stale tobacco smoke and sour sweat, a split second of fear, and then the fist laid her flat with one blow.

# OYSTER SHELL

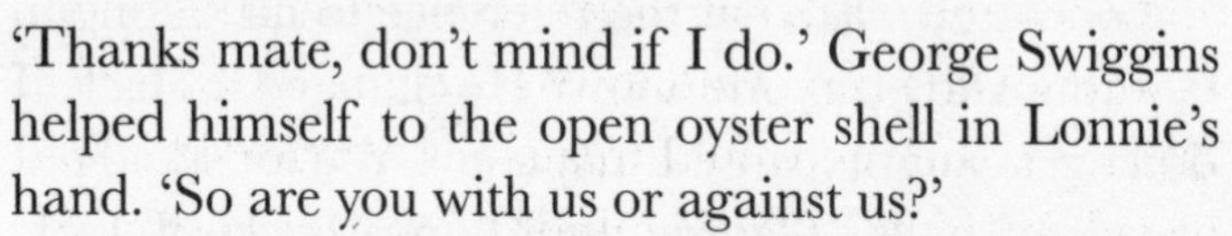

## Item No. 27

*One of many discarded shells found. Takeaway food of the era, but still something of a luxury.*

'Thanks mate, don't mind if I do.' George Swiggins helped himself to the open oyster shell in Lonnie's hand. 'So are you with us or against us?'

The leader of the Push lounged against the lamp pillar. He was nineteen and had an air of instinctive danger about him. He looked like a spiv, dressed like a spiv, and acted like a spiv. His dark hair licked to the back, oiled down sleek. His hat tilted at an angle, shading eyes where a reckless animal lay caged and ready to pounce. When he flashed his smile it was enough to make a girl stop short in panic. His tight jacket was cut away sharp at the hip. The trouser legs, with their fourteen-inch bottoms as narrow as pencils, had creases keen enough to slice fingers. The silk neckerchief was too bright and there was enough shine on his shoes to see his own face in.

'Come on, George. I'm not exactly built like a brick dunny, am I?' Lonnie replied, cautiously sidestepping the offer to join the gang. He wanted neither to be with him, nor against him.

This was not the answer George wanted. He bent down to flick an invisible speck of dust from his shoes. 'It's the pimpernel in you we're looking towards. You got a knack of never being caught. Could use a bit of that skill in our gang.'

'I don't get caught 'cause I never do anything.'

'Not what I heard. Word's around you outran one of Payne's watchdogs.'

Lonnie grimaced at the reference to his outing in Carlton. Did everyone know? He changed his tack. 'I don't get caught 'cause I'm a loner. You lot stand out like dogs' balls.' George gave him a back-off look. Lonnie shuffled uneasily; being frank was one thing, but knowing when to stop with the smart prattle was a lesson he had yet to master in life.

'Let me spell it out. I'm looking for a *yes* from you and I'm not known as a patient man. Tell you what, we'll even let your mate join as well.' He nodded at Carlo, who had come in with Lonnie and was keeping a low profile in the corner.

Carlo gave a nervous look around and muttered, 'Leave me out of this.'

To their relief, George didn't press for an answer. He strode over to his gang who were busy entertaining themselves by showing off, marking a bottle as if it were a footy over the heads of the people scurrying past.

'Let's beat it,' whispered Carlo. 'If we stay any longer there's bound to be trouble. Pearl's not going to show. You'll have to catch up with her later. Don't forget we still have to sort Auntie's stuff before we call it a night.'

Taking advantage of the shortest possible route, Lonnie and Carlo bolted in and out of the lanes that took them in a matter of minutes to Cumberland Place. The midnight backstreet seemed soundless and dark. While Carlo attended to things inside, Lonnie waited at the end of the row of houses. At the appointed time he waved his dark lantern in an arc. When his mate's cart turned the corner, the sound of iron horseshoes rattled over the cobblestones. Making haste, they rescued the bulk of Auntie Tilly's belongings.

The last thing to do was collect Auntie Tilly. Linked between the boys' arms to hold her steady, she climbed onto the cart. As she took her seat she was as stately as any abdicating queen. 'Never does to look back,' she said with finality, as though she might not see them again in her lifetime. She dabbed her glistening eyes with a handkerchief but her tight smile didn't falter.

''Course you will,' said Lonnie. 'When it's all blown over we'll be sure to come and see you.'

'We can't do without your oatmeal rounds for too long,' added Carlo with a shaky grin.

She gave a warm chuckle and clipped them both

on the earhole. 'Just mind your manners until then, duckies.'

The boys rode a little way on the back of the cart, seeing her off safely before jumping down. Their walk home was sober. The thought of no longer having Auntie Tilly where she'd always been was unnerving.

The day had been a long one. When Lonnie arrived home there was one final thing for him to do before nodding off for the night. Making sure his mam was fast asleep, he wrapped the watch in a handkerchief and placed it in the bottom drawer of the dresser. He was too tired to deal with anything more. Better for the time being to leave the watch hidden and stay silent. It had been a full and eventful day and early tomorrow he was due at the stables.

# HOOP HANDLE FROM A TRAPDOOR

## Item No. 2018

*Round, circular handle*
*used for raising and lowering a trapdoor.*

On the other side of town not far from Little Lon, at about the same time as Lonnie was settling down for the night, Pearl came around in a cramped, dark place beneath the floorboards of an old building. Her cheek was sore and she felt the burn of vomit in her throat. In spite of all her guile, the worst had finally happened. She groggily recalled the violent arm that had grabbed her and the thump which had left her insensible.

She tried to sit up. There was barely enough room to straighten her back so she shuffled to the side and lay down. She stared into the darkness of her premature grave. Tears splashed like fiery splinters on her cheeks as she imagined what was in store for her.

Sometime later a trapdoor lifted open from above. Pearl made out the twisted face of Annie Walker.

'Didn't think you were being watched, did yer?' she barked. A ghost of a smirk flitted across her thin, mean lips. 'Did yer think yer were invisible and no one could see yer out there working for Madam Buckteeth? Next you'll be toadying across to that Missy Do-Gooder Selina Southern and who else after that, I wonder?'

Eyes blotted with spite examined her. 'This is it, girlie. Sort out what yer owe because until yer clear that debt, yer my goods. That means keeping yer pussy away from that sour-faced hag, yer understand? See how easy it was for me to have Jack bring yer in.' She clicked her fingers. 'He can do it any time and if there is a next time, there'll be no holding him back. Not from you, not from yer friends, not even from Saint Selina herself. No bit of scrawny flim-flam can cross me and get away with it.'

Pearl shrank back from Annie's hissing anger. She felt a sob rising from her belly, but held it in. 'I've been trying to pay you out. Only I need more time.'

'But yer crossed me, girl. I don't like being taken for a fool.'

'Let me out.'

'Yer can rot here till yer mean what yer promise. Ungrateful muff. Let's see how yer do without my help.'

The trapdoor slammed shut above Pearl and darkness overwhelmed her.

# WORK BOOT

## Item No. 19

*One of a pair.*
*Brown leather, well-worn toe.*

'Steady, boy.'

Lonnie leaned down and patted Trident. The sun had hardly made its way over the nearby hills, turning the clouds into orange wisps, but already the day was turning into a busy one. On top of the stable duties yet to start – mucking out, laying clean straw, bringing fresh water for the horses and the grooming – it was open day at Golden Acres. The forthcoming auction meant other stables would be showing their interest. And although he loved it, the call for extra track work meant Lonnie had more than enough to do for his day's wage.

Crick was on Lightning. There was no doubting it was a magnificent horse. But the beast beneath Lonnie was a little beauty, too. Oh to be a horse owner like the Cricks; he would consider buying Trident for himself. Lonnie had no real pretensions that his boss was seriously trialling him as a jockey. He knew he had to be satisfied with what track work he could get, keep stealing every opportunity to ride horses, and hope against hope that one day he would have a real chance to make it.

'Open Day at the Acres' the sign outside read. 'Inspections welcome for the upcoming horse auction. Open to all offers'. Ned, the foreman from the Glen stables over Flemington way, was taking early advantage of the invitation. He made his way unannounced through the arched iron gates and wandered over to the practice track, taking a private opportunity to check some of Golden Acres' horses at work.

Two dark shadows were on the rise of the hill. As they galloped he noted the sheer elegance of their silhouettes against the carroty sky, in particular the poise and balance of the second rider.

As Crick and Lonnie brought their steaming horses back, Lonnie immediately recognised the man standing by the rails as the foreman from the Glen. He must have come along to check over the yearlings, but was here far too early. That would rile the Cricks. Track work was always a secret business. Horses were not to be timed by bookmakers or outsiders; their abilities exposed to the world, thus ruining odds and spoiling bets before a race meeting. He wondered what the Glen's foreman had made of them as they raced over the crest.

'Here a little early for the open day? Doing a bit

of scouting, are you?' It was about as much of a greeting as Thomas Crick could muster.

The slight was not lost on the Glen foreman. 'We can all learn, Mr Crick. Actually I'm here to look at your yearlings, sadly not at you, sir. There are a lot of studs to visit before the auctions. I have to start somewhere.'

Lonnie detected the cutting tone of the reply, but it passed over Crick's head like a horse clearing a hurdle.

'Well then, be my guest. McGuinness, earn your keep, help Ned see the yearlings before you groom these two.' He dismounted, tossed Lonnie his reins and swaggered over to the manager's office, leaving them alone.

'McGuinness, is it?'

'Aye, sir.'

'I was watching you this morning.'

As Ned was talking to him Lonnie felt his big toe sticking through the hole in his boot. Without fuss he eased it back into comfort. 'You were?'

'Why don't you come over to the Glen for a quiet word?'

'A word, sir?' Lonnie wondered if he dared think what this could mean. 'I mean, of course, anytime,' he added.

'Good lad,' said Ned, 'but give me a chance to finish buying our yearlings before you call over.'

Lonnie tried to stifle his excitement as he swung

down off Trident, keeping in mind that he still had a job to do, which was to show Ned the horses on offer.

# SKULL

## Item No. 1834

*Human skull.*
*Adult male. Identity unknown.*
*Has undergone forensic examination.*

The former draper's shop had been a front for many a trade, including a furniture mart and a fancy goods dealer. Old Postlethwaite, recently retired from pulling teeth, had lately taken up residence, opening a phrenological shop. To passers-by the chief attraction was the skull in the front window, covertly donated by an acquaintance who worked in the back rooms of the Melbourne hospital where skeletal remains were stored for medical study. Now proudly exhibited, the skull advertised the belief that the analysis of its shape helped to understand the workings of the mental powers.

Daisy's nose pressed flat to the window as she intently considered the centrepiece. 'Do you think it's human or monkey?' she asked Lonnie. Mapped out on the head were the continents of Animal and Moral, subdivided into countries called Combativeness, Vitativeness, Benevolence and Hope. 'What do they all mean?'

Lonnie answered with a shrug. 'Who knows? You're not seriously going in there and letting that quack's old fingers play a tune on your head?'

'I am and so are you.'

Lonnie threw her a disgruntled look. 'Having your bumps read won't help with nightmares.'

'Employers in the rag trade often check out their workers' skull shapes before they employ them,' she sniffed, 'so it must work or else they wouldn't do it.'

'Postlethwaite's an old shyster,' warned Lonnie. 'We'll be wasting our time.'

'What harm can he do? Come on, it's worth a try. Besides, you gave me your word.'

'I didn't think you were serious.'

Daisy folded her arms obstinately, a stance Lonnie had lost many a battle over. She was a headstrong girl and would never take no for an answer.

'Okay, Daise,' he relented. 'But I won't stand for any messing around. If Postlethwaite tries anything creepy, we're out of there.'

With a loud snort of victory, Daisy grabbed his hand and pulled him through the doorway before he had a chance to reconsider.

The self-proclaimed phrenologist, Alfred Postlethwaite Esquire, as the nameplate described him, was an earnest dabbler in all the sciences. His shop counter was bursting with bits of glassware and equipment – pipettes, tubes and crucibles, basins and burners. Arranged in glass cases were tweezers, forceps, scalpels and saws. Fungal colonies and spores were putting out shoots from bowls, ripening for closer examination. A collection of organs and animal specimens floated in formalin. Like any amateur's dream, Postlethwaite wished to make a great healing discovery without killing the human body in the process.

The sign behind the counter read: First Consultation Only $6^{d}$. No one need go untreated!

'Count me out,' Lonnie muttered, as Postlethwaite bundled Daisy into a chair and set about outlining a portion of her skull with his fingers.

The phrenologist stopped at several bumps and deliberated with a swift tap, chattering away as if he was dictating notes to an imaginary person. 'We are measuring the extent of this region to indicate the little lady's temperament.' His fingers continued their soft-shoe journey across her skull.

Suddenly he swept up a pad of papers and placed a tick against a word here and a phrase there. 'Such scientists as Charles Darwin,' he instructed knowingly, 'have been most keen to promote this science. A slight knock here will enlarge the reflective section and encourage our little lady's Agreeableness.'

'Daisy's agreeable enough,' muttered Lonnie. 'It's her nightmares she's come to find out about.'

'Ah, I see.' His hands circumnavigated Daisy's skull. 'The moral sector is well defined. You have a great amount of Spirituality.'

Lonnie was growing impatient. More likely the old fraud had seen Daisy jiggling her tambourine and wearing her Sally's uniform.

Postlethwaite moved his hand to the back of her skull. 'Here is the section we call Fear.' He tapped hard on the site.

'Ouch!'

'Steady on, mate.' Lonnie gripped Postlethwaite's arm. 'You'll do her an injury.'

'I'm merely working on the area of her trouble. If you wish to remain for this consultation then I insist you show less impertinence.' Postlethwaite brushed down his sleeve and resumed his map work across Daisy's skull. 'There are of course other possibilities for repair. Say we drilled here,' he said, pressing his thumb down hard on Trepidation, 'we may destroy the part of the brain which contains the important background to the fear. Only a small indentation will be left. Very easily fixed.' He gave Daisy an encouraging smile.

Lonnie grabbed hold of his friend and hoisted her out of the chair. 'That's enough, Daise, no one's drilling holes in your head.' He glared hotly at the phrenologist.

Postlethwaite was as aggravated as Lonnie, who turned his back and strode to the door, dragging the protesting Daisy along behind him. The scientist rushed after them. 'Now see here, wait a minute! What about my payment?'

Lonnie reached into his pocket and dismissively tossed a sixpence in his direction. 'Daylight robbery, mate.'

Outside Daisy ripped her hand away from his. Her eyes were grey specks in a stormy sky; the tempest was coming. 'What did you do that for?'

'He's demented. I told you so in the first place. Gives me the creeps.'

'In. The. First. Place.' Daisy sounded out each word as brutally as the force of an executioner's axe. 'Who said I can't speak up for myself? Am I mute? Do you think for one moment I'd give permission to anyone to drill into my skull, or for that matter I needed you to rescue me? I thought you knew me better, Lonnie McGuinness. And in the second place, who says you're right? Mr Postlethwaite may well have helped. So now you've dragged me out, have you any other bright ideas about how I'm going to stop my nightmares?'

'Come on, Daise, I didn't mean it. Postlethwaite's an old fool.' Lonnie trailed off, lost for words. There was no doubt about it, if anyone knew her own mind it was Daisy Cameron. He should've known better than to get on her wrong side. 'We'll find another way of sorting this. Let me think it over. I promise I'll help.'

'Be careful you don't make promises you can't keep,' warned Daisy sternly, but then relented and slipped her arm through his. 'Walk with me to number four. Let's see what Pearl's up to. I haven't seen her around for ages.'

'Good idea,' Lonnie said, relieved that Daisy was no longer cross with him. 'The little shirker was supposed to meet me at the oyster bar the other night, but she didn't show.'

# BROKEN HINGE

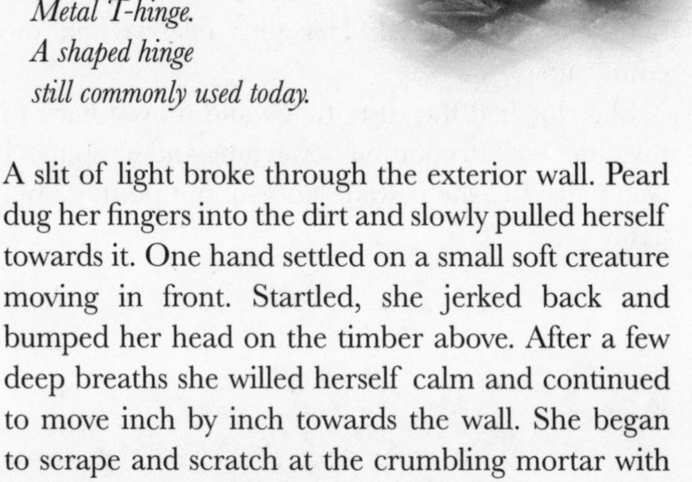

## Item No. 654

*Metal T-hinge.*
*A shaped hinge*
*still commonly used today.*

A slit of light broke through the exterior wall. Pearl dug her fingers into the dirt and slowly pulled herself towards it. One hand settled on a small soft creature moving in front. Startled, she jerked back and bumped her head on the timber above. After a few deep breaths she willed herself calm and continued to move inch by inch towards the wall. She began to scrape and scratch at the crumbling mortar with a broken hinge she'd found in the dirt. If she could gouge a hole large enough to squeeze through, then she could make a run for it before Annie cottoned on.

A squeak and a groan on the floorboards above warned her the trapdoor would soon be on the move. She hastily shimmied back to her place underneath the hulking door and lay still. Annie dropped a small, partially filled bottle through the hole. Pearl grabbed it and drank thirstily. With a feeling of disgust she threw it aside. There was more spit in her mouth than there was water in that bottle.

'Ungrateful slut, if yer never heard of again, no one will even miss yer,' snarled Annie. 'Yer depend on me, all I have to do is close this and forget about yer. That's how easy it is, girlie.' And just to prove her point she slammed down the trapdoor once again.

Dread enveloped Pearl. 'Don't let me rot down here,' she whimpered. Her plea dissolved in the empty air.

She clutched the rusty hinge and moved back to the outer wall to continue scratching and scraping. 'I won't give in,' she vowed. Not without putting up a fight.

# EMPTY FLAGON

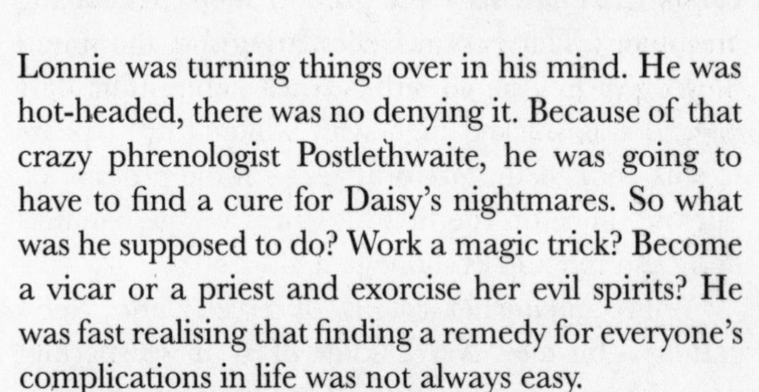

## Item No. 641

*Stoneware ginger beer or sarsaparilla flagon. Found in cesspit.*

Lonnie was turning things over in his mind. He was hot-headed, there was no denying it. Because of that crazy phrenologist Postlethwaite, he was going to have to find a cure for Daisy's nightmares. So what was he supposed to do? Work a magic trick? Become a vicar or a priest and exorcise her evil spirits? He was fast realising that finding a remedy for everyone's complications in life was not always easy.

He stifled a yawn. It was still early, barely sunrise in fact, yet he had already worked several hours. At least it was a short shift. A few days had shot by since the Glen's foreman had asked him to call over. Even though Lonnie had half convinced himself he might be offered a job, he wondered deep down if anything would come of the meeting. The prospect meant a lot to him, maybe a real chance of becoming an apprentice jockey. Lonnie McGuinness wearing silks? Now that would be a complication he welcomed. Still, it would have to wait.

He finished up at work, dusted off his trousers and set off to meet Carlo. Here was another promise to keep. Next time he was going to keep his big mouth shut. Not that he really minded helping out Carlo every now and then, if only for the reason in the shape of Rose Payne.

'Do ya reckon she'd ever walk out with me?' asked Lonnie, when the boys met up outside Carlo's house. Bella, ready to pull along Carlo's festively-painted cart with its new blue and yellow canopy, was taking an interest. Her ears swivelled around at the sound of his voice. Lonnie stroked her mane. The cart behind was stacked high with winter fruit – pears to sink your teeth into, oranges with the promise of bursting juice on the first bite, firm yellow bananas and crisp red apples shone to a gloss.

'You're making her jealous,' observed Carlo. 'She's getting a bit toey. Needs some of your whispering; those horsy things you do. Beats me why the girls all seem to like you, but. Even Bella! But you got no chance with Rose Payne. Too stuck up. Ordinarily that is. Too dangerous a name for the likes of you.'

'She can't help who her father is.'

'It's in the breeding. Stick to the girls around here. There's Daisy for starters.'

'Daise is like my kid sister.'

'Pearl's sweet on you as well.'

'Come off it, she's only a mate.'

'Hey, you going blind or what? Why do you think

she came to see you about the horse race?' Carlo couldn't resist a chuckle.

'Wrong again, mate. I went to her. She didn't come to me. If she's so keen,' Lonnie replied in self defence, 'why did she stand me up at the oyster bar, and where was she when Daise and I went looking for her?'

'Probably done a bunk. Scarpered for a while. You know how flighty she is. Besides, you can't look after every skirt in Melbourne, even if they all fall for you. You'd be a bit strapped for cash with the lot of 'em on the go. Better choose one and be done with it.'

Carlo had a point. Lonnie had to admit he was showing more interest in girls than ever before. Well, if he must, he decided to settle long and yearningly on the unattainable Rose Payne. Out of his league or not.

'I'm telling you, mate, she's too uppity. Reckon it'd empty the coffers taking her out.'

Lonnie was not to be deterred. 'But say I did, where'd I take her?'

'Can't see you doing the Block with the toffs on a Saturday arvo. And the Federal Coffee Palace won't let the likes of us through the door. Guess ya could walk around the Eastern Market. But you'd have to protect her from all us riffraff.'

'Take a lot to keep her entertained. I'd have to keep her laughing,' mused Lonnie, 'and stop her spending too much of my money.'

'You're dreaming, mate.'

Lonnie sighed and picked up a flagon from a stack on the wagon. 'New line?' he asked.

'Ginger ale. Heard it's selling well so thought I'd carry some. See how it goes.'

Lonnie inspected the stoneware jar with its corked lid. There was no doubting Carlo was a go-ahead. 'With all your enterprising, bet you'll be living with the toffs yourself before too long.' Carlo was already an owner-driver and determined to make enough to build an ice works factory. Lonnie fully expected Carlo would take his place on Collins Hill one day, where the houses of the wealthy, three storeys tall, lined the street behind wrought iron railings and raised garden beds. 'So long as you don't let those building societies nab your profits.'

'My stash is staying under the mattress. Best bank in Melbourne right now. Rumour's going around the Macquarie is about to close. That'll make nearly all of them shutting this year.' Everyone was having to tighten the purse strings. It was a sobering thought.

'Say I marry Rose Payne,' Lonnie said. 'Say we lived at her place on Collins Hill, you could be rich enough to set up next door. Do you reckon the nobs get more sleep than us?'

'Not if they stop off at Mrs B's.'

Lonnie laughed. As Bella plodded through the back lanes towards the main thoroughfare he murmured quietly to her. He became aware that

Carlo was grinning smugly. 'Just making sure her heart's not broken.' It was a double-edged truth. He had an intuitive understanding of horses, knowing well this was the way to give them confidence. You had to learn how a horse was feeling, anticipate what it was thinking, then work with it to bring out the best. Up until recently the most placid of the Benetti family, old age was catching up with the good-natured dobbin. The time was drawing nearer when after a day's work Bella would be sent to the glue factory instead of the stableyard. It would be a sad and sorry day for them all.

They headed for Melbourne's answer to the boulevards of Europe, an area where roads were lined by young elm trees and cobbled in timber and bluestone; where tramcars rattled downhill; and on a Saturday morning well-dressed young men and women were inclined to shop in the arcades, then stroll in the afternoon along the sheltered walkways, a pastime they fondly called 'doing the Block'.

On the street corners barrow boys were already setting up their loads. Coals warmed in their braziers ready for roasting horse chestnuts and potatoes. Flower sellers made ready their posies of pansies tied around with pale ribbons. Large bouquets trailed wild ramblers. There was a clatter of noise as the handcarts and wagons rolled into place and the traders dropped down the timber sides, showing off their heavy-skinned vegetables for sale. Everywhere the fruit was so fresh it could have fallen from the trees straight into the crates. On seeing this fat, rich fare it was hard to contemplate how some folk were already going hungry.

As they were setting up their fresh produce, Lonnie took the opportunity to tell Carlo about his recent track work on Trident. 'Reckon I could have beaten Crick,' he said. 'There's more to Trident than meets the eye.' He suddenly stopped short, as if he'd had second thoughts about something.

If Carlo picked up any slight hesitation on Lonnie's part, he failed to show it and the remark passed by without much of a comment, Carlo more concerned with his own prospects. 'Sure way to lose your job, but could be a good thing,' he declared. 'Then you'd have to come work for me full time. 'Bout time we went into partnership.'

'Can't, mate, may have some new prospects at the Glen.'

'So are ya telling me the Glen may steal you first? Talk about loyalty!'

A surge of customers descended into the main thoroughfare. Rings of young ladies stood twirling their umbrellas. They made a fetching sight, all buttoned up against the wind, their plumped-out bustles making each pinched waist even slimmer. Carlo caught sight of a particular girl heading their way. 'Here comes Lady Muck.'

Lonnie shoved Carlo aside, nearly knocking him

off his feet. 'Quick, let me serve her!' He brushed himself down, put on his brightest smile and started to spit and polish an apple.

The sixteen-year-old beauty walked towards them. Lonnie could not take his eyes off the few dark curls that escaped from beneath her blue bonnet. A padded jacket of the same colour squared off her slight shoulders. Buttons made of mother-of-pearl pinned the collar tightly around her neck and ran like cameo rainbows down to her tiny, drawn-in waist. On this bracing winter's morning, she looked like the dazzle of a Melbourne summer sky, warming Lonnie through to his very bones.

It was hard to believe that a scumbag like Henry Payne could have fathered her. It still made Lonnie furious to think of poor Auntie Tilly having to leave Little Lon because of Henry Payne. That man caused nothing but grief. As Lonnie imagined her as a baby swapped at birth, Rose greeted him with a fetching smile. Lingering in the crisp air around her was a delicate fragrance of dried rose petals and lavender. 'Do you think I should try a red or a green apple today?' she asked. Her heart-shaped lips shot arrows of desire at him with each softly formed syllable.

Ping, ping, the arrows hit. 'The red ones are crisp, freshly pinged, I mean picked,' he stammered. 'The sweetest, too.' *Like you*, he wanted to say, but he kept the thought private. He took a bite. 'See.' He offered her another of the same.

She giggled behind her hand then accepted, the tip of her glove making contact with his skin. She bit lusciously into the fruit, all the while staring squarely at him, her eyes sparkling a challenge. Ping, ping, more arrows hit. There and then, as she held the fruit to her mouth with those half-open lips, there was no other girl in the world for him. He was lost to her forever. If it had been summertime and he had offered her ice-cream, it would glisten transparent in the sunshine, and Rose's rosebud lips would open, and her tongue would lick and melt the cool ice. Ping.

'Delicious.' She interrupted his daydreams, undid a silver clip on her beaded purse and pulled out a coin.

Lonnie reached over and lightly brushed a hand that he was certain felt as charged as his own. 'No cost.'

She pulled her hand away. 'You mustn't do that.'

'What?' Ping. 'Do what? Why not?'

She glanced over at Carlo, who was keeping track of the exchange. 'You're supposed to be selling them. Won't you get in trouble from your boss?'

'He's not my boss. We're partners.'

Carlo's eyeballs nearly popped out and fell on the ground. He coughed, trying to stifle a laugh, and quickly diverted his attention towards Bella, who was happily shoving her nose into an oat bag.

'Ooh, I see. Well, you'll never be rich if you give away your fruit,' Rose said. 'Or if you eat it.'

'Let's say we want your valued custom. Once you've tasted our apples, you'll be sure to come back. Carlo calls it marketing. He's a real go-ahead.'

'How very sure you are.'

Before Lonnie could think of another clever reply, a snappily suited young gent, the last person in the world Lonnie wanted to see, all butterfly collar and starched cuffs, strolled towards the cart and tipped his hat to Rose. The toffs who did the Block were as elegantly dressed as the ladies. They wouldn't be seen dead without their top hats or their ebony and silver-finished canes.

'Thomas, how nice to see you.'

Glumly aware of his own worn trousers, brown waistcoat and workman's cap, Lonnie wished he could swipe the walking cane right out of Thomas Crick's hand and whack him hard over the head with it.

'Do try one of these delightful apples,' Rose chirped. 'They're crisp and fresh. By far the sweetest in Melbourne. You're allowed, it's marketing.'

Lonnie spat on an apple and slowly rubbed it into a shine on his sleeve before passing it to Crick. 'The lady's right, they're the best in town.'

Eyes brown as mud fixed coldly on Lonnie. 'I don't care to buy from street vendors.'

'Not even for me?' Rose asked.

Thomas scowled. With his white-gloved hand he picked another apple. 'This one.'

He glowered at Lonnie and Lonnie glowered back. 'That'll be sixpence.'

'A ridiculous price for one apple, McGuinness.'

Rose looked from one to the other in surprise. 'You two know each other?'

'The boy's a stable hand. Maybe not for long. We don't allow moonlighting. Can't afford to have the hired help too tired to put in a decent day's work.' He reluctantly handed over a sixpence.

Lonnie knew a threat when he heard one. So did Rose. 'Thomas, how very unfair,' she protested. 'Mr McGuinness is obviously only helping his friend out as a favour.' She looked anxiously at Carlo who was busy serving another customer, but was less than amused at the turn of events. Quarrels were not good for business.

Lonnie had never liked Crick and he liked him even less now that he was trying to humiliate him and move in on Rose. 'Even if I had three jobs, I could still do my work and ride as well as you, or as well as any other man.'

'Don't flatter yourself. Are you forgetting you're paid to muck out? You may ride fair for a trumped-up stableboy, but you don't compare with a true horseman.'

Rose looked shocked. 'Thomas, don't be so rude.'

Lonnie felt his anger rising. 'The only horse I've seen you win on is Lightning. Even a monkey could win on the back of a champion like him.'

'If you believe you're a better man than me, how about proving it in a real race?'

'Which race will that be then?'

'You're both so quarrelsome. I'm going,' snapped Rose to neither one in particular. 'Don't bother escorting me, Thomas, I shall take myself.' Without a second look at either, and although it wasn't raining, Rose unfurled her umbrella and walked off in a huff.

'A race you'd only know about if you could be trusted to keep your mouth shut,' Thomas said, once Rose was out of earshot. 'A heavily wagered race.'

Lonnie gave it some quick thought. It could only be the fixed one. 'I'm listening,' he said.

'There's a gentleman's race coming up shortly.'

'So I'm a gentleman now, am I?'

'I merely want to prove,' Crick hissed, 'that a monkey can ride better than you. So I'll be better than fair. You'll get a good mount to ride and I swear I'll still beat you. Let's see, I'm willing to put you on …' He paused for a moment as if he was contemplating a list of possible horses. 'How about Lightning? Then there'll be no doubt left as to who is the man and who is the ape.'

Lonnie knew full well from his conversation with Bookie Win that no jockey had yet been named for Lightning. 'So which horse are you riding?'

'I'll ride … let me see … I'll ride … Trident. He's never beaten Lightning so when I win that should convince you.'

'As simple as that, eh?'

'There is one condition.' Crick eyed him frostily.

*Surprise, surprise*, thought Lonnie. 'And what's that?'

'Like every contestant you'll have to place a ten pound entrance fee on yourself. Winner takes all.'

'As if I have ten pounds!'

'To prove how fair I'm being, I'll put it in for you, but if you lose you'll have to stay clear of Rose, do you understand?'

It gave Lonnie a smug satisfaction to think Crick considered him a threat. He couldn't let it pass. 'And if I win, will *you* promise to stay away from her?'

'Take it or leave it,' Crick snarled. 'If you agree, I may forget about telling my father about this moonlighting job. Still, with all these apple sales you won't have much need for a winner's purse.' He took a bite of the apple. 'Although I dare say you'd need to upgrade your selection of fruit from this inferior quality.'

Carlo was not known to react kindly to slights about his produce. Recognising his friend was ready to take a slog at Crick and being of a singular mind in this respect, Lonnie reluctantly shook hands over the deal.

Once Lonnie had agreed, and thinking he had the upper hand, Crick made an effort to be less snarly. 'The winner's purse is about seventy pounds, more than you've ever seen I imagine. It would put you on the way to buying yourself a horse. Could even snap one up like Trident for a hundred guineas or so.' Without another word he walked off.

No sooner had he left than Carlo blurted out, 'Are you mad? He's setting you up good and proper.'

'Don't I know it,' Lonnie answered.

'One more word from him and I would have flattened him. He had it coming.'

'He always has it coming,' Lonnie said. He got to thinking. 'So I'm on Lightning and Crick is riding Trident. According to Pearl, Lightning isn't going to win, which means I'm on a loser. Then again, if I did win we'd have more cash in hand than we make in a year. Set us up for life.'

Carlo wasn't so optimistic. 'Only if you win, mate. Besides Crick's not the only mug you've upset. Stop giving free apples away to the customers. You'll send me broke.' He held out his open hand. 'I reckon you need to square up for starters.'

'Do you realise how good it was to get one over on Crick for a change? His sixpence more than paid for Rose's apple and well you know it.'

Carlo grinned. 'So are you serious about coming in partnership with me? I'm not kidding you, mate.'

'I've always fancied life in a saddle, or else I definitely would. I'm afraid that'll have to do for now,' Lonnie told him as he threw an arm around his friend's shoulder. 'So mate, do ya reckon Rose Payne'll walk out with me?'

# PERFUME BOTTLE

## Item No. 4

*A single decorative container divided into two compartments, one for perfume, the other for smelling salts. Dutch blue glass with gold caps on either end. Purse size.*

Rose Payne was only going through the motions as she paraded the length of the covered arcades that ran off the main street. Like all the daughters of her father's friends, doing the Block was supposed to be her favourite pastime, but those two battling over a silly apple had gone and spoilt her day.

The way they both boasted like babies about their horsemanship was thoroughly irksome, each trying to outdo the other while stealing looks at her. Rose sighed at the thought of two suitors vying for her affections. Taking little notice of anything in particular, she stared vacantly into a bow-shaped window displaying its range of feathery bonnets and imagined being swept off her feet. She was sixteen, flirtatious and longing for a declaration of love.

It took her by surprise that Thomas Crick was not the one who came first to mind. It was that shock of ginger hair, that wicked curl of a lip, those green eyes flecked with tiny brown dares, the face full of mischief. It was how she had looked back into that bold stare from Mr McGuinness for longer than perhaps she should. How she felt his hand send a tremor along her arm when he so sweetly made a gift of the apple. A reckless rush of feeling at the possibilities washed over her until she could barely grab her breath. She leaned against the shop window to steady herself. Whatever was coming over her, when boys as rough as that stable hand or barrow boy, or whatever he was, succeeded in making her heart race so wildly? If only it had been a summer's day, she could blame the heat stroke.

From her purse she drew out a delicate glass bottle and breathed in the calming vapours. Once the world regained its colour and texture and she felt composed enough to take a turn, she made her way into Allen's Music Store. Browsing through the latest sheet music, but perhaps taking a few idle moments longer than she needed, her fingers came to a stop at a song called 'Narcissus'. She crossed her fingers in the hope it was not an omen.

Outside she found herself staring at a group of larrikins milling around the corner lamp post. Before they could send their catcalls and whistles her way, she turned stiffly and hurried off in the opposite direction. What if her father saw her talking to the likes of larrikins or barrow boys? What if Thomas mentioned Mr McGuinness when the Cricks came to call as they so often did? Her father would be wild with anger.

Anything Thomas said or did seemed to have her father's blessing. There was no doubting he was the preferred suitor. Rose knew her father only wanted the best for her. He wholeheartedly believed Thomas to be a fine, upstanding young man who was going places. Prospects were important, as he let her know often enough. The Paynes and the Cricks had land speculation deals in common and they both shared an interest in the sport of kings. All in all, Thomas Crick was her perfect match, at least in her father's eyes.

Rose thought she would like Thomas Wylie Crick much better if he had followed behind her when she left the apple cart. She wondered crossly where he could be. Only last Saturday they had enjoyed doing the Block together. He had romantically stolen her glove as they strolled through Royal Arcade, and she dared to imagine he kept it close by that night as he slept. Afterwards, they visited the book arcade and wandered alone around the fernery. They laughed together in the monkey house, sipped tea in the tearooms and smiled at their own reflections in a wall-sized mirror. How worldly and ardent he had seemed then, while today he had been downright ill-tempered. She looked behind her. Where was he?

Rose slowed down her pace, waiting to see if she

would be seized by a similar swoon, but romancing Thomas Crick in her imagination didn't make her heart beat any faster. She stopped by the nearest window display and contemplated the dress on show. It reminded her of a spring flower. It was a darling, made of silk in a deep shade of daffodil with white sweetheart rosebuds, flounced at the bustle and nipped tightly at the waist; it looked her very size. Instead of smelling salts she started thinking of the first Tuesday in November, which would see her attend the Melbourne Cup. She should really start thinking about having a dress made for the occasion.

'Miss Payne?'

'What are you doing here?' she asked tight-lipped, not bothering to turn around. 'I thought you were working.'

'Finished for the day. You recognised my voice?'

'Don't flatter yourself. I see your reflection in the window, Mr McGuinness. You don't happen to know where Mr Crick has gone, do you? I expected him to be escorting me this afternoon.'

'You told him not to. I heard you myself.'

'Stop teasing. Gentlemen never forget their manners.' She was immediately conscious that her prickly voice had pointed out the obvious for he coloured up like a strawberry patch. 'I daresay Thomas didn't mention where he was heading?' she asked more gently.

'No.'

'Why were the two of you goading each other back at the market?'

Lonnie thought it over for a moment or two before answering and convinced himself he wouldn't be telling Rose Payne anything she didn't already know. Since her father was such a good mate of the Cricks, she was bound to have heard something about the race.

'Oh, Crick is such a scoffer. Do you know, he's so desperate to prove he's a better horseman than me that he's willing to pay my entry fee for a race?'

'That sounds very generous to me. And he *is* a good horseman. No one can question that.'

Lonnie was more than a little put out. 'Well, I'm better! And I'm putting good money on myself to prove it. You should do the same.'

'Well then,' she said, smiling. 'I shall have a little bit each way on the *both* of you.'

Lonnie plucked up the courage to ask, 'I could walk you home if you like?'

She picked up the nervousness in his voice. Conscious of where she was and how it must look to others, she was reluctant to answer. What if someone should see them strolling the streets? It would be a costly thing to be seen out with the likes of McGuinness. What if her father found out? He already thought her capricious enough.

Boldly, Lonnie offered her his arm. 'Won't do you no harm.'

◈

Overlooking the same street, from a sweatshop where row after row of girls were making beautiful hats and dresses for the likes of the women doing the Block below, Daisy Cameron paused from the drudgery of her sewing treadle and gazed out the window.

Instantly she recognised the young man in workaday clothes standing in front of the shop opposite, speaking to a pretty, well-to-do girl.

'Well, well, Lonnie!' Daisy muttered. 'Here's how to make a fool of yourself.'

She watched the girl refuse his arm, hesitate, then turn back towards her friend and nod.

# JINGLE FROM A TAMBOURINE

## Item No. 7332

*Metal disc from the circular frame of a tambourine.*

Oompah! The Salvation Army brass band shrieked into action, their horns and bugles of glory waking up Little Lon and its surrounds. Amongst the good people inviting divine attention, Daisy fervently shook and jingled her tambourine for the Lord.

A window flew open outside the Big House. Madam Buckingham's voice roared out above the music. 'Pack it in, you yelling maniacs.' She spotted Daisy. 'Glory be girl, you making that racket, too? At least there'll be a bit of reasoning to be done then. Over here, I want a word.'

Daisy caught the eye of the solemn-faced Drum Major and swiftly exchanged her tambourine for his collection tin.

'See, I have no bones with the Army, but it's a problem you all being here at this particular time.' Madam Buckingham spoke in that contrary way she always did when addressing Daisy, with a tinge of kindness that bordered on annoyance. 'Sweetie, there's a matter of a few important parliamentary personages about to depart my fine establishment, who do not care to be recognised by the good Major over there. See if you can get the Army to move on, will you, pet? Quick smart, then you won't hold up the gentlemen any longer. They're running a bit late as it is.'

Daisy rattled the tin close to Madam's face in an action no one else, not even the Drum Major, would dare to do. 'But we've three more hymns to play.'

Madam Buckingham flashed her a wry smile and pushed four coins into the slit. 'This should hurry you along.'

'Or is it two hymns?' Daisy jiggled the tin a few more times.

The madam dropped in another coin. 'That's all you're getting, Daisy Cameron, or I'll tan your hide. Taking advantage of my own sweet heart, you are. Just like that scallywag friend of yours, disappearing without a word. If she thinks she can go back to Annie Walker without so much as a how's your father, then I don't know what the world is coming to. Tell that missy Pearl, if you see her, when I catch hold of her she's getting a what-for she won't forget in a long time.'

Daisy wondered what Madam Buckingham was going on about. When had Pearl gone back to work for Annie? A wave of guilt washed over her. She hadn't seen Pearl for days. Apart from searching her out that day with Lonnie, of late she was in no mind to be visiting anyone. There was always too much to do. As soon as the morning's Godly duties were over she would make the effort to find her.

Madam Buckingham may have stopped her tirade against Pearl, but she had unfinished business with the rest of the Salvation Army. 'Go beat those drums and rattle your tins elsewhere. There's many a rich sinner with deeper pockets asleep on Collins Hill or in Carlton. They're more in need of the Lord's good messages than the likes of us poor, penniless souls.'

Daisy smiled candidly at the madam's wickedness. 'I'll see what I can do about moving us along. I think we're running a bit short of time, anyhow. God bless you then.'

'And don't you go forgetting the silks and the gloves, mind. We'll be needing them soon. And tell Pearl she better be back quick smart. If it weren't for my little Ruby and the other girls, I don't know how I would manage to make ends meet.'

'The dresses are almost finished,' Daisy reassured her, doing her best not to set Madam off again.

'You're a cut above the rest,' Madam Buckingham called. 'I always knew you'd be fine; even if your mother was a thieving hussy and your father a drunken fool.'

The window slammed shut after this harsh, but truthful, reminder of her childhood. Daisy slipped away for a quick and quiet word with the Drum Major. After one resounding chorus of 'Onward, Christian Soldiers', God's army marched off in the capable hands of Jesus to wage war against evil in a different street.

# CRACKED SAUCER

## Item No. 1198

*Spoil heap.*
*Fragment.*
*Residue of wax.*
*At one time used as a candleholder.*

In the gloom of the cellar Pearl lay curled in a ball of misery, having abandoned her plan of escape. She spent her waking moments listening to the pitter-patter of a rat scratching behind the wall, expecting sometime soon the little feet would break through and crawl over her skin, the teeth gnash into her ear and gnaw her cheek, then she would share the fate of all those babbies who fell asleep in their cradles never to wake up again in this world. Her eyes remained shut tight, true to the notion that anything she could not see would not hurt her.

Hunger had given way to numbness. Her face felt sunken, as if the bones inside were turning to powder. She could only guess how many days she had been captive and wondered how long a body could remain alive with so little water or food or light. She only knew that soon she would become a ghost child. Well, it would serve Annie right if Pearl's lingering spirit scared her half to death.

When her prison door scraped open one more time, she blinked and raised an involuntary arm towards the square space of light above. From an upturned bucket a torrent of icy water splashed over her, plastering Pearl's stringy hair to her head, the wet seeming to seep through her skin and form ice crystals on her insides. She felt her body shake from the cold. The thirst had overcome her so heavily she sucked at the hair ends, greedily licking the liquid from her hands and arms like the animal she had become.

'Look at the state of yer, filthy vixen, stinking like a wheel of mice,' Annie hissed. 'Clean yerself up.'

It was true. Pearl could smell her own skin, stinking foul from neglect and fear. Thinking that Annie meant her to climb out, she strained to stand upright. Her limbs had stiffened, almost set into rigor mortis. She forced her upper body to reach towards the opening and painfully eased her head and shoulders through the small hole. She blinked again, this time forcing her eyes to accustom themselves to the light, dim as it was. The room that came into focus was small and one Pearl recognised.

Across its timber floor she made out the glow of a clay pipe. A man on a makeshift bed of newspapers and old clothes sprawled close by, his hand twitching in a fitful sleep.

Annie's attention also turned to the groggy man. 'What've I told yer about smoking in that state, stupid old fool. Yer'll burn the place down.' She picked up the pipe and kicked the man hard in the ribs. Blacked out to the pain, he moaned and turned over.

Annie's voice ripped Pearl out of her stupor. 'Where do you think you're off to?' She pushed a foot hard against Pearl's shoulder and sent her hurtling back down into the hole.

Pearl screamed as she fell backwards, the desperate voice of a stranger, no longer recognisable as her own.

'Get a load of this, Lolly.' A blubbery girl, with rouge so plastered it could have been slapped on by a brickie's trowel, slouched sullenly alongside Annie, who pinched her on the shoulder and snarled. 'See what happens to girls who don't do as I say?'

Annie had more menacing words for Pearl. 'Stop yer squawking, yer rattling bag of bones. Yer only good enough for the likes of Slasher, because yer don't do as yer told.' Without a further word of warning she spat on Pearl, then let the trapdoor slam down.

Left alone, Pearl's body took on a dreadful, involuntary life of its own, her limbs shaking as if she had caught the typhoid. Surely to become a ghost child wouldn't be so bad, once the darkness took over completely. She felt detached from her body, a colourless wisp of air.

From beyond the exterior wall came a faint noise, a slight suggestion of music, enough to coax Pearl away from these morbid wonderings. She concentrated on the beat of the Oompah. As it became a little louder, she could make out the ring and clashing of the Sally Army. Hadn't Daisy been teaching her this same salvation song? She jostled her memory for the words 'Onward, Christian Soldiers, marching as to war, with the cross of Jesus … coming down before …' *No*, she thought, *that isn't right, I should have paid more attention*. Annie's voice filled her mind, *Yer a muddling slag, a smut of soot*.

A single tear spilled from her eye. If it was the works of her mind gone insane, well, it would be understandable. After all, she had suffered so miserably of late and couldn't be blamed for losing her wits. But what if the sound was a sign that Daisy was coming to find her? Daisy who was always kind to her, the way she always was with everyone. To be with Daisy would be safe. Daisy was good and kind and generous. Not scampish and wayward the way Pearl had turned out. Not stinking vermin. Pearl didn't do what she was told. Pearl was only good enough for Slasher. That's why Madam Buckingham was so good to Daisy, but wouldn't help her. Madam knew Daisy was an angel and Pearl was wilful. Daisy could reserve a place in heaven. Pearl had nowhere.

She strained to hear the Sally's song of prayer. Could she dare to hope that sweet, kind Daisy was leading an army of God's angels to save her?

A feeble shaft of filtered light crept through the gaps between the trapdoor and the floor joists, directing her attention to a cluster of objects which, obscured by dust up until now, had gone unnoticed. For the first time since her capture, the light was shining upon this particular spot, illuminating these remnants of someone's earlier stay.

The music of the Army softened. The band passed by. Pearl realised she would not be liberated this time by her angel from God. But neither would she become a ghost child. For a fragment of candle stuck to a saucer with wax was lit up by the light as if itself were burning. Two matchsticks left there could be no less than a sign. It was an eerie feeling to rise from the dead. She was convinced there and then that an angel must have been sent to lighten her troubles.

A sense of hope filled her, warm and soothing. Yes, she might remain at Annie's mercy, probably she would die soon, but she would have some respite from the dark and the rodents until then. She struck the two match heads together and prayed the way Daisy did, asking for a swift deliverance, a good feed before it came, and the most fervent request of all: that Annie Walker lose her footing over a cesspit, topple down senseless and be left to rot in the bog forever.

# HORSE BRASS

## Item No. 5439

*Brass ornamentation worn on a horse's harness.*

Over in the office at the Golden Acres stud farm, Thomas Crick stood pleading with his father over the plan to let Lonnie McGuinness ride in the upcoming street race. 'That impertinent stableboy called me an ape. He needs teaching a lesson. How dare he compare himself with me or the other jockeys? You have to consent to him riding Lightning.' For the umpteenth time that week he tried to make his point. His father must see it was a matter of pride.

'Have you lost your mind?' Crick said to his son. 'If anyone'll be able to tell there's something fishy going on, it'll be McGuinness.'

It wasn't proving easy to convince his father, but Thomas wouldn't be silenced. 'It's clear as day. When Lightning gets beaten in the race, everyone will be suspicious of us because we've made such heavy bets against it. But if we put McGuinness on Lightning we can blame its defeat on his bad riding. All we have to say is we put money on Trident because we knew McGuinness wasn't good enough. Our plan's infallible.'

As his father considered this new point Thomas realised he was wavering, which prompted him to advance the argument even further. 'We'd look even better if we say that we were trying to do those Little Lon scum a favour by letting one of their own ride the best horse in Melbourne. Think of the publicity for Golden Acres. You could even fix it so that the story gets covered by the *Argus.* He drew the headline in the air: 'Lightning luck for a Little Lon lad. We'd sure look good, helping out the poor unfortunates.'

'The *Argus*? Are you a complete lunatic? This is an illegal race! We can't go admitting our horses are in it.' Mr Crick paused. 'But your idea is basically sound. 'Course it'd have to be done by word of mouth. Only rumours mind you, nothing official.'

Thomas could see from his father's expression that he was at last winning the argument. 'It's a perfect ruse, Father. Explains why I'm not riding Lightning. We just let slip about my bet with McGuinness and how, through the kindness of my heart, I'm letting him ride the "best" horse. Trust me, it'll work, I know it will.'

'Just make sure you win.'

With his father's permission, Thomas immediately sent a message to Bookie Win to change the details on the list of runners and riders. Lonnie McGuinness was to be added to the betting sheet as the rider for Lightning.

# PADLOCK

## Item No. 7765

*Heavy metal lock.*

Lonnie arrived early for work with only one thing in mind for the day, to search out Lightning and Trident and check them over. Soon the whole place would be crawling with trainers and jockeys. A quick inspection confirmed the horses weren't in their usual stables. He tried to think where he might hide them if it was he who was going to mess with one or both.

He strode across the soft mud ditches, systematically checking every outer building on the property. He liked the mud. Liked where the ground fell in when his boot marked the earth, mixing with the tracks of the other riders and the scores of horseshoe prints that were stamped everywhere.

A magpie warbled from the corrugated iron roof of a stable that was used nowadays to stack hay bales. Its mate landed and joined in the rowdy hoohah. They were plucky black and whites. Clever, too. Lonnie looked sharp in case they swooped.

A further inspection revealed a brand new, heavy-duty, iron lock fitted to the doors of the old stable.

He gave it a swift rattle but it held firm. The wind blew straight through the gap in the timbers. He peered through. The fresh smell of horses hit him. The semi-darkness of the interior made it difficult for him to determine exactly what was inside. But his ears singled out a frisk of movement, the rustle of straw, an intake of steamy breath.

A gruff voice roared from behind. 'What're you doin' here so early, McGuinness? You're not supposed to be startin' yet.' The stable foreman was a Neanderthal of a man, thickset with forearms not unlike Lonnie's own thighs and hands like shovels.

He needed a good excuse and fast. 'Aren't I supposed to be riding Lightning or Trident at track work? Only I can't find them in their stables.'

'Well, you won't find 'em here. Go muck out until you're called,' the foreman growled, shooting him a fierce warning glare. He pushed a pitchfork into Lonnie's hand. 'Be quick 'bout it, you're not paid to stand 'round doin' nuffing.' Lonnie sauntered away, much too slowly for the foreman's liking. 'Move yourself, lad,' he grumbled.

Lonnie picked up pace, pretending to head away. When he felt he was out of sight he backtracked, this time determined to see what was inside the old stable. If he'd guessed rightly, he already knew what he would find.

He snuck down the side of the old stable to survey the whereabouts of the foreman. He was still there, seated upon a water barrel with his back to Lonnie, guarding the padlocked door like a sentry.

Hastily Lonnie withdrew, nearly tripping over a rickety wooden ladder which lay almost buried in long grass. He was lucky not to cause a ruckus and have the foreman come running.

# EPAULETTE

## Item No. 1841

*Ornamental shoulder piece
of the type worn by a Russian military officer.*

There was no better place to be on a Saturday evening than the Eastern Market. Lonnie was feeling mighty pleased with himself that Rose had agreed to walk out with him. He could barely fathom her sudden change of mind the day he'd strolled home with her. Must have laid on his charms better than he thought. He felt like tonight was going to be a splendid affair, one of the best outings he'd ever have. He was dressed like a dandy in a yellow waistcoat and scarf, a hat cocked over one temple. Carlo's one set of good clothes fitted Lonnie like a glove.

Rose was catching everyone's eye. She was a classy girl all right in her silk dress and blue hat. Everything matched. Even her eyes were blue-bright and sparkling. Three dark curls tumbled over her forehead. When Lonnie handed her a posy of pineapple sage and grandma's bonnet tied around with ribbon she gave him such a smile. For the first time in his life, he told himself, he had a sweetheart.

Light rain was falling, so the pair took shelter under the canvas awnings. Overhead, a dozen of the newest electric lamps spluttered out a haze of evening light. The wail of dogs and other animals mixed in with the hum of voices around them: Moon, the Syrian seller, his lips coated with sticky sugar, spruiking his Turkey Lolly; the mission preacher standing on his soapbox and yelling out a message of damnation and hellfire; and what Lonnie liked best of all, the loud good-natured din of the crowd.

They ventured through the archway towards the flower stall, which burst with the sickly sweetness of yellow jonquils and pink carnations. Rose breathed in the heady fragrance as it laced the chill night air. The stall took up one full corner, a wooden sign swinging the dealer's name back and forth: Gilbert Smale, Flower Seller.

Catching sight of a pair of lovebirds offered for sale on the neighbouring stall, Rose said excitedly, 'Do buy them Lonnie. Then we'll set them free.'

Trust a girl to become all soppy. Still, he wished he could oblige Rose if only to impress her, but he didn't have the money. 'Over here,' he said, steering her away, 'come see the shooting gallery.'

At a canvas-covered booth a band of young lads pretended they were on the battlefield. They took aim at the large belly of a wooden Russian soldier. A hail of shots rang out at the target and the riflemen moved on, having happily saved their country from the Russians for the cost of a halfpenny a shot.

Rose was keener to watch the Punch and Judy show. 'Father has never allowed me to come here,' she said in wonderment, as the puppets battered each other mercilessly with clubs and chairs, while the children cheered them on with squeals and jeers. Rose looked giddy and light-hearted. Her eyes sparkled with the thrill of the evening.

She had never before in her life dared to venture into the notorious Eastern Market, scared off by her father's threat of lice lurking in the shadows of the floor straw and sawdust, ever waiting to march upwards under her dress. As a child, she'd had nightmares of the lice soldiering their way along her legs. Worse was the menace of catching scabby blisters and sores from the slum dwellers who brushed past.

Startled by these curdling thoughts, she scanned the faces in the crowd and, just to prove her point, settled on a lad watching the puppets. In the corner of his mouth was a sore, bloated with pus. When he moved on, Rose saw he had a limp. In turn he spotted Rose staring open-mouthed as he plopped up and down, nearly stepping straight out of his oversized boots. He grinned cheekily back at her and poked out his pale tongue.

Rose averted her eyes, repulsed by the sight of him. Her heart beat a little flustery and she wondered if she were about to swoon. No, she vowed, she wasn't going to let some bothersome ill-bred child blow over her like a cold wind. Not tonight when this was her one and only chance to experience a different, lesser side of life. Until this moment it hadn't fully hit home that Lonnie was one of these simple and backward people. She took another look around her, relieved to see no one she knew.

Lonnie misread the changing expressions on Rose's face. Deceived or not, all he could absorb was her admiration, which filled him with pleasure. Here with Rose it was easy to believe they were indeed a couple.

'What stall would you run if you had a chance?' he asked.

She didn't answer immediately. Lonnie stroked the faint auburn tuft of hair on his chin, wishing it would hurry up and thicken, mark him more as a man. He remembered his outing with Daisy and decided to put it to good use. 'Okay, I'll start,' he volunteered hopefully. 'What about a lumps and bumps stall where you can change character? You know, "Come right up, find the right bump!" Then get hit on the head with a hammer. Make the bell ring.'

Rose seemed genuinely impressed. 'How clever! Test the phrenological hammer. You could say something like, "Want to be more like Mr McCubbin or Mr Streeton or Mr Roberts?" and then knock them on the head with the hammer on the right bump for Artistic Temperament. I love it!'

'McWho?' asked Lonnie, wondering what she was rabbiting on about.

There was a polite silence. Finally she replied, 'You know … the cigar-box lids.'

Lonnie looked as blank as a sheet of white notepaper.

'"One hundred and eighty-two small panels painted on cigar-box lids"? Their "nine by five" exhibition in eighty-nine? Mr Frederick McCubbin? *A Bush Burial*? "Like a little poem without words"? You must have heard speak of our famous artists?' Rose waited for him to acknowledge the Impressionists whose work had been taking Melbourne by storm these past few years. Her father had just added two paintings from the Heidelberg school of artists to his collection and was keen to purchase a Roberts.

Lonnie shrugged. 'Never heard of anything like that. I was only thinking of Postlethwaite's shopfront.'

A look of realisation crossed Rose's face.

This serious about-turn in her mood was not in Lonnie's plan. He hastily set about to remedy it. 'Are you up for some fun?'

'What sort of fun?'

'We could take a glass at the skittle saloon.'

Rose eyes widened in horror. 'Father says the skittle saloon is built on the foundations of a leper hospital. I'm never to go near it.'

'There aren't no lepers there.'

A scowl swept her face. She shook her head.

'We could stop by the coffee stall for a cuppa and a bite o' plum duff,' he offered.

'I won't drink from those filthy cups. Father says they rinse them in the open drains.'

Rose's withering look told Lonnie that no decent lady would even mention what they contained. He only ever thought fondly of the coffee stall outside the market, with its huge boiler, shining brass nozzle and spout. How it kept the water piping hot on a pan of charcoal. How much he enjoyed stopping off to drink the steaming coffee from those thick heavy cups. And if you were early enough, grab one of the plum puddings or Chelsea buns, although he wasn't as partial to the buns – the currants always reminded him of dead flies.

'Flies' graveyards,' he found himself commenting out loud.

'What do you mean?'

'Them buns.'

At the suggestion Rose threw out her lower lip in a childish sulk.

Lonnie was at a loss to know why she disapproved of everything he said. Self-conscious to the bootstraps, he mentally prepared for his next move. *Keep her entertained*, a little voice inside barked.

'How about I take ya somewhere you've never been?'

'Where?'

Not willing to chance another rebuff, he said,

'Wait and see. If you're game.'

Rose stared him steadily in the eye. She had never felt so daring in her life. Marvelling at her own bravado, considering she already risked disease by being here in the first place, she said, 'Of course, I'm game.'

Deep down she knew she was being her father's 'capricious little girl'. She crossed her fingers and fervently hoped she would not come to regret the decision.

# PIECE OF BENT WIRE

## Item No. 1035

*Oddly shaped wire.*
*Strong.*
*Opinion is divided on its use.*

Melbourne was located too close to the South Pole for all but the most adventurous traveller. After the gold boom a few decades earlier, the town had grown into itself marvellously. Buildings were draped in filigree and clambered skywards, crying out for recognition. On the central corner, the Australian Building was the tallest in town, boasting its twelve storeys northwards to the boulevards of Paris and London, aspiring to be equal to any place there. Come one, come all!

Lonnie led Rose along a dimly lit laneway towards the much plainer rear entrance to this gigantic building. The shop windows on the ground floor were barred and shuttered, while the upper floors with their multitude of offices were abandoned for the night. Apart from the clattering of a hansom cab around the corner, the place was silent. Deaf and dumb. Deserted. Lonnie removed a piece of oddly bent wire from his jacket and nimbly released the tumblers on the lock securing the oak door, the way he had done a few times in the past. He slipped in through the opening and pulled Rose inside.

She wrenched her hand away and swallowed nervously. 'Are you mad? This is burglary.'

'We're not here to thieve anything. Only to play the lift.'

'Do you think I've never ridden a lift before?' She surveyed him with a cold stare.

'But have you ridden one in the tallest building?'

'No.'

'Ever been in a lift that works without cables?'

'No.' Rose turned away as if she couldn't bear to look at him. She waited a moment before speaking again. 'Well, is it safe?'

Lonnie was becoming desperate to impress her. 'Safest in the world, so they say. The latest hydraulic engineering. A steel ram pushing up and down.'

'Don't be a bore,' she said imperiously. 'Show me the view from the top and then let's get out of here.'

Before she could change her mind, Lonnie rushed forward. 'Come on then.'

As the decent-sized lift rattled upwards, taking them to dizzying heights, the Glass and Bottle Gang prowling the streets below discovered the open rear door of the building.

Lonnie drew Rose closer and gingerly placed his arm around her waist.

She pushed him away. 'We really shouldn't be here.'

Nothing was going to plan. Rose was acting all snaky. She should have been swooning in his arms by now; the way Pearl did when she wanted to practise falling into the arms of her clients and Lonnie was ordered to catch her so she wouldn't fall to the ground. He wondered if he had gone too far. After all, Rose wasn't like Pearl. He set the lift in a downward motion, hurt by her rejection but determined to do the respectful thing. 'No worries. We'll leave right now if you want.'

Silently the gang filed in, darting into the darkened corners as soon as they heard the lift descend, more than ready to meet the nightwatchman doing his rounds.

As the lift settled onto the ground floor, Lonnie sensed Rose and he were no longer alone in the building. Slowly, he eased open the cast-iron gate. Turning to Rose, he whispered, 'Stay there,' and heard her gasp.

A hand on the other side blocked Lonnie's exit. Billy Bottle leered through the grill at Rose. 'So, McGuinness,' he said. 'Who's your scrag?'

'Leave her be.'

'Or else?'

Billy was the sort who did not think twice about

smashing a bottle then thrusting it full into a man's face.

'I'm warning you,' Lonnie said. So far he had avoided a bottling, but didn't fancy his chances the way things were going. He clenched his fist, bracing to thump the gang leader.

'What ya going to do, eh?' Billy turned to his Glass and Bottles who were yelping around behind him like a pack of bulldogs. 'We know a threat when we hear one, don't we, lads?' The rest of the gang was eager to join in. From their point of view, nine onto one made a fair fight.

Lonnie's bravery was short-lived. He was no match for the burly larrikin, who sent a huge set of knuckles crashing into his cheek. He sprawled down onto the lift floor. Billy continued with his jibes. 'Caught you cold did I, McGuinness?' With one rough hand the gang leader grabbed Rose's waist, slipped the other into the neckline of her dress and ripped off a button. He moved his fingers suggestively along the open seam. 'Soak up this bit of silk,' he said, letting out a whistle as he pretended to feel the cut of the material. He jerked her towards him to the lip-smacking catcalls of his mates. 'Give us a kiss then, sweetheart.'

Still groggy from the punch, Lonnie caught her terrified scream.

'Think I'll give her a lesson in not playing so hard to get, hey, lads?'

Two glass buttons fell to the floor, exposing Rose's pale vanilla throat. Billy's dirty fingernails worked their way up and across her mouth.

For one fleeting moment, Rose Payne became a box of fireworks and resisted for all she was worth. Billy let out a yelp and sprang back. He checked the bite on his hand. With a smirk, he licked up a smear of blood and wiped his hand down his belly. 'Maybe she'll have more fun if you're not around,' he said, ordering one of the gang to take Lonnie back up the twelve storeys.

Lonnie attempted to stand, but his legs gave way. As a last resort he jammed one foot in the way of the gate, struggling with all his might to hold it back.

Billy fought against him to slam it shut. 'You're a cocky little runt, aren't you?'

Out of nowhere came a rush of feet. The foyer of the Australian Building was suddenly packed with angry young men and their unfinished business.

A familiar voice called out, 'You know how to pick your weight, Billy Bottle.' The words swirled around Lonnie like a spinning top. The Push, who had been tracking the Glass and Bottles all evening, had been waiting for a chance to pounce. This was even better; to catch their rivals unprepared and outnumbered as indeed they were. George Swiggins pulled out a brass knuckle from his pocket, spat and shined it on his well-tailored suit. 'Beating up on little girls now, are we?'

The rival gangs squared up to one another.

Billy never shirked a fight. 'Looks like we're set for a fine time tonight, lads.'

Rose broke away. To the sound of smashing bottles, she scrambled over to Lonnie. He managed to drag himself to his feet. They linked hands and struggled past the brawling men who were battering and pounding each other, and taking much delight in the blood sport.

As soon as they were out of immediate danger, in a darkened doorway across the road, Rose jerked her hand away. 'I hate you. I hate you,' she screamed in a voice shrill with hysteria. 'How could you?'

'I never meant to put you in so much danger,' Lonnie protested feebly.

'Well, you did,' she snapped back. Rose calmed down enough to notice the blood streaming from Lonnie's nose. 'You're bleeding.'

'I'm okay,' he said, 'it's nothing.'

Rose gave a great gulp. She seemed to have lost her earlier fire and tugged vainly at her dress in an effort to cover up. 'It's ruined. That man, he was … he was going to … I was supposed to be playing piano for father's guests tonight … I lied, made an excuse to be late … I hate this place. Please take me home.'

Lonnie knew he must make amends. He took off his jacket and placed it awkwardly around her shoulders. 'Sorry, Rose, I should never have brought you here in the first place.'

She shoved his hand away.

Across the street Lonnie caught sight of a nightwatchman running at full speed in the direction of the police station. He must have seen them leaving the building, or heard the commotion coming from inside. The law was only minutes away.

'Look, I promise I will take you home, but first I need to warn George.'

'Don't go in there again,' she begged. 'Don't leave me alone for the sake of that scum.'

'That *scum* as you call them,' he found himself saying without apology, 'are the people I have to live with everyday. George saved you and me from a beating, maybe worse. We owe him. Believe it or not, we mugs from Little Lon do try to help each other. Keep out of sight. I'll be back in no time.'

Lonnie made his way into the foyer, dodging flying fists and pieces of broken glass. George was about to pile drive Billy's head into a solid counter. The sound of bone crunching against the timber sickened Lonnie in the gut. More than enough to knock any man unconscious, but Billy was a hard head, already trying to clamber back to his feet.

Lonnie raced up behind George and placed a hand on his shoulder, intent on warning him the Law was almost upon them. Expecting the hand-on-the-shoulder, fist-in-the-face move, George turned around swinging.

'Stop! Stop! It's me.'

George pulled his punch and grinned down at Lonnie. 'Thought you'd be long gone.'

'You gotta get out,' Lonnie warned. 'I've seen the watchman heading for the station.'

'Scramble,' George called, immediately ordering his men out.

'Had enough, have ya?' the swaying Billy yelled, unaware of the latest state of affairs. George and his gang fled via the back door, wedging a piece of timber beneath it, leaving the Glass and Bottle Gang locked in to await the law.

'Let's see 'em get out of that one,' George jeered. He winked over at Lonnie. 'Owe you one, mate. Nice bit of skirt by the way.'

The Push scattered in all directions.

Rose hunched against Lonnie, still sniffling, her face hidden against his chest as they approached the much darker lanes leading to Little Lon. Suddenly realising where they were, she pulled away from him. Her eyes were swollen. She raised her chin defiantly. 'You don't expect me to walk down here, do you?'

'You have to clean up before I take you home.' Not that Lonnie had clearly thought about how to deal with Rose when he got her to Casselden Place, or what his mam would say as he led her through the door.

She shook her head. 'Father says there are great

pits underneath Little Lon that swallow up young ladies.'

'Your father tells you a load of tripe!' he snapped. 'I know many a decent kind-hearted girl living here.' Daisy for one. Which gave him an idea. Rather than take Rose to his mam's, he decided to take her to the Leitrim where he would have a lot less explaining to do.

Rose continued her rambling, as if he hadn't uttered a word. 'And thieves and murderers who are captured and taken to be hanged at the gaol, their restless spirits left to wander through these dingy, nasty streets.' Her brow furrowed. She gave a violent shudder and went deathly quiet.

# SEWING BOBBIN

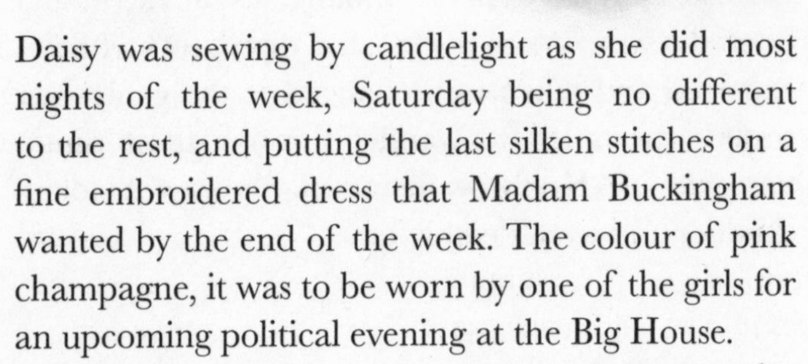

## Item No. 1446

*Wooden.*
*For silk thread.*

Daisy was sewing by candlelight as she did most nights of the week, Saturday being no different to the rest, and putting the last silken stitches on a fine embroidered dress that Madam Buckingham wanted by the end of the week. The colour of pink champagne, it was to be worn by one of the girls for an upcoming political evening at the Big House.

An urgent knocking at her door made her wonder if this was Pearl on a visit. It wouldn't be the first time at such a late hour. She recollected with a shock how long it had been since she'd seen her. Life was too busy these days and time had slipped away.

She certainly hadn't expected to see Lonnie standing bloody-faced in the doorway. 'Whatever's happened?' she asked.

At first, the girl accompanying him with her puffy, cried-out eyes, torn dress and dishevelled bonnet was barely recognisable as the pretty girl she'd seen with Lonnie outside the dress shop. With great concern, Daisy drew her into the warmth. At least the fire was still alight and the place cosy enough. It occurred to her the girl had probably never set foot inside a public house.

The Leitrim Hotel boasted nine rooms in its boarding house section, most hardly bigger than a closet, but Daisy had called it home for the past few years. She had made her small room pleasant enough. A sumptuous quilt, looped together by silken thread, velvety ribbons and braid, enveloped the bed in squares of violet and blazing red, leftovers from the many dresses she had sewn for Madam's girls. On the side table burned a collection of candle ends. Impish shadows danced over the walls. Several pairs of gloves were strewn across the button box, their newly attached beads gleaming like dewdrops in the light. If not for the open Bible, you could easily have forgotten this was the room of a devout follower.

Daisy made the girl comfortable in her only chair. She offered her a sup of broth from the hearth pot, passably warm and flavoured with beef bones and green cabbage. 'Put some strength into you. Breathe steady, love,' she said, willingly giving up tomorrow's dinner.

The girl pushed her hand away, having none of it. She didn't say a word. Daisy waited for an explanation from Lonnie.

'The Glass and Bottle Gang attacked us,' he said.

'What were you doing mixing company with the likes of them?'

'They found *us*,' Lonnie replied.

Daisy turned to the girl. 'Are you badly hurt, love?'

Rose refused to be drawn out of her misery. She stared glumly into the fire as if she'd been struck dumb.

'I think she's gone into shock,' said Lonnie, snapping his fingers in front of her face.

'They didn't harm her, did they?'

'Depends what you mean. Billy manhandled her a bit.'

'That's more than enough,' commented Daisy. 'Poor thing.'

'She'll need to clean up before I see her home. Can she borrow a dress?'

Daisy hesitated. Her only other decent dress, the brown linen one, was starched and pressed, but she felt too embarrassed to offer it. The young lady was far too refined. Then there was her Salvation Army suit, but she had to keep that for mission work. Daisy made a quick decision and ushered Lonnie through the door into the hallway. 'Be a gentleman then. She doesn't want you ogling her while she cleans up.'

Shortly afterwards came the call, 'You can come in now.'

Daisy was combing through the girl's thick dark hair. Rose was wearing the silk dress Daisy had been so carefully finishing off when they arrived. Frills cascaded from her waist like feathery fern fronds. The neckline, a little more revealing than she would decently wear, was embroidered in a chain of scarlet roses and revealed a pink scratch, the only noticeable sign of the attack. As Daisy made the final touches, pinning Rose's hair back tight from her face and tucking it inside her bonnet, Lonnie contemplated this tender picture. Rose was the most beautiful vision of a girl he had ever seen.

Daisy, fully aware of the meaning in his look, covered the girl's shoulders and throat with a shawl. 'Make sure she keeps wrapped against the cold.'

Lonnie nodded. 'Has she said anything yet?'

'Not a word.'

Daisy picked up a fragment of cotton fabric from her sewing box, dipped it in the washbowl and dabbed Lonnie's blood-crusted nose. 'I hope it's not broken.'

Lonnie brushed the comment aside, trying to be brave. 'It's nothing. Billy Bottle punches like a pussy.'

'I've a good mind to go and give Francis Todd a telling off. Thinking a change of name and a piece of broken glass gives you the right to terrorise every poor living soul.' Daisy whispered a string of orders to Lonnie. 'Once she's tucked up in her own bed, things won't seem so bad. Go settle her and don't leave until you've made sure she's safe. Will you promise not to let the dress be damaged? I need it returned quickly, please don't let me down.'

The silent girl showed no sign of gratitude. It was up to Lonnie to thank Daisy for her help and understanding. 'I'm sure when she's feeling better, she'll thank you herself. I'll see you soon.'

'You still haven't told me who she is.'

'Rose. She's Rose Payne.'

Daisy's mouth fell open as she looked from one to the other. 'God help us,' she spluttered. 'Whatever were you thinking? You'll be the death of us all.'

# BOTTLE

## Item No. 23

*Old soda or lemonade bottle.*

Not far away at around the same time, positive she had broken Pearl's spirit and certain the reptile would do exactly as she was told from now on, Annie Walker hoisted the weakened girl through the trapdoor, freeing her at last from the cramped space beneath the floor. 'See, there's nobody else out there who came to help, yer scabby tart. I'm the only one.'

Pearl's eyes stung with the light. Annie flung her a drink of dirty water, in an even dirtier bottle. Blind to the wrigglers squirming around the bottom, Pearl guzzled the liquid down her parched throat.

There remained one more punishment and humiliation in store. 'Slasher wants yer and he's impatient, so better show some gratitude. Consider yerself lucky he still likes that ugly face of yours, or he would've cut it from ear to ear.' She traced a fingernail sharp as a knife edge along Pearl's throat. 'Get cleaned up, yer ungrateful little slut. And don't forget who yer working for.'

Pearl's face set hard. Her physical freedom had

made her no less a prisoner to Annie. She was still trapped, as surely as if she remained locked in the cellar. She pulled herself together as best as she could and stumbled off to follow orders.

# FRAGMENT OF WASHBOWL

## Item No. 6531

*White and maroon earthenware made for everyday use. Staffordshire. From set of bowl and pitcher.*

With great commotion, her spectacles tipped cock-eye on her nose, Madam Buckingham charged through the door of number four Casselden Place and into the adjoining bedroom to find Pearl hunched over a washbowl of tepid brown water. 'You dirty mongrel. You dark horse.' A solid blow sent Pearl, along with a chunk of tar soap, hurtling to the floor. 'Seen fit to come back at last have you? My girls've been worked off their feet. If it wasn't for our Ruby stepping in and doing double shifts, we'd be in all sorts of bother.'

Her eyes narrowed. 'Look at the state of you, stinking like a cesspit. What you been doing then?' She didn't wait for an answer. 'I'll tell you where you've been – duck-shoving for that queen of scum!'

She delivered another mighty cuff to Pearl's ear. 'Or am I paying you so much money you're having a holiday? Doing the Block, ooh-la-la, skedaddling around Collins Hill!' She embellished every reprimand with a hard poke, a push, a slap. 'Scarpering for so long. Selfish and spoilt.'

Pearl covered her eyes and face to protect against the blows.

'Stop playing the high and mighty with me, you little cobbler, or else I'll give you a shearing you'll never forget,' the madam snapped. 'Mark my words, you're going to make up every missed bit of time. You can work every patch until you drop. The Big House within the hour. Then your spot at the Governor Burke. Finish outside the Princess.' She wrenched Pearl's hand away and pinched her on the cheek, squeezing hard. 'Fix yourself up. You look like the walking dead. No one wants a bag of bones with a pallor as grey as a tomb! Put a bit of colour on your face.'

With a start, Madam Buckingham visibly reined herself in before she did any more damage to Pearl. She wrenched her raging bushfire temper under control, almost as if someone had suddenly doused her flames. She fanned herself, sticky with sweat. 'There, you're looking better already. I'm mighty sick of it, my girl. You've been nothing but trouble for me. If I'd done a runner in my time, I would've had the hide beaten off me. Think yourself lucky I'm growing soft in my old age.' Abruptly she stormed off, the whole episode over in a flash.

The prospect of working for both madams, the

heaviness of her situation, came over Pearl like a blinding migraine. She was conscious of only one thing, to pay off Annie Walker. Maybe in time, with a little put aside, she could walk out of town over the Yarra bridge, away from the lot of them.

She wrung out the washcloth and sponged down her arm, repeating the motion over and over again, but the smell of her captivity and the hands of Slasher Jack clung to her like the odour of a rotting corpse.

# GOLDEN GUINEA

## Item No. 772

*Spoil heap – location unknown.*
*An unusual find in Little Lon.*
*Most likely dropped by one*
*of the wealthier patrons*
*who visited the area.*

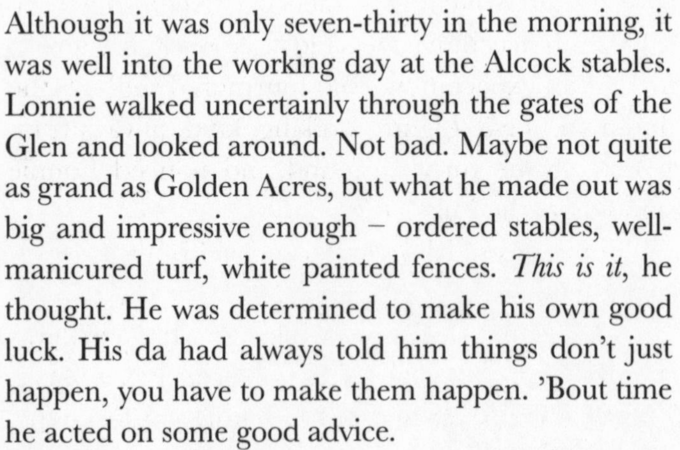

Although it was only seven-thirty in the morning, it was well into the working day at the Alcock stables. Lonnie walked uncertainly through the gates of the Glen and looked around. Not bad. Maybe not quite as grand as Golden Acres, but what he made out was big and impressive enough – ordered stables, well-manicured turf, white painted fences. *This is it*, he thought. He was determined to make his own good luck. His da had always told him things don't just happen, you have to make them happen. 'Bout time he acted on some good advice.

He crunched his way down the pebbly driveway towards a well-designed building. A right royal house for the gaffers, or for Mr Alcock himself by the size of it. Its many windows were catching the sunrise. As he approached the place he spied several Lonnies walking along in the pinkish reflections and took the chance to flex his muscles. *Still a weedy little carrot top*, he thought grimly.

A yardman walked over to him. 'What's your business?'

'Lonnie McGuinness. I'm after Mr Alcock.'

'Maybe I can help.'

'He asked me to call over – well, his foreman did.'

The man steered Lonnie in the direction of a nearby yard where the Glen foreman was attempting to saddle an unbroken horse. Lonnie placed his hands on the fence rail and accidentally knocked off a golden guinea, which fell to his feet. He bent and picked it up, watching in silence as Ned coaxed the horse into accepting the saddle. No easy feat for so foreign an expectation. Ned murmured softly to the unsettled horse. Lightly stroking, kind, always firm. Eventually he turned around and noticed Lonnie standing at the rails.

Lonnie cleared his throat and held out an open hand. 'Did you lose this, sir?'

'No, I didn't. But only a while ago Mr Alcock was standing there when he sold a horse for sixty guineas. I'm sure he'll soon find out he's only got fifty-nine. Thanks for your honesty.'

Lonnie hadn't even had a second thought about returning the coin to these good people. Had he picked it up at Golden Acres, it may have been a different story. He looked towards the horse. 'I reckon you've gained its confidence.'

'I have lad,' Ned said. 'But you've taken your time coming here. I thought you'd all but forgotten us.'

Lonnie stared at the ground in embarrassment, worried sick he'd left his call too late. 'I thought you needed more time, sir. You'll still speak to me, won't you?'

'Let me be frank with you,' the foreman answered. 'I've never been one to beat around the bush. If I've spotted you right you're a fair rider in the making and honest, too. So, how about starting at the Glen? You'll get a lot more riding to do here. Mind, you'll still have to muck out and do all the other jobs we ask, but you'll get a fair go and we'll pay you a bit more than you're used to.'

'I'd do anything to work here, sir.' Lonnie had never uttered more heartfelt words. He would be the most promising worker they'd ever had, muck out in his best suit if need be. A thought – well, more of a hare-brained notion – occurred to him. He wondered if he should raise it. For some unknown reason he couldn't even fathom himself, he went ahead and asked anyhow. 'Before I take the job, there's something I'd like to speak to Mr Alcock about.'

Ned's answer was no surprise. 'Tell me and I'll pass it on for you.'

Lonnie knew he wouldn't have a second chance. He'd have to see it through and hope for the best. He took a deep breath. 'Can't.' Now he'd gone and done it. Darned fool, risking his new job on a crackpot notion he'd only this tick dreamt up.

'I thought I'd got the oil on you, boy. Am I wrong? We're offering you a chance of a lifetime to ride in a stable second to none.'

'No, it's only …'

Ned cut off his lame efforts to explain. 'Look, I'm a busy man and Mr Alcock is much busier. Do you want the job or not?'

Well, he wouldn't have to worry now, would he? Lonnie had already overstepped the mark and spoiled his chances. Before he could make things right again, a voice interrupted. 'Who is it I don't have the time to speak to?'

Lonnie gave thanks for the luck of his own Irish ancestry. The tall brawny man striding towards them seemed jovial enough.

'Good morning, Mr Alcock. I was just telling the lad here how busy you are and to stop squabbling with me and take the job we're offering him.'

'Maybe you have a better offer?' Mr Alcock asked.

A shadow of confusion and disappointment passed over Lonnie's face. He was making a mess of this good and proper. 'No sir, I'd love to work for you. It's only …'

'Only what?'

'The lad's full of muddle, sir,' interrupted Ned. 'Won't give me a yes or a no. Won't speak to me. Wanted you in person. But he's as honest as the day's long. Just picked up a guinea he has, and handed it to me without a second thought. Honesty like that doesn't come along too often these days. If you allow me to speak on his behalf, I reckon he deserves a chance to have his say.'

'So do I,' agreed Alcock. 'Spit it out, lad.'

'I want you to buy a horse.' There. Lonnie had said it, plain as day, seeing as everyone wanted directness.

Ron Alcock pointed to his foreman. 'See Ned here. He's a very skilled and capable man who I pay a lot of money. And why do I pay him so much? Because it's his job to find me the best horses and riders around. If that's not good enough for you, young man, I'm intrigued.' He turned to Ned. 'Tell me again, what's this fellow's name?'

'Lonnie McGuinness.'

'The one from Crick's?'

Ned nodded. Lonnie didn't know what to make of the sharp look which passed between the two men. Ronnie Alcock placed an arm around his shoulder and led him a few paces away. 'Come on then, lad, let's leave Ned to his other business. Let me hear what you have to say about this horse.'

'He's real smart, Mr Alcock. Speedy, I mean. Exceptional. If you'd buy him, sir. And you should buy him.' Lonnie heard himself rabbiting on at full speed.

'Hold on, son. So this is what's too secretive for my foreman's ears; the same man I trust to find the best horses money can buy. How old are you?'

'Sixteen, sir.'

'And how is a sixteen-year-old going to convince me I should buy a horse on his advice alone? Especially a lad who should be jumping at the chance of a job here, but is more interested in selling me a horse.'

'He's not mine to sell, sir. The Cricks own him. But with the right training, this horse is a sure winner. I willingly admit I can't look at any horse the way your foreman can and know at a glance how good it will become. But I know the heart of this one.'

Lonnie knew he was fast losing Mr Alcock's favour, but he was determined not to give up. If he could only convince him. Lordy, he'd give it his best shot. 'Would you buy Lightning for a hundred guineas?'

'Lightning's not up for sale. And if he was he'd cost a lot more.'

'What if I say this horse is as good as Lightning, maybe even better?'

'I'd say you're still talking in riddles. There's not a horse around at the moment to compare.'

'A horse with spirit. A horse who is unproved, but I reckon could be the best. Real special. He hears me. I don't know why, but when I ride him he goes so much better for me than for anyone else. If you buy him I can leave the Golden Acres without a second thought.' Lonnie's own strong sentiment for the horse took him by surprise. He hadn't realised how attached to Trident he had become.

'If I thought for one minute you were saying that if I didn't buy this horse you wouldn't work for me, I'd kick you out by the seat of your pants. I'll not be blackmailed.'

Lonnie tried a final appeal to the Glen's business side. 'If the Cricks ever find out how good he really is, money won't buy him. But right now I bet you could persuade them to sell him for as little as a hundred guineas. That's what Thomas Crick said he's worth. It's a steal.'

The world seemed to slow down as he waited for a reply. Ronnie Alcock took out his pipe and lit it. Puffs of smoke dawdled upwards. In the distance a horse stood idly at the railings. Lonnie knew he had made an impassioned plea. Now he prayed it would work. Seconds ticked over. Any minute now the Glen owner would grab him by the seat of the pants and fling him out. He braced himself.

'Ned likes the look of you in the saddle,' Mr Alcock said, eventually breaking the silence.

Lonnie's face broke into a smile as wide as a barn door.

'Not so fast. There'll be one or two more things you'll have to prove. Talk to Ned about the job. Then I'll give some thought to your proposition about the horse.'

'But you'll buy him, Mr Alcock, sir?'

'By Jesus, you have a load of pluck, son. No

promises. I don't even know the name of this so-called superb animal.'

'Trident, sir.'

'What? Lightning's brother!' Mr Alcock shook his head in disbelief. 'He's tops to look at, but word has it he's a duffer. I'll have to think this one over good and proper ...'

It hit Lonnie like a brick that even if Mr Alcock did buy Trident, he could not start work at the Glen right away. There was too much riding on the street race. He must stay in the good books with the Cricks until it was over. Not that he could admit to Mr Alcock he was in any way involved in illegal racing. Anyhow, he'd jump that hurdle later. For now, he would go along with anything they said. 'I'll wait to hear from you then, sir.' Lonnie stood rigid, not daring to move away until he was given the all clear, a fact not lost on Ronnie Alcock.

'Anything else you'd like, lad, or shall I be off, leaving you to run the Glen by yourself?'

'No, sir!' Lonnie grinned, relieved, and sped off down the drive.

# HAIRPIN

## Item No. 6551

*Carved out of bone.*

The prospect of one day becoming a jockey at the Glen stables left Lonnie flooded with the idea of celebrating, and put him in the mind to drop by the oyster bar and pick up a bag as a treat. What's more, he'd check and see if Pearl was around. He'd heard she was back in her usual place by the Governor and was mighty relieved to think she had come back to Little Lon from wherever she'd scarpered off to. Some oysters would work wonders as her welcome back tidbit.

Treasured oysters in hand, he crept up on Pearl from behind, playfully pulling out one of the hairpins from under her bonnet. She turned around startled and Lonnie was shocked to find her face peaky, like a white dollop of sago pud, her cheeks hollow and gaunt.

'Lonnie, you gave me the fright of my life.'

'You're a bit jumpy. Been sickly or something? We thought you'd scarpered off from Annie for a while and found a hidey-hole somewhere.'

'Something like that,' she answered vaguely.

'Running a bit hot and cold. I'll be on the mend soon.'

'Fancy a bit of a celebration?'

'I'm working.' She cast her eyes around nervously, ever on the lookout these days. 'Anyhows, what are we supposed to be celebrating?'

'A bit of good news for one thing.'

'I told you I'm working.'

'You don't have to stay for long.'

'What if someone comes checking?'

'We'll lay low. How much is half an hour of your time worth, then?'

'Oh, so that's what you have in mind?'

Lonnie was relieved to see a glint of the Furies back in Pearl's eyes. 'Get away with you, Pearl. I'm not spinning you a line.' He held up the bag of steaming oysters. 'Even a working girl's got to eat.'

'Don't think I haven't whiffed them already, yer chump!' A final scan of the area reassured her no one was watching. 'I guess I can sneak a bit of time. What's the worst that can happen, eh?' She slipped her arm through his. 'I bags the bulk of them.'

# HARD RUBBER PIPE

## Item No. 455

*Various uses, including female contraceptive device used for washing out.*

Back at number four Pearl rummaged behind a pile of knickers, tight corsets, hard rubber pipes and glycerine bottles to uncover her stash of blended wines. She passed a bottle over to Lonnie and swigged long and hard from another. 'This'll warm our toes.'

'I stood at the oyster bar for over an hour waiting for you last time,' Lonnie reprimanded her. 'Where'd you disappear to?'

'You know how it is,' Pearl said in a roundabout way. Her face clouded over. No sense in telling anyone the worst of her time spent beneath the floorboards. She pushed an oyster into her mouth and swilled it down with a few more mouthfuls of drink. 'Never you mind what I've been up to.'

'Go easy, girl, you'll be giddy.'

'I can handle it.'

'Well, it makes my head thick. Watch out Mrs B doesn't catch you pinching her good wine.'

'See if I care,' replied Pearl defiantly. 'She can rot in hell.'

'Come on, mate, lift your spirits.' He could sense Pearl was really out of sorts. 'Hey, wanna know more about the horse race?'

'Found something out, have you?'

'Turns out I'm riding in it.'

'How'd you manage that?' She took another swig. 'You'd better win.'

'I did some checking. The two horses weren't in their stable. No one's been exercising them, at least not while I've been around. I'm gonna check some more, but I reckon I already know what they're up to.'

Pearl emptied her bottle and took another.

'Slow down. You'll get in all sorts of strife.'

'I already worked out why we're celebrating,' she said with a smile, raising the bottle and clinking it against his.

Pearl couldn't have heard about his job offer. He'd only just found out himself.

'It's the ninth,' she said.

Lonnie gasped; he'd completely forgotten. Fancy, the ninth, and he'd not even remembered. He recalled telling Mr Alcock he was only sixteen, but couldn't be blamed for an honest mistake.

Pearl giggled. 'Get drinking, seeing it's such a special occasion.'

They carried on sharing the bottles and drinking

to each other's health. Fast becoming sloshed, Pearl toasted everyone's birthday and anniversary, even Annie Walker falling and breaking a leg. Lonnie was feeling a little under the weather himself. Out of the blue she clutched his arm. 'Let's do some more snooping about the horses. I'll be lookout.'

'I dunno,' he said. There'd be some nifty climbing and fast running to be done. He wasn't sure of their chances. 'Thought you had to go back to work.'

'Men are bad for my health. They make me sick.' As a way of proving her point she burped loud and long. She looked at him accusingly. 'Lonnie's a scaredy-dare.'

'Save your bull,' he answered. 'It won't work on me.'

'You weren't a scaredy-dare the time we stole the empty bottles.' She nestled into Lonnie's shoulder and swilled some more wine. 'Remember?'

How could Lonnie forget that lark, where she'd helped him pinch empty bottles from the back of the Traveller's Inn and then carry them around the front, all the while pretending Lonnie had been out collecting them. They'd almost taken a good payment for returns from the publican.

'I was a good cockatoo,' Pearl said. 'I warned you in time, didn't I?'

'Got chased all the way down Spring Street,' Lonnie replied good-humouredly. Carlo's warning – 'She's trouble with a capital P' – drifted like a mist, in through one ear and out the other. But even when Pearl was carted off and threatened with prosecution, she never dobbed him in. 'Course Pearl was a good cockatoo. Why not the two of them go out on a midnight venture like old times? Especially tonight, being the ninth, even if the drink had made them a bit bleary-eyed. He could do with a little excitement on his birthday. As long as Pearl stayed cool-headed. 'I'm up for it if you are.'

Before the words even tripped off his tongue, Lonnie was beginning to regret them.

# IRON FILIGREE

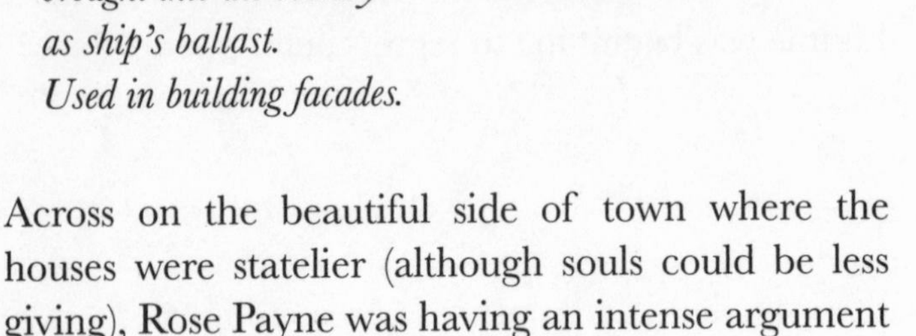

## Item No. 3080

*Moulded ironwork.*
*Fashioned from bars of pig iron*
*brought into the country*
*as ship's ballast.*
*Used in building facades.*

Across on the beautiful side of town where the houses were statelier (although souls could be less giving), Rose Payne was having an intense argument with her father.

'But, Daddy –'

Henry Payne glared angrily at his daughter. 'You know as well as I do, Lonnie McGuinness is one of those half-witted sons of Little Lon. Tell me if you dare that he doesn't loaf with other undesirables on the street corners of an evening.'

'But he's not a larrikin.' Who had told her father about him? Thomas, she supposed. Even as she made her defence, Rose thought dismally back to their encounter with the Glass and Bottle Gang and of her unlikely rescue by the Push. She couldn't deny that Billy Bottle and George Swiggins both seemed to know Lonnie. However, she pushed the thought aside. It was too horrible to consider he was one of them.

Henry Payne was far from finished. 'Moreover, my girl, he may well be the thief who robbed our Carlton house. Boys like him are a scourge; can't step over a lump of bluestone without seeing it as a missile and smashing it through the nearest window. The die's cast, his sort will never change. If I prove he's to blame, I'll haul him up to the magistrate's court in a flash. No daughter of mine will be seen with the likes of that ruffian, do you understand? I'll hear no more of it.'

Rose went cold at the sternness of his words. How dare he speak to her like that? However, she was well schooled in her father's threatening tone. 'Yes, Father,' she said, biting her tongue. It was pointless to argue.

Upstairs and out of his sight, Rose stomped up and down in her room. 'I hate you. I hate you. I'll see who I want to see.' Wasn't she old enough to make up her own mind who she saw, whether he was Lonnie McGuinness or even … even … Ned Kelly, if she had a mind to?

But was it possible Lonnie was a member of the Push? Those larrikins all seemed too familiar with him. And what did Daddy mean by calling him a thief? She knew he was capable. She'd been with him when he'd worked that lock.

The evil of that night resurfaced: the monster Billy Bottle mauling her; the dark squalid alleyways of Little Lon; the maid in the grubby room that looked like a whorehouse; that common dress she had been forced to wear. The same dress she had hatefully ripped off on her return and bundled into the cupboard where it had remained untouched for the past week.

And even though Rose Payne resolved never to set foot again in a place fit only for thugs and dirty girls, she was still vexed at her father. She would see who she wanted. But if ever she did see Lonnie McGuinness again, whatever would she do? She had never felt so out of sorts in all her life.

She pulled out the dress and in her temper tore the neckline and side seams. Then believing she would be better rid of it in case her father made the discovery, she made up her mind there and then to send it back with the coachman immediately to that hateful hotel. What was it called? The Leitrim?

# DARK LANTERN

## Item No. 903

*Badly damaged remains of a lantern.*
*Squashed and flattened.*
*Found in area that had once been a cellar.*

'For goodness sake, Pearl, shut it.'

She sounded like a drunken navvy. The dark lantern in her hand bobbed along, marking time to one, two, three, loud belches. Pearl threw Lonnie an apologetic look. He grabbed the lantern from her and held the light towards a shutter at the stable, half-hanging from its hinges. It was the obvious point of entry. He went in search of the ladder he knew lay in the grass, located it and propped it against the stable wall. 'Dog out for me here,' Lonnie ordered. Pearl would probably break her neck if she tried to climb. Better leave her outside.

He climbed the ladder with the ease of a possum, leaving Pearl at the bottom to keep watch while he scrambled through the opening to disappear amongst the hay bales. When he heard Pearl giggling, he reappeared, whispering, 'Find somewhere to hide and keep quiet.' A speedy change of mind decided him she would be better under his watchful eye. 'Nah, climb up here.'

'Make your mind up, yer chump.' She hiccupped.

Muttering a swift prayer that the moving moon of light he saw in the distance was nothing to do with the Cricks, he hung his own lantern on a nail and hoisted her up, preventing her from falling backwards. 'Lordy, hurry up, girl.' He half-dragged Pearl through the opening. 'Someone's coming.'

They were bound to spot the ladder. He knew he had to take one more chance at revealing himself. Leaning forward, he pulled for all he was worth. The ladder scraped against the sill as he dragged it inside. 'Douse the lantern before we're seen,' he whispered.

Still larking around, Pearl swung the lantern and made futile attempts to snuff out the flame. 'Make a birthday wish.'

Lonnie grabbed the lantern before she could burn herself or set fire to the stable. He smothered the flame and hauled Pearl across the straw, settling on an old horse blanket near some disused tackle. Below was the sound of restless horses shuffling and nosing the stalls, impatient to run.

Pearl was still prattling on. 'Lots of straw here. For bedding. For a wedding. How about it, you and me? I'll let you marry me.' She snuggled up close. 'I know you want it, Lonnie.'

'Will you shut up?' He pressed his finger hard on her lips.

Pearl swiped it away and nestled into his neck. 'Give us a kiss, yer chump.'

He broke free from her embrace. 'If you make any more noise we'll be in real strife.' Capital P – Carlo wasn't far wrong. Lonnie forced her to crouch low amongst the bales, praying she would keep quiet. Then he held his breath and waited.

There was a sound of approaching voices, the clunk of the iron lock being removed. The doors creaked open. The disturbed horses were jumpy. The swish of a tail, a mane. A settling pat on the flank. Lonnie wormed his way deeper into the straw. 'Keep down,' he whispered, throwing his arm out and muffling Pearl's mouth with his hand.

He felt what he thought was Pearl's leg brushing against his own, still playing games. One swift look down told him it wasn't her leg, but a filthy rat. If Pearl saw it and started screaming the place down they'd be done for. He nudged it out of the way, dislodging a small amount of hay, which floated down and settled onto the shoulder of a startled Mr Crick.

'Something's moving in the loft.'

The rat was back again, this time trying to claw its way up Lonnie's trouser leg. Instinctively he lashed out. His boot connected with the rodent and sent it flying.

As it hit the floor the stable foreman grumbled, 'Damned rats're everywhere round here!' He struck out with his foot. Missed. The rat scuttled between the men and out the door.

Satisfied they had discovered the source of the noise the men went about their business. Lonnie's nervous heart thumped so loud he was sure it could be heard below by the three men in the world who, tonight of all nights, he least wanted to meet – the boss, his son and the Neanderthal.

'No one's been snooping around here, have they?' questioned Crick senior. The tone of his voice was threatening enough to make even the Neanderthal edgy.

'I done exactly what you said, Mr Crick, guarded this place day and night since we set up the horses here.'

'And?' Crick raised his eyebrows questioningly.

'Once I caught McGuinness hangin' around, but I sent him packing.'

Thomas Crick joined in. 'McGuinness? What's he doing sticking his nose around here?'

'I don't know why you got him involved in the first place,' his father snapped back. 'I should never've let you talk me into it.'

Lonnie's ears were burning as the men moved around below. To his relief Pearl lay motionless, the drink having finally knocked her out.

'Can you tell 'em apart, sir? Can you tell which is which?'

'No, you've done a fine paint job on them. I can't

tell one from the other. There's no way anyone else will either, especially in the dark.' He turned to Thomas. 'See to a bonus for him. On the understanding he remains quiet, that is.' There was a veiled threat behind the words.

Everything now made sense to Lonnie.

It seemed like an eternity before he heard the men leave and the padlock secured once more. He peeped down. Safe now to go below for a closer look and confirm for himself what they had been up to. He checked out where it was safest to jump and shook Pearl awake.

Lonnie jumped first, stumbling off the hay bale that was meant to break his fall. He regained his footing and stacked a second bale for Pearl to land on. She managed to get down without breaking her neck and they approached the two horses.

# BROWN PAPER

## Item No. 4642

*Shopkeeper's brown paper used for wrapping goods.*

On Daisy's return to the Leitrim she found a package had been left for her with the publican. She waited until she was in her room away from prying eyes to open it. Sitting on her quilted bed, she undid the brown paper. Inside was a mass of crumpled pink fabric, torn around the neckline and muddied around the hem. Spread out on the beautiful quilt it resembled the trawled-up remains of a once glorious sea creature.

'And she calls herself a lady,' Daisy said fiercely, at the very thought of returning a dress to anyone in such a shabby condition. Her eyes drifted across to Rose Payne's blue silk dress, which was draped neatly over the chair, having been lovingly repaired, sponged, dried and pressed. She rolled up her sleeves and lit another candle end. There was stitching to be done if she was to have this working dress ready in time for Madam Buckingham the very next morning. So much for Lonnie and his promises. He'd sworn the dress would be returned safely, but he had let her down.

In the early hours, there was a frantic thumping outside her room and the call of 'Police raid, open up.'

'Not again, Lonnie,' she complained through the door. 'I'm dog tired. This isn't funny!'

'Open up, Daise, can't you take a joke? I've come to tell you some news.'

Daisy gruffly let him in, flicking her plaited hair off her shoulder. 'You've been drinking! You're a disgrace!'

Lonnie rolled his eyes, trying in vain to stop his words slurring. 'Settle down, you should be more free and easy like Pearl. For starters, reckon I've a new job at the Glen. What d'ya think about that?'

'If they see you in this state you won't last an hour.' She frowned. 'What do you mean, "like Pearl"?'

'Nothing.' Something in Lonnie's mind cautioned him it would not be a good idea to describe how on their return from Golden Acres the two of them had festively drained the last bottles of wine and then tossed the empties one by one into the old cesspit, loudly singing 'Around the Rick' until the shrieks of a neighbour sent the duo scarpering off in different directions. He wasn't sure how he'd ended up at Daisy's. 'Just thought you'd like to celebrate, too,' he finished off lamely.

'I wish you'd act your age.' She picked up the dress

that Rose Payne had sent back and held it out. 'Do you realise what state this was in when your lovely lady friend sent it back?'

Lonnie tried to focus, but all he saw was a pink haze. 'What's wrong with it?'

'Not a thing now! Since I spent the entire night repairing and cleaning it. You promised me!'

'Sorry, Daise,' muttered Lonnie, although he was not quite sure what he had to be sorry about.

'That's not good enough. It's not about the dress. Look at you. Look at what you've done lately. Just what were you thinking of drinking until this hour? Not to mention last week, getting mixed up with the Push and, worse, Billy Bottle. You know he beats his chest whenever he cuts people and he does it just for fun.'

'Why are you harping on about that? I was only riding the lift.' Lonnie's stomach rushed sickeningly into his mouth. If only the room would stop swaying. He tried to steady his feet against the next wave of nausea.

'Did you get in the same way as before? It's the police who'll be thumping at *your* door and dragging you off to gaol for breaking and entering.' Daisy was just warming up. 'And with Rose Payne of all people? Do you want to get yourself killed? You don't mess around with Henry Payne, especially not with his precious little girl. Not to mention how you've been stealing goods and smashing windows like a larrikin.'

'According to the likes of Payne anyone from Little Lon is a thief and a vandal.'

'And you're doing your very best to prove him right. Just how stupid are you? People talk. Everyone knows you were chased by his watchman, that bully who comes along with the bailiff to scare the wits out of people every time they fall behind with their rent.'

'Sometimes folk should keep their mouth shut.' The effect of the drink had turned Lonnie's mood sullen.

'Are you, or are you not the one who robbed Payne's house in broad daylight?'

'It wasn't like that.'

'I know you did it. I've known for ages. I dropped by your mam's ages ago and she told me everything.'

'Cut the claptrap, Mam doesn't know.'

''Course she does!'

Lonnie tried to unravel all the accusations Daisy was levelling at him. Come to think of it, his mam had been very quiet since the night Tilly did her moonlight flit, as if she were waiting for Lonnie to start a conversation. His mam could do that sometimes when she had a bone to pick. Keep silent, go for days waiting for him to admit whatever she thought he had done wrong. That silent treatment could be much worse than any screaming or yelling or clip around the earhole. And his mam only brought it into play for the most serious of things. She must've found the watch.

Daisy was shaking her head fit to snap it off. 'But what I really don't understand is why you weren't content to take the stuff and sneak off. But no, you couldn't help yourself. You had to smash those windows as well. Don't think I haven't heard. That's what larrikins do. Tell me, what does it feel like to be Billy Bottle? Does it make you feel big?'

'I told you before it wasn't like that. Wasn't broad daylight for a start; it was evening. And I didn't steal anything. I just took things back for their rightful owners when no one was looking.' Lonnie had enough wits about him to know how he was sounding. Like a tacker who'd been caught out. He didn't mean to sound peeved, but all the same he wished Daisy would stop acting like his mam.

'This is serious. If Payne has proof, he'll put you in gaol.' She eyed him squarely in the face, still persisting, 'I can start to understand the theft. I guess men like Henry Payne deserve all they get for taking people's belongings unfairly, but the law's on their side. You can't be Robin Hood, robbing the rich to give to the poor, even if you mean well. Smashing those windows was a senseless act. It's time to stop playing the fool. You have to be responsible or one of these days you'll find yourself in terrible trouble. And another thing, what will your mam say if she knows you're betting on a street race?'

Lonnie shook his head miserably. Was there anything she didn't know? He had a sudden urge to go home for a sleep, for a bit of peace and quiet.

'If she knows you're gambling all that hard-earned money on the outcome of a horse race … recklessness and gambling?! What are you turning into?'

Daisy was a no-nonsense girl, never one to avoid the truth. But tonight she had a sting in her tongue and her demand for honesty was too much for him. He could hear his own sarcastic tone before it left his mouth, regretting the words, but unable to stop. 'Better get your friends the Sallies to pray a bit harder for me and stop behaving like you're my mother. Come to think of it, you should be a better friend yourself.' Why did she have to go and put him in such a dark mood when he had only wanted to do a bit more celebrating?

'What do you mean?'

'What I mean is – Pearl lying for so long, sick as a dog, who knows where, and no one, not even her best friend, there to give a helping hand.' He saw Daisy's face pale over. It was a low comment. Daisy did not deserve such a cut. 'Aw, I didn't mean that, don't be mad at me, Daise. You're Pearl's best chum. And look at how you helped Rose. I only came here because I was in the mood for a bit of cheer. And to thank you,' he added, trying to make amends.

'There's nothing to thank me for. I'd have done it for anyone.' Daisy's sorrowful expression plainly made it known to Lonnie how upset she was. 'You better make sure Rose gets this back in one piece,' she said flatly. 'Here, let me fold it.' She laid the blue silk dress in tissue and brown paper, folding the edges carefully and binding it with string as a carry-all. 'Don't ruin it beforehand.'

'Rose will be ever so grateful.' Lonnie accepted the parcel, ready to do a runner. 'Time I went.' It was a miserable and sorry goodbye. All the girls he'd been mates with were starting to turn on him. He didn't know which way was worse, first Rose's grim silence, then Pearl's flirting and mucking about, now Daisy's telling off. There was only one left, his mam. Today of all days he would have to face her and square up about the watch, when he believed deep down it was really him who needed the explanation.

Daisy closed the door behind him, knowing her words had been harsh. Lonnie always rushed through life like a shooting star. Hadn't she told him often enough! And like that star, one day he would come back down-to-earth. In the meantime she wondered what other reckless acts he would find himself caught up in. Why, he was nearly seventeen: he should start acting more like a man. She wanted him to do so, for her sake as well. When would he realise how soft-hearted she was for him?

As for Pearl, Daisy was full of self-reproach over her friend. She prided herself on being pure and honest to even the smallest creature, yet had broken pledge after pledge to follow up on the wellbeing of her dearest friend. When all along Pearl had been lying ill in some stranger's bed with not a soul to feed her broth or wipe her forehead with cold compresses. The fact Pearl must have confessed these hurt feelings to Lonnie rather than to her, made Daisy's guilt even more overwhelming.

Wonderful. Insufferable. Nearly seventeen? 'Oh, Lonnie, that's why you were out celebrating. It was your birthday!' With a sudden realisation of the date, she leant her head against the door. And in the long silence that followed, Daisy gave in to her tears, letting them fall down her cheeks unchecked.

# FRAZER'S SULPHUR POWDERS' BOX

## Item No. 368

*Box for holding Frazer's Sulphur Powders. Medicinal. Promoted as good for the purity of blood.*

As Lonnie stumbled through the front door, a damp grey draught followed him inside. He wondered if his da had slipped in as well, to take a squiz at how things were going in the old family home. By the looks of it, he wouldn't be too pleased. *You shoulda got better, Da*, he thought miserably. He swallowed hard, but the lump in his throat would not budge. The long night and the grog had sapped his energy. His head was thumping. All he wanted to do was climb into his bed and have a kip.

His mam sat wrapped in a woolly blanket, fast asleep in her armchair by the hearth. Before the draught could reach any deeper into her bones he eased the door closed. Her head had keeled over, leaving her chin propped up by her chest. She must have been sitting there waiting for him, probably all night. He felt scummy, treating his poor mam this way. Only thirty-four years old and look at her. Scrubbing and washing for that toffy lot had dried out her hands and ploughed lines deep into her face. A crying shame. Daisy was right about one thing. Starting tomorrow, he was going to be more of a man. With Da dead and buried, it was all up to him.

The fire had burned low. Lonnie was thankful he'd been a squirrel in the months leading up to winter and stocked up on firewood. At least that was one thing he'd done right for his mam. There'd been plenty for the taking from work sites. Only throw-outs. He could almost hear his da's reprimand: 'Not the most honest path, son. Not one I would've favoured.'

By rights he should set his mam comfortable, but he elected to leave her be. Lonnie tried to tiptoe past the chair. His mam snorted, drifting up from the depths of sleep. The blanket slipped down and there in the little hammock formed by her nightdress was the watch. Her eyes opened. She gave a start.

'It's only me, Mam.'

She saw him looking at the watch. 'Time we talked, lad. Where did you find it?'

Lonnie shuffled nervously and did what he always did when he knew his mam was going to give him the what for – he reversed the questioning. 'Where did you lose it, Mam?'

His mother looked reproachful. 'I never intended you to know.'

'Why not? I would've got the money.'

'The very reason I didn't say anything. You always take the law into your own hands.'

'But giving them Da's watch, how could you?'

'Do you want to be homeless? They promised I could have it back when I put the money together for the arrears. They said they'd done everything lawful, kept the property for ninety days before they sold on.'

'Those dirty mongrels. They never sold on. They stashed it.'

'There's no argument with the law. I didn't have a leg to stand on.'

'The law's one thing, but people should stay inside decency. You should've told me.'

'And what would you have done? Raided a building society? Remember just before your father died? How he needed those sulphur powders to purify his blood? And you went along to Mr Salvadore's. Remember what happened?'

Shamefaced, Lonnie followed his mam's meaningful stare. On the side table laid out as if his da would be picking them up directly were medicine jars and powders, a razor strop, tumbler and brush. Neither of them could find the courage or the desire to remove them from permanent display.

Lonnie knew full well what his mam was on about. His thoughts returned to the day when he had gone into the corner shop hoping to get the powders on tick. When Mr Salvadore refused, Lonnie argued the point with him. 'You know our word is good. We always pay up.'

The shopkeeper replied, ''Course I trust you. And I trust your mother, the way I trust all the decent people around here. But everyone's in the same boat these days. I'll be broke soon if I don't watch out. Last week another building society failed. Today the price of wool dropped again. We all have to make a few sacrifices.'

'Come on Mr Sav, my da's real sick and he needs that medicine bad. We'll have the money next week. Only one more time, please.'

'Sorry, lad, but you'll have to wait until next week to buy them. Look, I have work to do out the back, so off you go and close the door behind you.' Mr Salvadore walked around to the back of the shop, leaving Lonnie to his own devices.

Right there and then, Lonnie knew it wasn't one of his brightest ideas, but grabbing the opportunity he jumped the counter and helped himself to a box of Frazer's Sulphur Powders. 'Sorry, Mr Sav,' he muttered as he raced out. 'I swear I'll pay you back next week.'

His mother's words sliced through his recollection. 'Remember how you told me Mr Salvadore had given you the powders on tick. But there wasn't any credit.' She held up the watch. 'You're too old to go taking things when you feel like it, even if you think it's the right thing to do.'

'I did go back and pay.' Lonnie fell silent as his thoughts returned to the day he'd made payment. It was exactly one week after he'd light-fingered the powders. True to his word he'd laid the correct price to the halfpenny on the shop counter.

'I know you eventually paid for them, but it was wrong to take the powders in the first place. You were fortunate Mr Salvadore didn't call in the police.'

It was true. Mr Sav had a good heart. When Lonnie went back to apologise, Mr Sav told him those failing banks were doing bad things to good people. There he was himself, sending good customers away, while Lonnie, who wasn't such a bad lad after all, had been turned into a thief in order to help his ailing father.

'If I had waited, it would've been too late. Da died that same week, Mam.' Maybe it was the guilt of what he'd done, or the excessive drinking of the evening that finally caught up with Lonnie. He cursed the bottles of wine, regretting his angry words to Daisy, knowing full well he had shamed his mam, his friends and himself by his behaviour, hating himself as each thought clamoured for attention and forgiveness. Above all, he regretted the grief he had given and the fact that his poor da was lying dead in the Melbourne cemetery and there was nothing at all he could do to change any of the whole stinking lot.

'I know your heart is in the right place, son. You do know why I kept one eye open for you tonight.

Did you think I would forget?' She pressed her husband's watch into his hand. 'Happy birthday, son. Seventeen years old. Your da would have wanted you to have this. And I know deep down he would have been proud of you.'

# TIMBER POLE

## Item No. 221

*Traces of blue paint still evident.*

As the week wore on Lonnie let himself believe things were not so bad after all. Nothing was broken that couldn't be fixed. Like the way Carlo had fixed his wagon again and was busy painting the poles that held the new canopy. His wagon was getting fancier all the time. The poles were a barber shop trio in swirls of maroon, blue and yellow. 'Gotta catch the public eye,' he said, proudly standing back to admire his own handiwork.

'Got some more news about the race,' said Lonnie and proceeded to fill his friend in on exactly how the Cricks were planning to fix it. 'Lightning and Trident are full brothers; the same sire, the same dam. They're almost identical but for a small, white, lightning-shaped blaze on the forehead of one and a scar on the neck of the other.

'Bet Trident has the blaze!' Carlo chuckled.

Lonnie smiled. 'Very funny. You'll be hitting the stage soon, doing a bit of stand up. Seriously, mate, it's a simple bloody horse switch! All those crooks've done is stain out the white blaze on Lightning and blanch one onto Trident. Not many people even know about Trident's scar, you wouldn't know it's there unless you felt for it.'

Carlo was unconvinced. 'They'll never pull off a cheap trick like that.'

'Ordinarily no. But think about it. This isn't the Melbourne Cup; it's a street race, run at night, after dark.'

'Well, that's dandy,' said Carlo. 'Crick gets to ride Lightning disguised as Trident, while you get to ride Trident disguised as Lightning. And you still lose.'

Lonnie shook his head. 'Not so simple, mate.'

'Then you plan to swap 'em back?' Carlo pressed, taking Lonnie's silence as tacit agreement. 'Call me backwards, but I don't understand why the Cricks need to cheat. They own Lightning, the fastest horse in Melbourne. Thomas Crick may well live up to his name as a pain in the neck.' Carlo paused for Lonnie to crack a smile at his joke, but Lonnie didn't budge, so he continued. 'But even you can't deny he rides well. So tell me why they would bother fixing a race they can win fair and square?'

'Odds! And greed. Running as himself, Lightning will pay much less than he would running as Trident.'

'I still don't get it. Do we put our money on Crick then, is that what you're telling me?'

'If you back him you'll lose.'

Carlo shook his head. 'Mate, you're confusing me.'

Lonnie tried to reassure his friend. 'There's more to it, but for now just make sure you get all our bets over to Bookie. I was hoping you'd drop by Pearl's too and pick up her wager. Thought you both might have a friendly get-together for a change. Haven't you got a bit of making up to do?'

'Gee thanks, a great mate you turned out to be.' Carlo grimaced in mock horror. 'S'pose I'll go. First let me get things straight: there's this horse race, but we don't know when it's happening, we don't know which horse is which and we don't know who we're betting on.'

'All you need to know right now is the race'll be coming up soon, it'll be on a Saturday night, I'll let you know when, and you're betting on me.' Lonnie knew there was still one important detail he was keeping up his sleeve, and for now that was where it was going to stay. He gave Carlo a secretive wink. 'By the way, I put you down as my strapper.'

# SLATE PENCIL

## Item No. 3577

*Fragment of child's slate pencil.*

When Carlo gave his word he kept true to it. There was a Benetti philosophy in life that his family tried to live by – it's not what you say that matters, but what you do. So as promised he intended to collect Pearl's wager, then hightail it out of there before he had time to dwell on the gloomy prospect of speaking to her. He hoped Lonnie knew what a favour it was, especially since he and Pearl usually ended up arguing. Somehow Carlo was the one who always ended up with one foot set firmly in his mouth, and blamed for the honour.

'What're you doing here?'

He could see by her greeting that Pearl was equally as delighted to see him. 'Lonnie asked me to pick up your wager for the race.'

'So why didn't he come?'

Carlo was straight on the defensive. 'Dunno. Busy.'

'All right, but stay here.' Pearl's reluctance was as obvious as a swollen thumb. She looked back over her shoulder, before going to the back room and returning with a purse, which she emptied into his hand.

'Is that all you're putting on?' Carlo asked bluntly.

'What d'ya mean? This is all I've got. D'ya reckon I'm made of money?'

'If it's all you've got, you should keep hold of some for a rainy day.'

'All right for those who can afford to,' she replied. 'But you gotta know when it's raining. Right now it's coming down in bucketfuls for me.'

Carlo half-heartedly slipped the money into his pocket. He was full of doubt. 'We shouldn't really be betting on this race anyway.'

'Why are you so worried?'

'I'm laying out good money too, you know.' He knew he was being defensive, but there were too many things about this race that were uncertain. Maybe Pearl knew something he didn't. 'Lonnie's my best mate, but sometimes I don't know if he's being full-on honest with me. He doesn't seem to care which horse he's on. Half the time I think he'll be riding Lightning, while the other half of me reckons he'll be on Trident. He's so cocksure of himself, he'd believe he could beat Crick and Lightning on the back of Bella … or even the milkman's horse.'

'Bet he could, too,' Pearl remarked, scowling at Carlo.

'You must be sweet on him if you reckon that. It's all right for you girls to do all the romancing, but this is real money we're laying out. It could make or break me.'

'So what do you want me to say? Lonnie's no fool. He must know what he's doing. Why else would he be saying that barring an accident he *will* win?'

'But what if he's just mouthing off? He wants to get even with Crick at all costs. I don't wanna risk all my hard-earned cash on his silly pride.'

Pearl gave Carlo a withering look. 'I, for one, trust Lonnie. He can have all my money. He's never let us down. Anyways, I was with him at the stables.'

'He told me that much. Did you see him swap the horses back?'

'Quit tormenting me. Ask him yourself,' Pearl scoffed, trying to tally in her head how many bottles of wine she had guzzled in the haze of that night.

'You must know if he swapped them back or not? And what if the Cricks found out and re-swapped them? Lonnie's not telling us everything. Ever since he took that dare he's been acting sneaky.'

'That's the difference between you and Lonnie,' sniffed Pearl, her heart flaming up at Carlo's pressing questions. 'He's not a stick-in-the-mud, snooty lordy-lord who's running down his best mate right this very minute to one of his other best mates. You're panicking over nothing. You're still a scaredy-dare and always have been. No wonder you were Miss Siddy-bow-tum's favourite at school,' she said snidely, emphasising the syllables of their old schoolteacher's name, knowing full well how this would rile him.

Carlo's face disintegrated. The girl had a tongue and a half. And here he was trying to be fair and polite. All she had to do was answer some simple questions, but no, she had to bring up that story again. As if he could ever forget the day when at a tender age he'd gone to school for the first time. Together with Pearl, Lonnie and Daisy and all the other ragged children of the neighbourhood, Carlo had assembled for the first class at the Wesley hall, which they would attend mornings until they were eleven years old. During those few brief years they were expected to knuckle down and learn the three Rs, in the hope of avoiding any future rendezvous with Melbourne's police force.

When the teacher had told the class her name, Carlo's attention had been wandering out of the window and onto the street, where by now the littlies were playing marbles or spinning tops. A little while later, upon realising he'd been drifting, he had tugged on Pearl's sleeve and whispered, 'What's her name?'

To which Pearl had answered from behind her hand, 'Sidebottom. Miss Sidebottom.'

'Thanks.'

'Quiet, you two down the back.'

In all fairness, at this point the schoolmistress had not seriously reprimanded him at all. She'd merely remained perched behind the rostrum at the front of the class, her watchful eyes and monotone voice disciplining them all on the etiquette of good behaviour; stressing how they must never utter a peep while she was instructing. But Carlo preferred the way he remembered it – being singled out, made to stand up, the terror he felt when the teacher threatened to march him out of the classroom forever, the puddle of water forming on the floor between his legs, the sniggers and the ticking off, and before he knew it he was close to tears and blurting out, 'Sorry, Miss Sidebottom.'

It wasn't his fault she had blown up all red and blue and purple in the face. He wanted to run home there and then to his own loud but effusive mamma – who saw no wrong in her children – and snuggle into her bosom, let her wrap her arms around him and hold him close to her until he could barely breathe, even though there would be five other littlies clamouring for the same right and he would have to wait his turn.

A murderous scowl on her face, Miss Sidebottom thundered straight for him. Without another by your leave she clapped him hard around the earhole until it was ringing: 'My name is Miss Sid-dy-bow-tum, my lad, and you'll do well to remember. Sid-dy-bow-tum!'

After the walloping, Pearl wouldn't even look his way, although he had watched her cup her hand trying to cover that stupid grin. For the rest of the day he silently fumed, not daring to say another word. Later when his mamma asked him what he had learnt on his first day at school, the only two things he could think of were how to properly pronounce Miss Sidebottom's name in four syllables, and to never ever again in his life believe a single word Pearl said.

It was pointless trying to be civil to her. He turned away from the door with an abrupt 'Seeya.'

She called after him, 'Wait on, yer chump, I was only teasing. Don't be so peppery. Lonnie's our mate, we can trust him.'

Carlo wanted no favours. He was jack of being the butt of her jokes.

# PIECE OF STRING

## Item No. 7543

*Short length of hemp string.*

Lonnie tucked the parcel containing Rose's dress inside his coat and buttoned up tight against the inclement weather, determined to keep the brown paper wrapping and string secure until he delivered the dress as clean and neatly folded as Daisy intended. He would do her proud. She was a rock all right and did a good job of everything she put her mind to. Look how she had attended to the dress. Rose was bound to be full of appreciation, especially when she saw how carefully Daisy had mended the tears for her and sewn back the buttons. Well, he would keep it neat as a pin.

How delectable Rose had looked that evening at the Eastern Market. How invitingly vulnerable. She was a girl who needed his protection. It seemed to Lonnie that she was dusted in fine icing sugar. All he wanted to do was wrap his arms around her and lick up her very sugariness until he was filled with the powdery white.

Surely she would understand that none of the mauling was his fault. Returning the dress would help make things right between them. He summoned a picture of Rose, happy with her dress all sewn and pressed, letting him make up for that bad turn of events with the Glass and Bottle Gang by taking a tour around the Carlton Gardens on his arm. He imagined brushing a shy kiss across her cheek.

It did not reassure Lonnie to see the heels of her dainty boots board the open tramcar the instant he turned the corner into Collins Hill. Nor when he saw her pay her threepence to the conductor, then bob down into a seat at the very moment he called out her name. Rose surely must not have heard him, for she was barely seated before she stood up and moved further out of view. He yelled an appeal to the lever guard. 'Hold on!'

The guard doffed his cap and gestured back. 'Too late.' With a clang of the bell the tram jerked to a start, before picking up speed and rattling down the hill.

Lonnie tried to catch up, but it was difficult to maintain even a walking pace along the footpath. At this hour of the day, everyone in Melbourne seemed to be stepping out and obstructing his way. He pushed through the crowd. A bevy of young ladies glided along in his direction, their noses snubbed in the air as they did their best to show him they were scandalised. It was certainly not his good looks that had caught their attention, rather his screaming the name of their acquaintance, Rose Payne, at the top of his voice, completely unabashed.

A weedy larrikin with small eyes singled out the prettiest girl and spat on the footpath. This was a signal to the tight-fitting suits and polished boots who congregated around a lamp pillar to yell out, 'How's about a smacker then, love?' The girl shot them an outraged glare, lifted her skirt free of the dirty path and primly tiptoed past, happy at the very least she wouldn't be the target of the latest gossip surrounding a certain Miss Rose Payne, the next time *she* did the Block.

The tram continued to rumble downhill, sounding its bell to alert pedestrians and taking Rose almost out of Lonnie's reach. Droplets of rain started to fall. Lonnie kept his head down, threading his way around verandah posts, dodging the red and white barber's pole, a pawnbroker's sign projecting over the walkway with its three balls hanging like a chandelier, cases of books, hanging bells, wire cages and sea chests. He felt like he was playing a game of blindman's buff.

Raising his head, he caught a glimpse of a clear space by Mackinerny's Billiard Hall. As he broke into a run, a gang of youths spilled from the hall. They were laughing loudly and pushing each other around as they crowded onto the footpath. Lonnie couldn't prevent himself from bowling straight into them. He bounced clean off one of the lads and, with the wind knocked out of him, crumpled to the ground.

It took a few dazed seconds for him to register the cut of the two-tone shoe near his face, a signature one of shiny cut leather, the heels high, and so tight the impress of every toe was visible.

A strong fist grabbed him by his coat lapels, lurching him upwards to his feet. 'What's the hurry, me old pigeon?'

The face of George Swiggins grinned down at him. The leader of the Push seemed friendly enough, quickly letting him go and slapping him heartily on the shoulder. George had never bothered Lonnie – in fact he had often been quite sociable, like on those few occasions when he had invited Lonnie into Mackinerny's to lose a few games of billiards to him. However, there was a shadowy quality to the young man's behaviour that made Lonnie break out in a cold sweat. An air of self-importance and danger. George was too poker-faced, his forehead too low. He was too fast speaking, too quick-minded and lively for the constable on the beat and much too shrewd for the law. He was a young man not to be meddled with, nor, as Lonnie thought, one to run smash-bang into.

He brushed himself down nervously. 'G'day, George.'

'Still chasing the girls? They're nothing but

trouble, especially those toff-nosed beauties you keep chasing after.'

Lonnie gave a weak grin and started to move off, but some of the Push lads cut across his path, ambushing his escape route.

'Hang on a mo,' said George. 'Reckon Billy Bottle'll be wanting a spill of your blood after the other night. Better be looking over your shoulder from now on. But let me tell you something, me old pigeon.' George nodded across to the rest of his lads. 'The Push here owe you one for giving us the nod about the Law.' He studied Lonnie for a moment. 'So are you up for it, mate? Joining us?' He dropped his voice conspiratorially. 'I could do with a few more brains around the gang.'

Over George's shoulder, Lonnie heard the tramcar's gong and saw the vehicle take leave of its stop.

'Lost something, have ya?' A pointy-chinned lad with drainpipe legs picked up the package Lonnie had dropped in the collision. The string had loosened. The paper was damp and crushed, open at one end with an edge of blue material tucking out from one corner.

Lonnie went to grab the parcel. Before he could retrieve it the holder mashed the wet lump into a ball and tossed it to one of the others.

'Give it here.'

Dodging Lonnie, the lad passed it to another Push

member who tossed it on again, until a stern nod from George's direction sent it flying into Lonnie's hands.

'Only having a bit of fun. Can't you take a joke? Now don't keep me waiting too long for your answer.'

Lonnie's main thought was that when Rose discovered her dress soiled, she would not be in the mind to walk out with him ever again. And if Daisy knew, she would murder him. And how was he going to explain to George Swiggins that he had too much on his mind to think about joining his gang? The rain had started to bucket down. Cursing his misfortune, Lonnie pulled up his coat collar, nodded at George and strode off. Still, it was something to know he had the Push on side.

# WHITE GLOVE

## Item No. 906

*Men's dress glove.*

Rose Payne stepped off the tramcar outside the Federal Coffee Palace, brushing aside the offer of a young gent's helping hand. She raised her Parisian umbrella to guard against the sudden torrent of rain. Apart from a slight pallor around the cheekbones and lips, Rose did not show any visible signs of her distressed state of mind.

She tossed a quick backward glance over her shoulder then scurried inside the building. Without the least acknowledgement, she jabbed her umbrella in the direction of the attendant, spraying him with raindrops. She was in no mood to be pleasant.

The doorman's job entailed him to be polite and ignore any mistreatment from the wealthier townsfolk, of whom Miss Rose Payne was definitely one. He dutifully held out his gloved hand to take the brolly to the cloakroom, reminding himself as he shot it open to dry, that it wasn't worth losing hair over a prissy little miss, even if she did treat him like a toad.

Ignoring the six lifts, Rose fumed her way up the elaborate staircase to the first floor. She fired angry darts at people, through the salon, the smoking room, and the writing room, before eventually storming towards the family table in the dining room where she positioned herself away from prying eyes. There, safe at last!

This section of the Federal Coffee Palace was set aside exclusively for the most desirable patrons of Melbourne. Her father's table was always held in reserve. She chose a chair guarded by a potted palm and lush emerald curtains looped to the side by a heavy cord, where she sat distracted, rhythmically smoothing the damp folds of her dress. How dare Lonnie McGuinness trail after her like a slobbering mutt. After what he had put her through, how dare he not leave her in peace. She thought of him running alongside the tramcar like some escaped lunatic, down Collins Hill of all places where everyone knew who she was, shouting her name for all and sundry to hear. What a disgrace! She shuddered to imagine what people must think.

From outside on the street, Lonnie looked skyward at the seven storeys of the Federal Coffee Palace. He surveyed the iron-framed dome, as if Rose could be nesting up there with the pigeons and sparrows, working his eyes down the tower. His gaze moved past the turrets and gables, down the five storeys of bedrooms, the first floor where she most likely would be and finally to the ground, fixing his eyes on every window, anxious for a possible glimpse. He failed to spot her, but he had a hunch she was somewhere inside.

After one step into the foyer Lonnie found his way blocked by the same doorman who Rose had so rudely brushed aside.

'Hold on, my good man.' The attendant spoke through half-closed lips, which Lonnie swore hadn't even moved. His eyes took in Lonnie's muddy shoes and well-worn coat, made worse by the rain. There was no remote hint in their expression of regarding Lonnie as a 'good man'. More like his kind were better off using the kitchen entrance. The hand gripping his arm ready to guide him back towards the street was a dead giveaway.

Lonnie faced the doorman with as much pride as he could muster. 'There's a friend of mine here. Someone I need to see.'

'And is this "friend" expecting you?'

Lonnie gestured towards the staircase. 'She's up there somewhere.'

'Perhaps you're mistaken? Perhaps she went elsewhere?' His voice dropped low enough to be just audible. 'There are plenty of coffee houses more suitable.'

Lonnie glowered at the man. 'How about I take a

look for myself first?' he suggested defiantly.

'Are you a patron?'

Lonnie was losing patience. 'No! But I won't be staying long. If she's not here, I'll go.'

The man tut-tutted. 'Members only, I'm afraid.'

'I've as much right to be here as anyone else. And if I want to see Rose Payne, I will.'

At the mention of her name, a visible nerviness settled on the doorman. To allow entry to a larrikin scruff like this lad could cost him his job. But to disgruntle Mr Payne or his family was worse. If he trod on their toes he would never again hold down a job in this town.

Lonnie noted his hesitation. It convinced him Rose was upstairs. 'Let me have a few quick minutes. I only have to deliver this parcel.' He started to unwrap the paper. 'It's her dress, see. Then I'll be on my way.'

The attendant looked at him wide-eyed and accusing, not able to disguise his own suspicion. 'What are you doing with Missy's dress?'

Lonnie knew he had the advantage. The doorman wasn't going to risk a scandal here on the premises.

'Wait over there.' The man pointed to a dark recess by a service door. 'I'll see what I can do.'

Much as it shamed Lonnie to be stood in the corner like a dunce in a classroom, he did as the doorman asked. Anything to see his Rose.

The doorman returned soon after with a look

of triumph. 'The lady will accept the parcel, but is unable to see you.'

'Go back and tell her it's Lonnie.'

'We don't want any trouble, lad.' The doorman scrutinised the crumpled brown paper, with its dangling string tie and peep of blue silk. 'Better give me the thing, then leave.'

Seeing he would make no more headway, Lonnie reluctantly handed over the dress. The doorman held onto it with his thumb and forefinger, making a show of not soiling his white glove.

Outside, Lonnie made up his mind to wait for Rose if that's what it took to see her. The rain was still falling. He sheltered in a small alcove across the road. Shivering, he pulled up his collar and fixed his eyes determinedly on the entrance.

He was already planning how to win her over. After all, she couldn't be blamed for not wanting to see him. First, after he apologised, they would take a stroll, her hand linked through his arm, towards the Princess Theatre. There he hoped to impress her with a glimpse of Sarah Bernhardt arriving for her concert. Rumour had it the great French actress had brought along a whole host of pets, including a pug dog, a native bear, even a cage of rainbow parrots. If Rose and Lonnie didn't see her in person, chances were they'd spot her menagerie, which would be just as good in Lonnie's opinion, seeing he couldn't afford the two pound ticket for the concert. Instead he would woo Rose with a stroll through the Carlton Gardens, stopping at the fountain, where he fully intended wrapping his arm tenderly around her lovely waist and apologising once more, most indulgently, for the uproar the other night at the Australian Building.

Lonnie was daydreaming of the romance ahead when a hansom cab came to a halt in front of the Federal. Thomas Crick stepped down, dusted off his lapel, corrected his bowler hat, settled one arm behind his back, placed a hand firm around a walking cane – set to impress, Lonnie thought sarcastically – and swaggered inside the building.

Thirty minutes passed. Still no sign of Rose. Or Crick. Lonnie felt his blood boil. If that backslapper was anywhere near his Rose! Restlessly, he paced up and down. The doorman had better have delivered that parcel in the first place. What if he hadn't even told Rose that Lonnie had come looking for her?

While Lonnie was deliberating whether or not to return and have it out face-to-face, the door of the coffee palace swung open for the eighteenth time; Lonnie had counted every single entry and departure. Thomas Crick stepped outside, accompanied by Rose. In one hand she held her umbrella; the other was tucked behind her back. Lonnie saw her eyes scanning about. She would be looking for him. He took a step out to greet her.

A cab drew up. Crick spoke to the driver. Rose hesitated on the running board before climbing inside. Her hand let something unwanted drop into the gutter. As the horses pulled the cab away, the brown package caught beneath a wheel, spilling out its contents along the road in a trail of blue silk.

# WOOLLEN SOCK

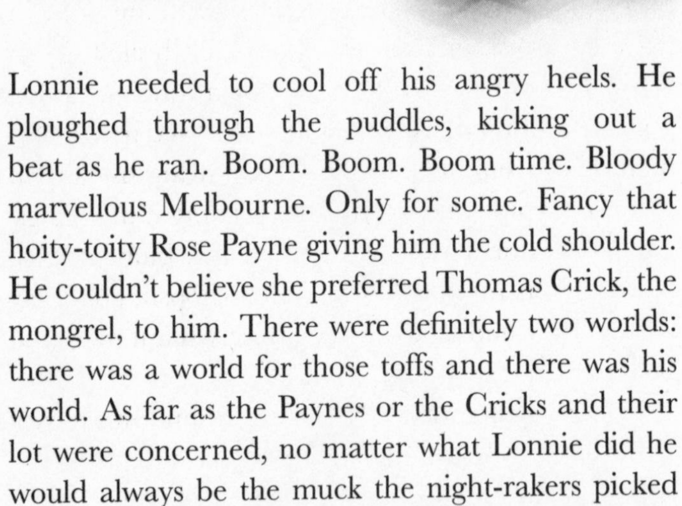

## Item No. 333

*Well-darned woollen sock.*

Lonnie needed to cool off his angry heels. He ploughed through the puddles, kicking out a beat as he ran. Boom. Boom. Boom time. Bloody marvellous Melbourne. Only for some. Fancy that hoity-toity Rose Payne giving him the cold shoulder. He couldn't believe she preferred Thomas Crick, the mongrel, to him. There were definitely two worlds: there was a world for those toffs and there was his world. As far as the Paynes or the Cricks and their lot were concerned, no matter what Lonnie did he would always be the muck the night-rakers picked up. He fisted the bricks on the wall alongside him. Wait until the horse race, he would show them all.

Heavy clouds lingered overhead, pulling the sky downwards. The water soaked through his boots into his woollen socks. He concentrated on how high the splashes reached up his trouser legs. *So what if I catch my death of it?* he thought dismally.

What a fool. All the signs had been there, but he'd been blind. Was he still such a lad, when all the time he had been thinking he was a man? Wasn't he trying to do the best by everyone? Daisy's rebuke was still troubling him. He hadn't seen her since their argument and it saddened him deeply that he'd been the cause of her tear-filled eyes.

He ran a fair way before he realised he was almost at the bridge over the Yarra. He slowed down his pace. Cupping both hands to his mouth, he drew in the cold moist air until his cheeks felt hollow. With lips like a puffer fish he blew out a long sustained flow of hot breath. A white plume formed in the cold night air. It reminded him of Da blowing smoke out of his clay pipe and his trick of turning it into rings. The white formation blew away in a bullying gust of wind – as rapid as his da's life, whoosh, gone. He wished they had talked more about what it meant to be a man.

Lonnie contemplated becoming a sundowner. Not a bad idea, to spend the rest of his days roaming the bush, picking up work and a bed where he could, calling at outback stations for a meal when the sun went down, seeing the country. Not a worry in the world anymore about ladies or landlords, or lugs like Slasher Jack, or George Swiggins, or Billy Bottle. Yeah, a swaggie, go on the wallaby and leave the lot of 'em to it.

The clouds chose this moment to burst open with a vengeance. Rain ran down the back of his neck. He pulled his collar high, tucking away his ears. He picked up the pace and headed for the bridge, intent on taking cover underneath.

From now on, according to Daisy and his mam, he had better pull his finger out. But one thing was for sure, and there was no escaping this fact: at seventeen years old, he'd finished once and for all with the ladies.

# FROZEN CHARLOTTE DOLL

## Item No. 6150

*Child's toy.*
*An unjointed, porcelain doll,*
*popularly known as a penny doll*
*or Frozen Charlotte.*
*Originated in USA.*

Pearl found herself below the bridge that spanned the Yarra river, standing alone on a grass verge under a great stone arch. Above her was a wide roadway, double tram tracks and two footways broad enough for a thick line of pedestrians. Normally the bridge would be a bustling place, but the rain had started to hammer down, sending everyone except her scurrying indoors for shelter. There wasn't a soul in sight, walker or cab.

Here she was, driven out into this dismal night instead of warming herself in the Big House with the pollies, sipping French wine from a crystal glass held in a warm hand covered by a pearl-studded glove. Out any longer and she would set solid from the cold and rain. Already she felt hard as a statue. Her arms and legs were as stiff as the penny doll she'd once found, cherished and then lost. Her hands and lips felt frozen over. She could have put skates on them and done a twirl or two. Fed-up was the word. Her new work dress, flowing ruffles of pink champagne and a neckline of scarlet roses all hand sewn by Daisy, was soaked through, already ruined for the boudoir, wouldn't even see her through one summer night. Her red, all-covered-in boots were caked with mud. She was tired of it all.

When the runner had delivered a message from Annie Walker that a client would arrive for her down by the Yarra bridge at eight o'clock, and she would earn a good sum from it to help pay off her debt (but if she didn't show she'd be sorry for many a year to come), she had no choice but to clear out of the Big House and make her way hastily downtown. So where was the chump?

Once Annie's lug had turned up, she intended to make a speedy end to this whole dark sorry episode and get back to the Big House before she was missed. If Madam Buckingham should discover her gone; if she ever found out that Pearl was at this moment doubling up on her shift and cheating her on account of Annie, she would face a hiding and a half. Hopefully, dear sweet Ruby the goody-two-shoes was covering for her, under the cloud of Pearl disclosing to Madam a few eye-opening truths about that little she-devil herself. Life was all a game of bluff.

Whatever was she thinking? The reality hit her in the face like a wet flannel. There was no end to all this, whether it was over at the Big House with the silver spooners from Parliament, the speculators and the doctors, lucky enough to be born in the right bed, on the right side of Melbourne; or on the corner by the Governor, where the theatre patrons and the passers-by beckoned her over; or in the laneways, where the drunks and the bully boys were too rough and demanding, some of them only lads themselves. Every time she shared herself, when she horsed around, teased and taunted – every time – they took a part of her away with them; small fragments, a penny for her laughter, sixpence for her charms. The debt was never-ending. Eventually she would be ripped apart; there would be nothing of any worth left to sell.

Her mind toyed with the shadows. Sounds of water amplified the night, the plop of rain falling from high above the bridge structure, the slosh of water running along channels into the river. She could hear the scuffle of rats. Filthy creatures. Gnawing the skin to the bone. A scrawny tom doddered by, too old to catch the lively rodents, more intent on scavenging through the muck by her feet. Pearl kicked out savagely. In return, the old cat arched its back and set about wailing threateningly. They both felt the same helpless rage.

She began to think about what to say if a constable

passed by. Say she agreed to being a parlour girl, he might take her to the cells at the gaol. Even the cold stone walls would be warmer than this icy river bank. At least she would be dry. Say that did not work, she could pretend to be a lunatic. But then Madam Buckingham would find out. And if she didn't meet this client for Annie, she'd be a goner.

Pearl's tiny hand buried into a hidden pocket to search for the coins that should be there – nothing. Momentarily she panicked, and then remembered she had given all her money to Carlo to put on the race. Maybe Lonnie would win her a small fortune. Then her luck might change.

A sense of a presence from behind came too late to save Pearl. A monstrous arm lifted her until her feet cleared the ground. She screamed against the force and was suspended like a rag doll under the arm of a vengeful child. A brutish palm covered her face, trapping her nose and mouth, muffling the cries but not her terror. She was carried off into a darker section further under the bridge. The coarse tweed of the man's coat scratched against her skin, the size of him, the stink of his body – she had known even before she heard his menacing threats, who this man was. This prowler abroad at night. The dirtiest of maulers.

Slasher Jack's hand left her face and forced its way downwards, filthy, foul fingers creeping down her body and between her legs.

She found her voice. 'It'll cost you,' she demanded.

A rush of foul breath brushed past her ear like a spectre of death. 'You'll not get a penny from me, slut. You're the one who has to pay.' With his giant hand around the back of her neck, he forced her down roughly.

While his free hand pulled at her clothing, Pearl forced herself to imagine she lay in warm linen sheets. A light-headed feeling overcame her. She was transported to one of Miss Selina's beds at the mission house, tucked up safely. While Jack twisted her arm and kicked her legs apart, she only felt her face being gently stroked. Her fingers interlocked with others, sweet smelling and warm. Her head sank lower and lower into the feather pillow.

A grey heaviness of rain hit Pearl's face bringing back a faint stirring of comprehension. Slasher was gone. Her body felt stiff. She had refused to be his victim, but there was no Miss Selina, nor sweet-smelling hands, nor feathery pillows to alleviate the hurt. She pulled herself up into a half-sitting position and leaned against the side of the arch, staring out at the river, the raindrops hitting the water in a vicious stampede.

Once on a sunny day she had gazed into the same section of the river and seen it ripple and glisten. The thought now occurred to her that if you looked a bit harder you saw straight through the shiny surface to the dark and predatory. Larger fish ate smaller fish, which in turn ate the weed. Below her was a world of violence and resignation, the same one she was living in. There was no escape.

Her leg ached. Her neck was pinched. All she could sense was the stink of Slasher and his hands upon her. She straightened up her clothing as best she could and forced herself to climb onto the bridge spanning the river, where she clung to the iron railing. A bridge made for the princes of the empire. Half their luck.

When would Annie stop having this revenge on her? Was there ever to be an end to the ordeal? The road ahead would take her away from this stinking place. If only her legs would do as they were told she could keep on walking right out of Melbourne, for good. Far away from this pitiable life. Anywhere.

Pearl stopped short, her vision of the future obscured. Where to? Where would she go? Where *could* she go? Who had come for her when she was being held captive by Annie Walker? No one. Not one soul had come looking. Not even Daisy or Lonnie had missed her. No one cared whether she was alive or dead. Annie was right, no one was going to help some scrawny bit of flim-flam like her. She shuddered at the thought that there was no one to reclaim her; neither brother nor sister to apply to someone like Miss Selina or the rescue brigade from the mission hall for help in bringing her home. No family waiting. No home. No welcome. No protection. At the very extent of her hopelessness, misery spilled from her body and over the bridge like a waterfall.

A hansom cab splashed its way across the bridge, swaying violently in the wind. The driver reined in the horse as he navigated through the pouring rain. The unlikely sight of a soaking-wet girl leaning over the handrail, when everyone in their right mind should be rushing for shelter, drew his attention.

At first glance she looked about the same tender years as his own cherished daughter and he wondered what on earth the girl was doing, playing out in a storm. It did not take him long to realise. Still he found some empathy for her. He slowed down the horses and was about to call her out of the rain and onto the backboard, when a gruff voice came from the comfortable dryness of the cabin. 'Be swift, man. It's already past the hour.'

It was a voice Pearl would have recognised – the voice of Thomas Crick – had her mind not become a brown swirling torrent, daring her, drawing her into a raging darkness. She paid no heed to the cab driver or its occupant hidden in the blackness of the cabin.

The river was calling. A siren's song. She did not have the energy to walk away. How easy to end her life; over and done with, once and for all. Not a surrender, but an escape. She wondered what it would be like to lie beneath the swollen waters and how long it would take for her to die. Would it be painful? The idea of dying scared her. She thought about Biddy's babe. 'Do we have to be dead to be cradled in Heaven's arms?' she asked aloud, looking skywards. 'Are we ever truly safe?' If only one person cared, she would have a reason to live, a reason not to jump.

A sheet of grey rain blew horizontal, biting into the face of the warm-jacketed youth who rushed over the bridge. As he approached Pearl, she moved back from the railing and raised her head, indifferent to the downpour, staring at him wild-eyed, a shivering fragile girl in a dress so flimsy it glued itself to her body.

The young man who approached her was ripping off his jacket to cover her shoulders. 'What are you doing here, all dripping and drenched through? Lordy, it'll be the death of you. Take my coat. You're grey as a ghost. Even Mrs B can't expect you to stand out in this weather.'

'It won't be the death of me, yer chump.' Pearl's voice was faint. 'A little rain never killed anyone.' She gripped Lonnie's arm and turned from the bridge. 'Let's leave. I'm freezing.'

'Too right, I'm taking you home. Take it easy. Lean on me.'

As they staggered through the rain, Pearl kissed

him tenderly on the cheek. 'Out of all the people in Melbourne, Lonnie McGuinness, I should have known it would be you. I shall love you for always.'

Lonnie blushed up like a dark cherry. 'Get away with you, Pearl. Are you trying to embarrass a man?'

# DOORKNOB

## Item No. 718

*Cast iron. Front door.*
*Well used. Worn thin.*
*Located at site of No. 4 Casselden Place.*

The door at number four Casselden Place refused to open. Usually a welcome to any man who was half-cut and in need of a frolicking, the evening downpour had swollen the timber in a triumphant rush before spring came and made it stubborn.

Lonnie shoved his young strong shoulder hard against it, ramming the timber door open. 'In you go, my girl.' He hurriedly ushered Pearl out of the pool of water in the doorway and into the front room. 'Warm yourself up, then put yourself straight to bed. I'll pull the door hard-closed as I leave.'

Pearl's voice was almost a whisper. 'Don't leave me, Lonnie.'

Lonnie swallowed hard and gave Pearl a quick nervous look. His words came out hoarse as if he was almost talking to himself. 'I should be going.'

Pearl touched his sodden hair, letting her fingers linger. 'Please don't go, not yet. Please stay. Don't you want to stay?' She looked at him appealingly. There was desperation in her voice. She didn't care. Wasn't Lonnie her saviour? She didn't wait for the bashful reply that would surely follow, but took his hand gently in hers and wandered inside the darkened room. 'You're soaked. Let me at least dry you before you leave.'

At the touch of her hand Lonnie felt a warmth flow through him, an intensity of which he had had little previous experience. The vow he had made to himself earlier in the evening, to be done with the girls, rose in his mind but was soon diminished by thoughts of the nearness of Pearl. How she was making him feel. Like that inadvertent brush of an elbow against a woman's bosom that time in Bourke Street. Well, he had Carlo to blame for that sly manoeuvre, catching him unawares with a swift side push. And the gush of desire he'd felt when he'd walked through the Eastern Market with Rose Payne as if they were a couple. A careless arm loosely placed around Daisy's slender shoulder; but that was only a friendly gesture between mates. All over again he was having a rush of feelings, wanting to be close to a girl. To Pearl. There was an explosion in his head as the vow blew to smithereens.

As he allowed her to seat him on the *chaise longue*, his knees tottering and his emotions spinning, one part of him wanted to run. Maybe he had the wrong end of the stick. Maybe she did only want to dry him and see him comfortably on his way home. Pearl knew this game. She would easily realise he'd never been with a girl before.

The fireplace was stacked with screwed-up old newspapers, small kindling and a good-sized, red gum log. Pearl set the fire ablaze and slowly dried herself in front of it; then slipped from the room, returning dressed in only a silken shimmy that fell in frothy volumes to the ground.

Silently Lonnie sat, his eyes fixed on her. She seemed to be transforming into a fairy child, a winged butterfly, a white rose.

The flames were taking hold. Sap oozed and spluttered from the log, boiled by the licks of the kindling flames, until it evaporated and all that remained was a heady eucalyptus fragrance wafting through the room. The fire gave off comforting heat. Soon they were enveloped in orange-yellow light.

Pearl moved across and began to dry him, towelling his hair, softly rubbing the back of his ears. A warm feeling moved up from his toes. His eyes closed tight, the way they used to when his mam dried his hair. There was something soothing in the rhythm and the touch. A safe haven. A coming home.

Pearl's strokes settled into slower caresses. She was thinking of Lonnie's shy innocence, wanting to thank him for caring, for saving her life. He would never know she had had every intention of leaping from the bridge. If she was to love Lonnie in the way she planned, she must be the instigator, take her time. She changed her attentions to his chest, moving unhurriedly.

At her female touch, Lonnie's excitement grew. She moved in even closer, folding her arms around him, tenderly drying his back. Her breasts ever so lightly brushing him. 'Take this wet thing off, yer chump. You'll catch your death of cold.' The faint echo of the words entranced him. He felt himself weakening. She didn't wait for the inevitable refusal, but began unbuttoning his shirt. 'What about these?' She tugged on his pants. 'You should dry them by the fire.'

Lonnie swallowed hard, his words croaking out. 'They're nearly dry.'

'Say you like me, Lonnie.'

''Course I do.' He felt edgy and shy at the same time.

'I mean, do you really like me?'

'I just told you so.'

'Will you kiss me, Lonnie?' She waited for his answer, catching his embarrassed stare. Still in part such a boy! She could see he wasn't sure how to react. 'It's okay to kiss me.' She pushed back lightly on his shoulders until he laid full length on the hearthrug. 'Come on,' she said, easing his belt loose, 'time to get these off.'

With delicate eagerness, Pearl sketched the lines of his body, moving inch by inch along his shoulder-blades, over the curve of his chest, deliberate and slow. She lay her body towards him, bringing her face closer to his. Her lips opened, her tongue making its way into his unknowing mouth. Taking his hands into hers she traced the contours of her own skin.

Tonight this invitation, this generous offering, was a gift.

# TATTERED PIECE OF PAPER

## Item No. 3947

*Part of an agreement for the sale of a horse.*

Midweek and it was well past the period the racing fraternity had set aside for buying and selling yearlings, although there were a few owners and trainers braving the cold morning here in the Golden Acres saleyard. One man in particular stood out alone, and it did not take Thomas Crick long to notice him.

'Back for another look at the yearlings? Couldn't find any finer than ours, I suspect,' he said, by way of a greeting. It was a testy statement, much more than a simple question thrown at Ned.

'Oh, there are plenty of good yearlings around. But the Glen's more interested in young stayers like Lightning,' he replied.

'Lightning's not for sale and even if he was,' Crick said, involuntarily pulling on his horse's rein and less able than most to mask the scornful edge to his voice, 'I think he'd be a bit out of your price range.'

Ned always kept a clear head and an upper hand. He continued with a cool smile pressing at his lips, 'All I can say is good job you've got him, for the rest of these youngsters look like an ordinary bunch to me. I'm not here to buy Lightning, you'll be pleased to know, but his brother's ours now.' He stared Thomas out. ''Course you'd know already. Or at least he soon will be. I'm only here to do the formalities and hand over the money.'

'What are you talking about, man?' Thomas was confused. 'Trident's not for sale. There's some mistake.' What the devil was going on? Father wouldn't sell Trident without telling him. Not with the race coming up.

Ned grinned, taking a great deal of delight in the young upstart's discomfort. 'No mistake. We're taking delivery of him sometime in the next fortnight or so,' he replied cheerily.

With a curt by-your-leave, Thomas rode over to the office, dismounted and threw open the door.

'Father, we have to speak.'

'One moment.' Crick senior waved his hand at his son's interruption. He finished putting pen to paper.

Thomas rocked impatiently from foot to foot. 'It won't wait.'

His father paused. The Crick eyes were alert, intelligent, but cold like steel. 'What's so important you come bursting in here like a larrikin? Is this the way a Crick behaves? Speak up then.'

'Tell me it's not true that you've sold Trident?'

His father's nod signalled the horse was indeed going.

'How on earth can we fix the race without him?'

'Hold on, lad, nothing's going to change. We'll just give them the horse on the Monday after the race. Simply scrub him back to his old self and send him off. No one will be any wiser.'

'But why sell him?'

'We don't need him. He's had plenty of chances. We've got a good price from Alcock, much more than he's worth. And we've got many other pacemakers to run with Lightning. But think, lad! If Lightning and Trident do ever race against each other in the future, as I fully expect they will, everyone who remembers this street race will bet on Trident. They'll remember the race the way we want them to. And that's with you riding to victory on Trident, over the unbeatable Lightning. The only speculation left for the mugs out there is whether Lightning would have won with you aboard and not McGuinness. No one will ever know we swapped them. There's absolutely nothing to worry about.'

Thomas realised his father was talking sense. From what he had seen at track work, Trident would always finish a couple of lengths behind Lightning.

# EIDERDOWN

## Item No. 445

*Bed coverlet,*
*stuffed with the first feathering*
*of the eider duck.*

There was no denying it, Lonnie had actually done the deed. From now on, Pearl was his girl. He couldn't wipe her full-bodied charms from his mind.

Still he wished he hadn't been such a great gormless goose. He recalled the long silence when it was all over and done with. Well, he'd been as mopey as a wet rooster, hadn't he, only able to gasp out a breathless, 'Thank you.' Pearl seemed faint or something, no doubt swept away as much as him. He brushed away the inkling she might say a mumbled 'My pleasure' to all her punters.

There was only one thing for her to do and that was give up the game. About time she became an honest woman. From now on he'd look after her good and proper. As far as he was concerned they had sealed their union.

His chest was bursting. There was nothing he could not do. He felt ready to face anything. Even the horse race coming up soon. The way he was feeling,

Thomas Crick wouldn't stand a chance.

True to form, being the fair sportsman and gentleman that he was, Crick had forbidden Lonnie to be anywhere near his mount. All he had been told was to meet under the elms at the Carlton Gardens at an appointed date and hour, which they wouldn't disclose until nearer the race. At least Crick had had the decency to put in the entry fee of ten pounds on his behalf as promised.

He supposed he should be grateful, but he couldn't help the swipe. While he was expected to fully honour his part of the deal, there was no question of him doing any training. No track work. No favours. No arguments. And definitely no Rose Payne. Good riddance. From now on, there was only one sweetheart for him, so Crick was welcome to Rose any day, win or lose.

Lonnie was mulling over these details and what declarations he would make to Pearl, when he bumped into Daisy hurrying down the bluestone steps from the Wesley hall. Lonnie had not met up with her since their argument. Before he could make up, she planted a warm, sisterly kiss on his cheek.

'Lonnie, your birthday, I didn't mean –'

'Wasn't your fault, Daise. I've been meaning to come over and apologise.' He scrambled for the right words to express what he wanted to say. 'I've been thinking about what you told me about being a man. 'Course you were right all along.'

Daisy smiled forgivingly at him. 'I'm never mad at you for long. Guess it isn't the first time, won't be the last either.'

'Wanna go to the skittle saloon and knock over a few pins?'

Daisy shook her head, dismissing the idea. 'Can't, I'm on my way to see Miss Selina.' She seemed agitated.

'What's up?'

'Something dreadful's happened. About Pearl.'

Lonnie felt his face flame up over his evening with Pearl. Lordy, his girl hadn't gone and blabbed already?

Noting his expression, Daisy continued with a baffled whisper, 'Wait till you hear the truth of it. She's been in such a state. The horrors she's confessed!'

What was Daisy on about? He hadn't manhandled Pearl. If anything he'd been shy and nervous.

Daisy hesitated. 'I probably shouldn't be saying this to you. I did promise not to tell.'

'I'm her mate, too,' he fished. He had a right to know. Pearl was his girl now, good and proper.

Daisy's head swung uncertainly from side to side. If she had a horse crop she would soon be thrashing her own back.

Lonnie wasn't going to let it go. 'Are you gonna tell me?'

She gave a huge sigh. 'I guess secrets between friends should never be kept when they're so sinful and cause such sorrow.' Not allowing herself a change of heart, she spilled out exactly what had happened, all the sordid details of Pearl's story, starting with the babe born and dead to some poor girl on the night of the wild storm, how that was the reason Pearl had left Annie Walker's employ in the first place; her kidnapping and captivity under the floorboards; having to double up for the two madams; and the latest violation committed under the bridge of the Yarra river.

'The bridge?' A memory surfaced of Pearl leaning against the handrail, the rain soaking her to the skin, her deep sense of melancholy, her emotional plea. Ice flowed through his bones.

'Seems it started ages ago when Annie sent Slasher after her.'

But if Slasher hurt Pearl on the same night, why hadn't she let him know? Why hadn't he realised her state of mind himself? Lonnie's stomach turned over at his own short-sightedness.

'Are you unwell?' Daisy asked anxiously.

The ways of women were much too difficult for him to understand. But one thing he quickly realised was that Daisy seemed none the wiser to the fact he'd been with Pearl or that she was his girl. And glad he was to keep that a secret.

Her own pain at Pearl's distress was obvious. 'I've let her down, I'm ashamed to say. All this time I've done nothing to help.' She flung both arms out fitfully, seeking confirmation from Lonnie about how wicked and uncaring she was. 'From now on, I'm not going to stand by and let her suffer on her own. She's in fear for her life. I only hope Miss Selina will know what to do.'

Both in the same mind, they set out heel to the ground in the direction of the Home for the Wayward & Fallen. They cut through Cumberland Place. New pots replaced Auntie Tilly's flowers in her window box.

'Hope Payne treats these ones better. Not likely though, is it? No one on Little Lon counts for much,' Lonnie said glumly.

'In God's kingdom we'll all be rewarded,' Daisy assured him.

Lonnie sometimes wished he was more of a believer; he could do with a bit of help these days.

They soon arrived at Miss Selina Southern's Home for the Wayward & Fallen, which stood directly across the way from the Carlton Gardens. Lonnie patted the mangy dog that lay on an old eiderdown alongside the doorway. 'Must be under Miss Selina's protection,' he said. 'Not such a bad life, fella.'

Three loud raps and the door opened.

'Is Miss Selina here?'

'And who may I ask is wanting her?'

'Daisy Cameron and Lonnie McGuinness.'

'I'll check if she'll see you.'

They heard the footfall of hurried steps. The

woman who came to the door was regimental and straight-backed, her sleeves folded neatly to her elbows. Selina Southern may have been military in her stature, but she had the kindest eyes Lonnie had ever seen. When she smiled, goodliness shone out like sunshine. The smile was for Daisy. Towards Lonnie she was stern. 'I hope you're not here to fool around, Lonnie McGuinness. This is not the time for one of your practical jokes. I'm very busy. A young girl's about to deliver.'

'Aw, Miss Selina, I haven't played a joke on you since I was twelve,' said Lonnie.

'And I still haven't recovered from the scandal. All those cream cakes! You neglected to tell me they were taken from Mr Chamberlain's store without his permission.'

'But the cream was a day old and he'd piled them outside to toss away. I just thought it may cheer you up, doing such good work and all. I'm not messing around now, honest. Pearl could get herself killed if we don't act fast.'

'Pearl?'

'She's in grave danger.'

'Still looking out for everyone I see.' Miss Selina's smile softened. 'Come in both of you. Let's see what we can do.'

'We won't keep you long, Miss Selina,' promised Daisy, as she explained the dangers Pearl had faced of late. 'You'll help her, won't you?'

'Can you bring her here directly? Then I'll do all within my means to help her.'

'I tried to talk her into coming, but she won't,' said Daisy. 'Can't you come back with us, bring her yourself?'

They could almost see her mind turning over.

'I'm afraid not. For one thing, I can't risk Pearl being injured because of me.' Miss Selina made clear how it would jeopardise Pearl even more if she was seen meeting on the street with a child rescuer. 'Only last week a girl was found dead. We'd been trying to steal poor Biddy away. They made it look like an accident, but it was a cover-up all right. Stopped her blabbing too much to the wrong people, you see. Where's the law when you really need them?' She sighed. 'I guarantee that once Pearl steps foot inside here she'll be safe. So the sooner you two persuade her to come, the better.'

'Isn't there anything else we can do?' Daisy asked, growing more and more anxious.

There was a scream from the first floor of the building, so piercingly high that Selina Southern looked heavenwards. 'I'm wanted upstairs. Sorry I can't do any more. I'm afraid you'll just *have* to convince her to come here.'

Dejectedly they took their departure.

'She'll have to do things Miss Selina's way or she won't have her full protection,' Lonnie argued.

But Daisy was definite. 'She won't.'

'She doesn't have any choice.'

'There must be another way to help,' Daisy said. They walked in silence, both tossing ideas over in their heads. Eventually Daisy came up with a suggestion. 'What about Madam Buckingham? She's always helped me.'

'Mrs B doesn't treat you in the same way she does her girls,' Lonnie reminded her.

A shiver ran down Daisy's spine. The reason Madam Buckingham had taken such an interest in her over the past few years, setting her up at the Leitrim, giving her sewing work, was indeed a mystery. Daisy always half expected to be sent to work in the Big House, but it had never happened.

Lonnie saw her shudder and sympathised. 'Someone must've walked over your grave.'

'Feels more like my coffin's been lugged out by body snatchers.'

They resumed their silence, both trying desperately to think of a speedy and absolute solution for Pearl.

Daisy threw him a troubled look. 'What if Slasher gets wind of us seeing Miss Selina and comes after Pearl again? He terrifies her and with every reason. He's an animal.'

Lonnie couldn't argue with her. Even if Pearl did agree to go under Miss Selina's protection, Slasher would always be a threat. What they needed more than ever was to protect Pearl from his torment. Her well-being, even her life, depended on it. But Lonnie knew he couldn't take him on single-handedly.

Suddenly an idea flashed up at him like sunshine shining on a leather shoe. A two-tone shoe. 'Maybe there is a way to fix things,' he said thoughtfully. The way he was thinking of needed more muscle than he had alone. He would need help. This was where the Push came in. It was time to call in a favour from someone with spiv shoes and a bit of strength behind him. But it was safer if Daisy didn't know all the details and even though she quizzed him, Lonnie kept his mouth shut.

# VELVET DRAPE

## Item No. 749

*Fragment of red fabric with a thick, soft looped pile, used as curtaining. One of a great number of artifacts found in close proximity to Madam Buckingham's establishment.*

Daisy had a scheme of her own. She headed straight for the Big House in Lonsdale Street, planning to see Madam Buckingham. There were two things she intended to set straight, one about Pearl, the next about herself.

She was surprised to be led so quickly through a curtained doorway to a room where Madam Buckingham sat filling in a ledger. The madam kept writing and didn't look up. 'Well, Daisy Cameron, to what do we owe the pleasure?'

'I've come to ask your help for Pearl.'

'And why would she be needing my help, or yours for that matter?'

'She's my friend. And she works for you. Aren't you concerned about her misfortune? Why are you being so unfeeling towards her?'

Madam Buckingham's pen halted mid-sentence

and she grew tetchy at the cheek. 'Insolent imp!' She had a mind to give that defiant tongue a different kind of licking. 'I'll tell you why,' she snapped. 'She's an ungrateful double-crossing slut who's sneaking off to work for that cow Annie Walker, so what am I s'posed to do? Send her flowers?'

'You have a duty to protect your girls.'

'Don't you go attaching blame to me. If Pearl lies with dogs, she's gonna get fleas.'

'I don't see why it's so hard for you to help.'

'Watch your lip, Daisy Cameron. It doesn't pay to mollycoddle girls like her. You've not lived her life. She's been taking care of herself well and good since she was twelve.'

'Can't you just help her out this once? She's no match for Slasher. I don't understand why you won't, when you've always been so kind to me.'

'What yer getting at?' Madam Buckingham's eyes were white-hot with suppressed anger. 'I do no more for you than for anybody else. Perhaps I'm spoiling you. Perhaps I should do less for you.'

Daisy's voice faltered. 'No, I don't mean …'

Madam Buckingham cut short Daisy's words. 'Do I have to keep every mewing waif in Little Lon who comes pawing at my door? If it wasn't for your pa …'

'What about him?'

Daisy's sharp question made Madam Buckingham's eyes narrow. 'Yes, what about your pa? You tell me, Daisy Cameron. I've always wondered what you remembered about the night he left.'

Daisy shook her head. 'I don't remember anything.'

'Nothing?' Madam Buckingham rose out of her chair and stormed towards Daisy. 'Well I'm beginning to think, missy, you know more than you're letting on. Get out! Scarper! Stop wasting my time!' Brusquely, she proceeded to shove Daisy out of the door.

Suddenly, her voice changed, springing from a kinder woman's mouth, all traces of her fury disconcertingly pushed aside, as if they had never been arguing, 'Daisy, me girl, I want you to make a new white dress for Ruby. There's another parliamentary party coming here in a few days time and they'll be expecting the best. Lots of frills and tucks, there's a pet.'

Daisy didn't know what to make of Madam Buckingham's sudden mood swing. She left the Big House wondering why God had suddenly done a runner. Pearl was still without help, and Madam Buckingham was asking strange questions about her pa. She sneaked a look over her shoulder, half expecting Burke to be following behind. What a pigeon pair she and Pearl had turned out to be, one afraid of Slasher, the other of Burke. 'Listen to me,' she heard herself saying aloud, 'waging war against the Almighty because I'm in such a frenzy.'

She should have taken heed of Lonnie's advice in the first place and stayed clear of Madam

Buckingham. At any rate, he had another scheme to help Pearl, although knowing him as well as she did, any solution he thought up was bound to bring its own share of trouble.

# LEATHER SHOE

## Item No. 5117

*Dress shoe.*
*Leather.*
*Two-tone.*

'So me old pigeon, what d'ya want doing?'

George Swiggins rested a foot against the shopfront, his arms crossed leisurely. His small round hat was tipped at a hard angle, shading his eyes. With only a vague interest, he waited for Lonnie to spell out his request.

What had occurred to Lonnie when walking back from Miss Selina's was that George Swiggins owed him a favour. The Push may indeed be the only ones who could help deal with Pearl's situation. So he searched out George and found him camped with his gang on a street corner. However, the bustling centre of Melbourne was not, generally speaking, the most secluded place to make such a dangerous request known.

'I was hoping for a quiet word. Alone.'

'Spit it out, mate. There's nobody around here listening except us, and my boys won't breathe a word.'

Lonnie's words came out like he was choking on a boiled lolly. 'I may need some help … that is … to sort out a … let's say difficulty … for one of my friends, er … that is, if you can help.'

The leader of the Push seemed sympathetic. He wrapped a firm arm around him and pulled him in so close that Lonnie's nose took in the fresh starch of a cleanly pressed shirt. One thing about the Push, they liked to be as spick and span as the wealthy. George sniggered and a trace of spittle appeared at the corner of his mouth. 'Another of your rich lady friends need rescuing? Hey, you never knocked her up?' His voice darkened into a murky, uncharted space. 'Is that what you want sorting?'

'No. I need your help with … Slasher.'

'Don't tell me you've started walking the streets for Annie Walker? Well, I knew times were hard!' George chuckled, enjoying his own joke. He stuck Lonnie a jab in the rib. 'Or has he had his way with your pretty pound-note girl, given her one in the loins to remember.' He jerked his fist at full throttle, loaded with insinuation.

The words hung accusingly in the air between them. It had been the wrong thing to come here. George was only having a laugh at his expense. It was bad enough asking the Push for a favour in the first place. All the reasons why Lonnie did not want to be a member of the gang came flooding back to him. 'Forget it,' he said, flustered and angry. 'It's a bad idea after all.'

George was not one to be put off. The suggestion of a bloodthirsty brawl with Slasher Jack had given his eyes a buoyant glimmer. 'So, you asking us to get rid of him?'

'Yes! No! Don't kill him or hurt him, only scare him off.'

''Course we won't hurt him. How about we send him a nasty letter instead? Can any of you write?' he asked, turning towards his mob. Jeers and vulgar suggestions poured in before George silenced them with a wave of his hand.

'Just keep him away from Pearl.'

George gave Lonnie a smirk. 'Our little oyster gem? Why didn't you say so in the first place? Thought you were doing it for that stuck-up bit of skirt you were hanging around with at the Australian Building. Leave Slasher to me, me old pigeon. I can take him with one arm tied behind my back.'

With George agreeing to the favour, another tremor of alarm passed through Lonnie. The Push were a sinister lot. They didn't do things by half. Committing murder was not inconceivable. So there was no misunderstanding, Lonnie felt bound to repeat his concerns. 'Just warn him off, agreed?'

'What d'ya reckon? Let's just say you won't hear from him again. Consider it done. But this'll make us even. No more favours. 'Course, if you joined the Push, you wouldn't have problems like this.'

Lonnie began to wonder what demon he had set loose. If Slasher died, and the finger pointed his way, he would be implicated, tried by a jury, found guilty and strung up alongside George on the gallows. The floor would drop beneath him, his neck broken; or worse, he'd be left hanging while his feet twitched and turned and he clung helplessly to life.

When they cut him down they would make a cast of his face, a death mask like Ned Kelly's to display at the Town Hall. A line of spectators would come filing past, some aggrieved – his poor old mam for one, Pearl, Daisy, Carlo, Ned and Ronnie Alcock maybe; others taking pleasure in his fate – the Cricks, Rose Payne and her father, Postlethwaite, even the man with the mongrel dog; and some who would care less – like Billy Bottle and his gang. His body left to rot in an unmarked grave behind the prison walls.

Lonnie's wild imagination took hold until his knuckles became tight and blanched, and his knees weakened and trembled to the marrow with the horror of his own death.

# RED BAND

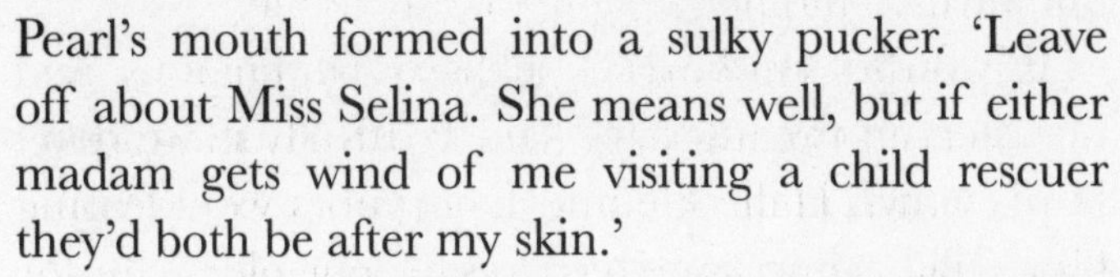

## Item No. 4

*Ribbon from a Salvation Army bonnet.*

Pearl's mouth formed into a sulky pucker. 'Leave off about Miss Selina. She means well, but if either madam gets wind of me visiting a child rescuer they'd both be after my skin.'

Daisy perched dubiously on the roll of the *chaise longue* in the front room at number four, listening to Pearl's refusal for the umpteenth time. She had deliberately dressed up in her navy woollen uniform and bonnet for the occasion; the red band and gold badge symbolising the force of the Army she had brought along with her as divine backup. Not such an easy task as things were working out. She sipped on a cup of tea, which had been left to stew in the pot until it was slap cold, tossing over whether a few more desperate, attention-seeking prayers would be needed in order to help Pearl change her mind.

'You know as well as I do, I can't go. At least, not yet. No matter where I hide, Slasher will come looking for me. He's a bogeyman. He'll sniff me out.' Pearl's thoughts rushed back to the bridge and the deep dark abyss of water.

Daisy touched her friend's arm. 'We're not about to stand by and let Slasher Jack do anything more to harm you.' However, Daisy knew as she spoke that what Pearl said was true. Her life was in jeopardy, putting even God to the test. Everyone in Little Lon knew Slasher attacked Annie's wayward girls in the dark of night with boot or knife. Look at what he had already done to Pearl. She was lucky to have come out alive.

'I wonder if we'll be chased by demons and monsters in the afterlife,' said Pearl. 'As if we don't have enough in this lifetime. Even you, a God-fearing soul, still have your nightmares.'

'We are loved,' said Daisy. 'There's always a guiding light.'

'I'd rather God do something more down-to-earth, like make Slasher disappear forever.'

'Pray to the Almighty. He always helps.'

'Let's hope he sends an angel.'

'He will. But I'm afraid God's chosen one isn't Madam Buckingham. I already asked her to help, but she refused.'

Pearl sprang up in a panic. 'You didn't let on I was working for Annie, did you? You didn't tell her about Miss Selina?'

'No,' Daisy reassured her on both counts. 'I kept quiet about everything. But she already thinks you're doubling up.'

Pearl's face went ashen. 'Madam hates Annie

Walker with a vengeance.'

'Steer clear of her temper. By the time I left she'd already started to turn. She was asking strange questions about the night I came to the Leitrim. Do you remember?'

As Daisy asked the question of Pearl she felt a sudden stab of fear in her chest. Her memory tumbled back to a moment from their shared past. She was ten years old again and waking up inside the room at the Leitrim. She must have fallen asleep for she had no idea how she'd come to be there. Pearl, still in the care of her own parents then, appeared like a little mother sitting by her side, anxiously stroking her hand. 'Hush now, it's all right.'

Daisy looked blankly at Pearl. 'Why am I here?'

'Don't know. I saw you brought here so I sneaked in. I overheard Madam Buckingham tell the others to keep you here until you feel better and then they're to take you over to the Big House.'

'Has my pa sold me?'

'Not that I know.'

'Where is he?'

'Haven't seen him.'

Through a crack of light, Daisy brought Pearl back into clarity as a sixteen-year-old.

Pearl was speaking to her, the words coiling through the air towards Daisy in slow motion. 'Do you ever wonder why Madam Buckingham has been so good-hearted to you, setting you up, seeing you comfortable at the Leitrim, not putting you on the streets like me or Ruby? Do you ever wonder why?' Pearl was rubbing her hand anxiously, a puzzled look on her face. 'Daisy, are you all right? Whatever's the matter?'

Daisy tried to readjust her thinking and bring her friend back into full focus. Her mouth felt as if she had swallowed gravel and her head was throbbing. She managed to say, 'I came over all giddy.'

'You scared me! You were in a stupor, staring out as if I was a ghost or something. Whatever were you thinking?'

Daisy shrugged. 'Nothing more than you being at the Leitrim and stroking my hand.' But her head was filled with the recurring nightmare – the short sharp pain, the strap, hands tossing her into the air, sliding, falling, tumbling, a crumpled body at the bottom of the steps.

She clutched at Pearl as enlightenment dawned. 'What if it isn't a nightmare? What if there really was a man at the bottom of the stairs? What if Madam Buckingham and my pa had something to do with a … a murder?'

'Don't speak such thoughts too loudly,' whispered Pearl, anxiously looking around the empty room. 'If they are true and Madam Buckingham gets wind of them, your life could be in danger. Say she did commit murder, it means she can get rid of you just as quietly.'

Alarmed, the two friends flew into one another's arms. Far from comforting each other, they sat pensively contemplating the murderous intents of those around them.

# MUG

## Item No. 558

*Fragments of an earthenware mug.*
*Blue and white pattern,*
*transfer printed. Staffordshire.*

When Lonnie turned up at number four, it was Daisy who opened the door. She assumed he was on the same mission to see Pearl and quickly whispered, 'She won't listen to one word about Miss Selina. See if you can do any better.'

Lonnie decided to keep his business with George to himself; no point in causing alarm.

Daisy glanced down at the small posy of dried-out poppies and gum nuts that he had lifted out of a blue mug on his mam's dresser and was holding in his hand. 'Buttering her up first?' she asked. 'Good luck, you'll need it.' She left him to it.

Once they were alone, Lonnie pushed the posy towards Pearl. 'You haven't told her, have you?'

She looked across at him with a perplexed look. 'Told her what? And what're you doing bringing me flowers, yer chump?'

'Did you tell her about us two? About the other night?'

Pearl's face broke into a smile. 'I never kiss and tell.' She hastily changed her mind. 'Anyways, not if I can help it.'

'I guess she's bound to find out eventually, what with you and me walking out together from now on. But I thought before we tell anyone we should set you up in a new line of work. Miss Selina could find you some laundering. I could go with you to see her now if you like.'

'Don't you start on me as well.' To be spirited off the streets by a well-meaning mission lady was one thing, but to spend the rest of her working days drudging in someone's scullery till her hands were raw from the soap was not Pearl's notion of a rescued life. The rest of Lonnie's words suddenly hit home. 'Hold on, what're you saying? We're not walking out together.' She took in the look of hurt crossing Lonnie's face and changed her tack. 'I'm sorry if I misled you into thinking such a thing.'

Embarrassment was setting like mortar into the frown on Lonnie's face. Without a word he took three steps backwards, making to leave. What more was there left to say when a girl had spurned a lad?

'Wait on, Lonnie,' Pearl beseeched him. 'Don't go. Not yet.' She reached for his arm.

'Where've I heard that line before?' he asked sarcastically, breaking away from her. Without another word, he strode off.

# SCRAP OF HESSIAN SACK

## Item No. 5786

*Probably used for hard wheat.*

At this late stroke of the hour, Little Lon was a place of shadows. It was not for the nervous or faint-hearted to be out and about.

George Swiggins had done his surveillance well; he and six of his gang were watching and waiting from every possible dark and secluded spot in the alleyway. When Slasher Jack came prowling – with a belly full of grog and in a frame of mind to slip a knife between a set of ribs faster and with no more sentiment than a butcher would have carved boiled ham – they struck. Appearing from nowhere like a lightning strike, six of the strongest with muscle and fist, their intention to kidnap him – one to wrestle each of his arms and legs, another to whip a hessian sack over his head, the last to bind him.

Not one to be subdued without a fight, Slasher thrashed like a wild animal. One mighty swipe from a loose right arm sent a luckless Push unconscious to the ground. Jack fought hard and dirty, gouging at eyes and biting anything unfortunate enough to get close to his head. Blood mixed with spittle and dribbled from his mouth.

The weight of numbers finally knocked the fight out of him. Jack cursed blue murder as the mob held him down. They tied his arms behind his back then dropped down the rope to secure his feet. When he was firmly hogtied they tossed him onto the hard boards of an open-backed wagon and covered him with old sacks.

George took the reins and guided the horse down the hill towards the wharf. The rest of the Push piled heavily on top of the bundle, which reeled up each time Jack tossed his head around and tried to roll off the rattling cart.

All seemed to be going as planned until the figure of a white-helmeted constable slowly formed, busy on his lone night rounds. He walked towards them from out of the darkness.

There was a lively commotion on the cart. The gang threw themselves forward and packed close together over their hapless victim. They launched into a bawdy song to drown out the muffled oaths coming from beneath them, trying to ward off any chance of the law recognising the deed for what it was.

'What you got there hiding under them sacks?' the constable inquired, gingerly pushing his baton towards the writhing mass. He was new to the beat and an unsettling meeting so close to the dark waters of the bay with a group of youths nearly his own age made him jittery. 'Some poor devil's pig, no doubt.'

George's laughter exploded out of him as if someone had lit a fuse in his belly. He uncovered the toe of Jack's boot to prove he was indeed no stolen pig. 'Wish him well, he's due to be wed in the morning,' he gave by way of explanation. 'We're making his last night of freedom one to remember.'

His light-hearted tone was convincing enough for the youthful constable, who was more than relieved to send them on their way with a piece of advice. 'Don't take your pranks too far and land yourselves in trouble. I don't want to find no poor lad tarred and feathered or tied naked to a pole on my beat, do you understand?' As he watched George suck in his cheeks to stop himself laughing and then drive off, he put it down to bachelor-night palaver. Keeping to his duties, he pencilled a few words about the incident in his pocket book.

The wagon came to a stop at a gloomy row of warehouses, dimly lit from the moonlight. The dockside air smelt of tanned hides and offal, and was damp and cold on the skin. Out on the bay a mist was sluggishly rising from the sea.

George jumped down from the wagon and nodded towards the waiting boat. 'Toss him in there.'

As the group manhandled Jack off the wagon, the sack ripped away from his blood-soaked head.

Realising where he was and what they were about to do to him, he filled his lungs and let out a murderous shriek. With every wild movement he used to try and free himself, the well-tied ropes cut deeper into him.

On George's order, one of the Push rammed a chunk of dirty hessian into Jack's open mouth and tied it fast with string. He was lucky not to lose a finger. The remainder of the gang set about removing the iron weights from the wagon. They bundled Jack onto the small boat, away from where the clippers on the tea run were moored and out of sight of prying eyes.

George Swiggins left himself the duty of relieving Jack of the purse from his pocket and the knife stashed in his boot. 'You won't need this anymore, not where you're going.' He held the knife close to Jack's throat. 'Nice one. Ivory handled. "Jack Smith". Don't tell me you had a sweetheart once?' He gave a hoarse and throaty laugh at Jack's muffled growl.

Slasher Jack acted like a man who knew his fate and was helpless to change it, but there were no prayers, no requests for forgiveness, no begging for mercy. He could only try to suck in some desperate, ferocious breaths of air past the suffocating gag, before George flung the sack back over his head, making his breathing even harder.

The water slurped around the side of the boat. Each stroke of the oars pulled them further from shore. A gruff voice broke through the misting air.

'Think we're out in deep enough water yet?'

'It's not the depth that concerns me,' replied George indifferently. 'I don't want him washing up on the morning tide. Take us out a little further.'

They continued to row out on the bay to a place where the mist was thickening into a heavy fog. One of the Push secured the iron weights to the ropes that bound their captive.

For the last time, George ripped away the sack covering Slasher's face. Two of the gang helped to manhandle him over the side. The weighted man pulled down heavily against their strong young arms. It was a merciless conclusion, but the Push leader wanted Slasher Jack to have a final view of his vanishing world.

'A favour well paid, I'd say. See ya later, Jack. With compliments of Pearl.'

# BLADE

## Item No. 1338

*Handle missing.*
*Double-edged, long, thin blade.*
*Dagger type.*

The night of the street race celebrated the event with one of those moonlit skies well suited to late-hour pursuits. By the time George Swiggins was making his way to watch the race, after leaving the billiard hall with two of his Push, the streets had all but emptied, leaving only a few night owls from the skittle saloon and the odd oyster bar patron who lingered on a street corner.

George was not intent on causing trouble. Indeed, he had left most of the gang still enjoying themselves at the tables. The Push had placed good bets on Lonnie and were looking forward to peacefully watching the race and collecting some quick money.

Billy and his gang had other ideas. They swanked their way along the street, looking for trouble, and nothing could have made them happier than when their full contingent of thirteen met up with the three Push.

'Good night for a blue, George,' challenged Billy,

as he and the rest of his gang began their ritual smashing of bottles against the stonework, keeping the razor-edged necks in their gloved hands.

George drew the ivory-handled knife he had wrested from Slasher Jack and held it towards his attackers. 'Don't you think it's a bit unfair; three Push onto a dozen or so of you?'

Billy's laugh came out as a whistle. A gaping black hole in his mouth exposed the result of a smacked-out tooth. 'Your tough luck.'

'Wrong, you great galah.' George smiled mockingly. 'It's *your* safety I'm concerned for. You won't stand a chance in hell against the three of us.'

At the jibe the Glass and Bottle Gang charged towards the Push.

'Run, split up, meet back at the billiard hall,' George commanded. A bottle thrown from one of the mob stung his hand and he dropped his weapon. 'You'll keep,' he yelled back over his shoulder, as he shot off to avoid further injury.

Billy picked up the knife that lay discarded on the ground. Having a scuffle, short-lived though it was, always gave him a thrill, especially when the Push ran away and he scored a trophy. He checked out the ivory handle and wondered who Jack Smith could be.

# RIDING WHIP

## Item No. 956

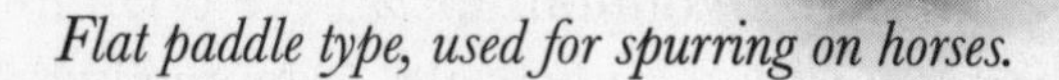

*Flat paddle type, used for spurring on horses.*

Over in the gardens the more cautious of a party of gentlemen were trying to conceal themselves in those same elms where, on that day several months earlier, Lonnie had tried to outwit the pursuing dog. The ghostly shadows of the trees blackened the gents' faces, but silver moonlight flashed over an occasional top hat, cane or beard to reveal some aspect of their identity.

A private carriage stood silent on the roadway. From inside the cabin, two dark curtains twitched open. Crick senior peered out from behind one of them to inspect the line up, while Henry Payne spied from the window opposite. On his good friend's advice, Payne had a lot riding on a favourable outcome.

For an illegal race, the line-up was impressive. Seven riders with their seven strappers and seven of the best horses in Melbourne, as good as any Saturday race could draw, had assembled on the lawn beside the white stone fountain and were waiting for the starter's orders. The horses were lean and muscular, ranging in colour from chestnut to grey, their ribs showing under shiny, well-groomed coats. Some wore blinkers and sheepskin nosebands. Without exception, they were at peak fitness, proud, showy and strong, their nostrils flaring in anticipation of the workout to come.

Like everyone here, Lonnie kept an eye open for a potential police raid. The law had been trying to clamp down on reckless riding though the streets. Only last year there'd been an outcry when a speeding street racer ran down Harold, a young night-raker. Poor boy had been cleaning the horse muck off the streets ready for the morning traffic, but for all his trouble had become a cripple. Not long afterwards, a pollie was trampled. What a big hullabaloo! 'Course, the scandal was fuzzed over by the *Argus* when they found out he'd left the Big House in the early hours and staggered across the road blind drunk straight into the path of the rider, with no one to blame but himself. Lonnie tried to put the risk out of his mind and concentrate. No good scaring himself over knocking someone flying. He'd be extra careful.

Lonnie drew the outside and carried the number seven saddlecloth. He was not in the least surprised to see Crick had the most favourable inside draw, number one. He stroked his horse's mane and spoke quietly in its ear. This may well be an illegal race, outside the bounds of officialdom, and in reality, the Cricks had done their best to fix it, but he was set on being the first across the line. At last, he had a chance to match his skills equally against six jockeys. Most of all he intended to settle once and for all who was the best rider.

As arranged, Carlo was here as Lonnie's strapper. They didn't have much time. Carlo quickly checked the reins, saddles and foot irons, going about his duties as if he was a second in a duelling match; the pistols ready, the powder dry. 'We're not the amateurs around here, mate,' he joked, enjoying his new role. 'Now all you've gotta do is prove it to them by winning.'

The other riders seemed in high spirits. Only Thomas Crick was out of sorts. When he grudgingly caught Lonnie's glance, he glared across and waved his whip arrogantly. Lonnie felt his mount tense noticeably beneath him at the mere sight of it. 'Easy, boy.' He leaned forward, once more stroking the horse's neck and shoulders.

Carlo had also sensed the horse's fear. He too began soothingly stroking its neck. His hand moved across scar tissue from an old wound and he gave a startled look up at Lonnie. But the time for explanation was lost to the sound of Bookie Win bringing the riders under starter's orders. Along with all the other strappers, Carlo hastily retreated out of harm's way. Lonnie knew his friend needed an explanation, but whatever had to be said would have to wait until the race was over.

Bookie Win hurriedly outlined the rules in his compact accent. As well as being the bookmaker, he was also the official starter. The race was to be run the distance of the Melbourne Cup, only tonight there were no handicaps or set weights. The fountain marked the start and finish of the race. All decisions would be final. The riders had to follow three main rules – all horses had a fair and even start, riders must follow the designated course through the town's streets and the race was to be run in a gentlemanly fashion. 'Plea, no short cut, gent-men.' When Bookie finished, there was a definite hum of excitement from the small crowd.

'Simple enough rules to follow,' scoffed Lonnie, irritated by the idea of what a gentlemanly race meant to the Cricks. For them the words gentleman and fair play were a contradiction.

Lonnie settled his feet firmly into the irons. He shuffled his backside into the saddle, making sure the straps were tight. He clutched the whip in his right hand. Satisfied all was well, he slackened the reins ready for the off.

The starting pistol cracked. Horses were off and running. Lonnie's mount began roughly, rearing at the start and almost throwing him from the saddle. He struggled with the loose reins, and then grabbed with both hands at the horse's neck, somehow managing to hang on. His whip fell to the ground. By the time he had recovered and settled the horse into an even gallop, he found himself trailing the rest of the field by a good eight lengths.

In stark contrast and much to the delight of the Crick dynasty, Thomas had begun the race well. Past Parliament House he was leading the field, his horse travelling magnificently.

There was a thundering of hooves as the seven horses swept around the first corner. Lumps of dirt went flying from the roadway. Lonnie was still the widest of all the runners. He knew he was riding a particularly timid animal; staying out wide and away from the others would give it a little more galloping room.

Riding hands and heels, he constantly whispered, 'Come on boy, you can do it.' As he did, the horse grew in confidence and he gently eased it forward, making up a little ground. Although still too far behind, he was unruffled, deciding it would be wise to remain out wide for the time being.

Still running last, but going much smoother, he rounded the next corner. Lonnie found time to have a quick look around the street. He spotted Billy Bottle and his mob beneath a sign on a wall. No Nuisance. What a laugh. They hooted and bawled at the riders, but when Billy saw Lonnie bringing up the rear, his larrikin shouts turned downright nasty, 'Move up, yer little runt.' He waved a knife menacingly. So Billy Bottle had backed him, great!

Tails swished. Manes flew. The nostrils of the

horses flared open, dragging in more oxygen. Their used breath blew out like hot steam. All seven riders were racing to win and soon Lonnie was travelling as well as anyone.

As his horse cruised past the second-last runner, his thoughts drifted back to the track work at the Golden Acres and the number of times he had secretly ridden this horse, always believing it was exceptional. He had been longing for the day when he could actually race, have the chance to prove himself.

As Lonnie moved up into fifth place, he thought about all his friends who had bet on him. Carlo would be nervous. His glance at Lonnie as the race began was a telltale one. More than likely, he would be pushing his way through the spectators to find the best place to witness the finish. He would be wondering what game Lonnie was playing. He'd been a little upset all along over this race. Say they did lose, Carlo would be heavily out of pocket. It would set him back a considerable way in his business ventures. There would be no ice works built for a long time.

Lonnie crept into fourth place and thought about Pearl. What a big mistake there, thinking she really wanted him as a husband. How wrong could he have been? They were an unlikely match. Not a mistake he'd make again in his life. For the time being he was going to stick to his vow of no ladies. But Pearl had been a mate a lot longer than she had been his girl. She was counting on him to win this race. He couldn't let her down.

He stole a look away to his left. The Push had regathered and was gleefully cheering him on. Was there anyone in Little Lon who hadn't backed him? He nearly dropped the reins at the sudden mental picture of Slasher laid under a layer of turf. Had George already made his move?

'Steady, boy.' Lonnie was not only talking to the horse. Beads of sweat formed like raindrops on his neck. He tried to readjust his thinking. All this extra weight on his shoulders mustn't get him down. He gained more ground and eased up into third place.

By the time they rounded the final corner and were heading up the straight in sight of the fountain, there was only one horse in front of him, ridden by Thomas Crick two lengths to the good. Crick belted his whip against the horse's hindquarters.

Lonnie recalled dropping his whip at the beginning of the race. He had no need, nor wish, to hit his horse. He could feel the power of the magnificent creature going along effortlessly beneath him. The horse's stride lengthened, reaching out, gobbling up the ground with each pace.

Crick turned his head. Lonnie reined in a little, allowing him to maintain his lead. He hoped above all he was not leaving his run too late.

Standing close by the winning line, watching the two riders engaged in their final run, it was more obvious to Carlo viewing the race from a distance, than it was to Crick on top of the leader, that Lonnie wasn't riding his horse flat chat. He seemed to be deliberately holding it back, leaving Crick in front. 'Come on, mate, come on,' he yelled, going hoarse with the effort. This wasn't the time to ease off. 'Ride hard, come on.'

With only fifty metres left to go, Crick again turned to check his lead. The smirk on his face hardly had time to fade, his whip scarcely time to be raised, before Lonnie's horse swept past and crossed the winning line, to win by almost a length. The third horse finished a good three lengths from the winner. The also-rans never got into the race and came in many lengths further back.

Never in his life had Carlo seen such acceleration from a horse at the end of a race, after running that distance. As soon as the track was clear he bolted over and threw both arms around the horse's neck. 'You beaut, you did it,' he gasped, looking up at Lonnie. 'We're set. We're fixed.'

Lonnie gave him a breathless grin.

'You nearly stopped my heart, mate. I'm beside myself. But you conned me, didn't you? You were on Trident, weren't you?' Carlo's excitement bordered on reproach. 'I felt the scar on his neck. You didn't switch horses back. You knew all along you were riding Trident and not Lightning, didn't you?'

'I won, didn't I?'

'How, I don't know, when Lightning is supposed to outclass every bloody horse in Melbourne. My heart's barely pumping. You're a dark horse. I thought I knew all there was to know about you. I may be your best mate, yet you're still keeping secrets from me.'

Lonnie laughed away his friend's ticking off. 'You're right, there's something I never came clean about. But I reckon you'll understand. I'll save it for later while we're doing a bit of celebrating.'

They were interrupted as some of the spectators milled around, slapping the horse and winning jockey in congratulations, before they hurried off to collect their winnings from Bookie Win.

Lonnie shook his head in amazement, now intent on sharing a rundown of the race with Carlo. 'What about when I missed the start? Bet you thought I was a goner.'

'When you dropped your whip!' Carlo gave a crow of indignation. 'Did the jitters get you or what?'

Before he could answer, Bookie Win approached them and stuffed a purse into Lonnie's hand. 'You save Bookie. I take big bet on Crick before race start. If he win, I broke.' Bookie Win had a puzzled look on his face, but he managed a secret smile. 'You very luckee to get ride. Best horse win.'

With a sly grin and a wink at Carlo, Lonnie answered, 'Yes, the best horse won. And as far as being lucky, I sure am.' His fingers gripped the bulging purse, Bookie Win's gift, which, on top of the winning bets and the prize money he still had to collect, added up to a handsome sum.

'Keep quiet about the money,' he muttered to Carlo as the beaten riders began to circle around on their horses, handing over their ten-pound bets and congratulating him. Thomas Crick, true to his colours, remained sulking in the background, a purplish blot of humiliation spreading across his face.

Spotting him, Lonnie couldn't resist a jibe. 'Aren't you going to shake my hand like a gentleman, Mr Crick?'

'Come on over and congratulate our new champion jockey,' Carlo called out.

With all the others observing, Crick had little choice but to ride forward and reluctantly shake the hand of the stable boy who had beaten him fair and square. Only Lonnie heard him say, 'You're finished at Golden Acres. I never forgive and I never forget.' He flung the ten pounds at Lonnie. Throwing his horse around, he nearly knocked Carlo to the ground as he rode off in a mad gallop.

'You can keep it if you let me see Rose again,' Lonnie called with relish, knowing his proposition had the desired effect of making Crick even angrier. As if Lonnie planned ever to cross Rose Payne's path again. Not in this lifetime.

'He's just riffraff,' Carlo said furiously.

'The likes of Thomas Crick don't bother me.' Lonnie slipped Carlo the purse to which he had added the winner's stake. 'This'll perk us up.'

'Sweet Jesus!' Carlo gave a snort of admiration, forgetting in the rush of excitement that he had faithfully promised his mamma never to take the name of the Lord in vain. He swiftly stashed the money into his pockets. 'We're loaded.'

'We've got more winnings coming.'

'More?'

'Yep, but it's your turn to collect. Reckon I've done most of the work up till now.'

The worry of picking up more money overtook Carlo's mood. There was no sign of his usual sharp efficiency as he floundered about like a landed fish. 'Where's Bookie? I better catch him while he's still got our money. Hey, d'ya think I need Bella and the cart to carry home all our cash?'

Lonnie smirked. 'I'd like to think so. Uh-oh, more trouble.'

Crick's strapper came striding towards Lonnie. 'Great ride, mate. Nothing personal, but I've gotta take the horse from you. Better follow orders or I'll be in for a roasting.'

Lonnie dismounted and handed him the reins. 'Be sure you rub him down well before you put him in the stables for the night.'

'Will do. Be careful. You gave it to the boss so bad he's spitting blood.'

Lonnie nodded and gave the horse a stroke of tranquil assurance. His feelings were mixed as he realised his favourite horse was being led away forever. Pride in their achievement. Regret about his loss. Trident was Crick's horse when all was said and done. There was nothing he could do. He wondered anxiously if the Glen had bought Trident. Because if they hadn't, no amount of money offered in the future would. *I'll really miss that horse*, he thought sadly.

He slung his arm around Carlo. 'Meet me at number four in about half an hour with the cash. We'll raid Pearl's stash of grog. I'll explain everything then.' He'd already decided he could pretend as well as Pearl that nothing had ever happened between them. 'Keep out of the back lanes and watch yourself. The strapper's right, I've made a few too many enemies here tonight and they know you're a mate.'

# HOBBLE

## Item No. 1616

*Spoil heap. Location unknown.*
*Fragment of a rope used to restrain an animal.*
*Commonly used for a quiet night horse,*
*kept outside overnight on a homestead*
*and used to muster the other horses in the morning.*

Lonnie should have listened to his own advice. He made his way alone down a street that had been in full life during the race. But in the early hours of the morning the air had turned chill, the windows were latched, the curtains drawn, the onlookers departed.

Life's changes were coming thick and fast for Lonnie and he wanted to do some hard thinking. The win had spelt an abrupt end to his working days at Golden Acres. All his attachments with those detestable Cricks were severed. Good riddance to the lot of them. All being well, Mr Alcock would let him start work soon at the Glen.

If Lonnie had been able to traverse distance and time, he would have understood the effect his winning ride was already having on the Crick dynasty; been able to eavesdrop on the dressing-down Crick senior was about to give his son – Thomas skulking into his father's office in the early hours of that same Sunday morning, not expecting his father to be there. Crick senior sitting in a chair by the fire, his head down, in apparent calmness. Holding his palms forward towards to the flames, rubbing them vigorously to warm them, repeating the action in mindless repetition.

Thomas removing his greatcoat and walking despondently towards the warmth of the fire. Standing by his father's chair. Breaking the silence that was hanging like a nerve end between them. 'How shall I face all my friends tomorrow?'

His father looking up in disgust and opening his mouth in one long and seething complaint. 'Your friends? Does the whole world revolve around you? Only an imbecile loses a rigged, unlosable race to a half-wit kid from the slums! I told everyone I know of importance to back you. Henry Payne lost a small fortune. And he put more on you minutes before the off. You've ruined our reputation. Our credibility's gone. No one in Melbourne will want to deal with us. All because of your blindness and stupidity. And to top it all off, you let me sell Trident to the Alcocks for a pittance.'

Thomas uttering a few miserable words in self-defence: 'I tried to stop you selling, you know I did.'

'You tried to stop me selling a nag for one hundred guineas. That would have been a good price for a nag. Only it wasn't a nag, was it? It's the horse who beat our champion. And you were too stupid to see. You wouldn't know a champion from a night horse.' His ranting temper moving to a crescendo: 'You dare call yourself a son of mine! Get out of my sight!'

If only Lonnie could have witnessed this carry-on for himself. But the reality was he was still making his way down the street towards Pearl's, and by this time feeling mighty proud of himself. One thing was for sure, his dream of becoming a professional jockey had taken a giant leap forward. Those riders were no amateurs. They were all first-class horsemen and gentlemen. Fancy little Lonnie McGuinness, the stableboy, beating the likes of them.

He chuckled, imagining a procession of trainers calling by and asking for the jockey named McGuinness, in the hope of engaging him to ride their very best horses. Maybe one day he would have the pick of their best stables. Maybe one day, with a bit more luck, he'd be dressed in cap and racing silks and bringing home the winner of the Melbourne Cup. Leading it into the unsaddling enclosure to the cheers of the crowd. Standing up in the irons victorious. Waving his whip in salute. He could even hear the unmistakeable sound of pounding hoofs – of horse and rider in full gallop, as if it were happening – closing from behind, closing in on him.

He spun around, the breath of a horse almost upon him. Too slow to recognise the danger; too late to avoid the rope tossed skilfully over his head and shoulders, the slipknot tightening around him, pinning his arms fast against his sides; too helpless to withstand the final power and momentum of the passing horse as it lurched him clean off his feet.

Lonnie was helpless, being dragged face down along the full length of the cobbled street. The roughness of the road drove like nails through his trousers, skinning his knees raw. The skin on his face was burning.

Just when he thought he was a goner, he heard the horse's iron shoes pull up. The rope loosened. He levered his head painfully upwards, trying to identify the rider. Nothing more than a black outline, a phantom. Lonnie clenched his fist, set for some hard hitting.

The whip cracked. The horse moved back and forth, restless and uneasy. An angry order urged it to trample. Disobediently, the horse reared. Such a murderous act wasn't instinctive. The rider spurred the horse away, spinning it hard around, galloping back up the street.

Lonnie waited for the inevitable: his assailant coming back for another go. The frightened animal would have little or no choice but to obey the command. He wasn't wrong. The rider was already turning his horse around and heading back towards him. The anticipation turned the noise into a pounding echo. Lonnie threw the loose rope over his head. Too injured and weak to even crawl, he rolled himself into a ball and covered his face with his arms. With the side of his head half buried in the dirt he could feel the vibrations of the approaching hooves. He braced himself for the impact.

So this was how it would end. Not from any mongrel dog or pickaxe handle; no Uncle Dick with his screwed neck and sucking blood, nor bodies lying around the rick; no stabbings by Slasher Jack; no cut by Billy Bottle; no swinging at the end of a rope in the Melbourne Gaol alongside George. Of all things, he was going to be trampled by a horse in the shadows of Little Lon. His thoughts flew to his mam and how she would receive the news of his death. He would trust Carlo to see her right from the winnings. There was enough to tide her over for a while.

Lonnie felt a whoosh of air above him. The disobedient horse, still unwilling to trample, had launched itself high and long into the air, clearing him with ease. A vicious crack of the whip made the horse rear. Whinnying in terror, the stallion stood almost vertical on hind legs. It tried to dislodge its tormentor from the saddle. Lonnie heard a venomous curse. The whip cracked again. The rider was too experienced and strong a horseman. He subdued the resentful animal. When the horse was finally standing quietly, the rider dismounted.

Lonnie tried to drag himself out of the way. The footsteps closed in. A savage kick landed in his lower back, another drove into his shoulderblades; no mercy shown, the man was intending to teach him a lesson.

Lonnie was swept away on a cloud of impressions entirely disconnected from his own body. Scream, after scream, after scream. The pounding of a galloping horse. The rush of feet on stones. A soft hand brushing his face. A cold wind blowing over him. He caved into an overwhelming desire to drift away.

# FLAT IRON

## Item No. 21

*Heavy cast iron.*
*Heated and used to smooth*
*freshly laundered clothes.*

A light touch on Lonnie's face sent a rush of feverish heat through his cheek. As gentle as it was, it felt red hot, as though someone had pressed a flat iron down hard.

From far away in the distance, a voice that sounded dimly recognisable was asking him a question. 'Lonnie, can you hear me?'

He longed to reply. He worked his way through a range of words as if he were speaking them aloud. *He came from behind, lassoed me*, he was trying to say, but the words forming deep inside came out only as dribbles of air and blood.

The voice sounded annoyed. 'Will you stop blubbering and give me a hand, you cowardly custard.'

'But he looks so heavy,' came the answer. 'I can't carry the poor lug all the way to Casselden Place. Leave him be. We have to get back.'

'You brainless scallywag, we can't leave him here.

Anyways, we only have to get him through the door, past the curtain and up the stairs. Help me, or I swear I'll tell Madam about how you've been drinking the French wine, and watering it down. And don't think I haven't seen, because I have, you moocher.'

'But you told me to do it and you're the one adding the water.'

'Then you won't mind me telling Madam how much you've been drinking, will you? Last week alone I counted five missing bottles. We'll see who she believes the most.'

While Pearl cast a crafty look at Ruby, Lonnie started to count five empty bottles standing on a mantle. But where had he seen them? A childhood voice trilled at the back of his head. 'One, two, three, four, five, once I caught a fish alive.' Pain was a peculiar thing. It turned solid into liquid and slowed down time; split body and mind; changed the here and now into the imagined.

'You wouldn't dare.'

'Try me. Stop loafing like the dense lump of lard you are and help. Mind you lift him gently.'

Lonnie's vague attention drifted to the hands he could feel pressing and cradling his armpits, attempting to lift him. He stared blankly at those butterfly hands. He felt a flutter and a tickle. He could have been laughing. His insides hurt. A moan came rattling from his chest.

'Easy does it, Lonnie.'

If only he could place the voice.

'We'll take him upstairs. Don't let Madam see.'

'If she does, I'll blame you,' Ruby snapped.

'Just do what you're told!' Pearl fumed back. 'Carry him inside before he bleeds to death all over us.'

Ruby shot her a terrified look. 'He won't, will he? What if he does? What if his insides spill out over my dress and his eyes pop out? What if his heart bursts open?' Her voice went shrill at the horror. 'What if he dies?'

'I swear you better shut up before I punch your podgy brain out with my own bare hands.'

To the sound of Ruby heaving and puffing and ever complaining, and before they had taken three unsteady steps, Lonnie heard the sounds of their argument blur. He spun down into a deep dark well of nothingness.

# VELVET COVERLET

## Item No. 6772

*Purple coverlet.*
*Blood stains.*

Carlo had an uneasy premonition about leaving Lonnie by himself after the race. An awful feeling that crept up on him as if a black cat had crossed his path. Like he'd broken a mirror and was facing seven years' bad luck.

'What's happened to him?' he yelled, when he came upon the two girls struggling to carry his injured mate up the steps into the Big House.

'Shut your trap or Madam'll hear us,' gasped Pearl. 'Take over Ruby's end. She's about as useless as a cart without wheels.'

Pearl sent Ruby ahead to dog out, which the girl happily did, more than willing to trade places with Carlo and be out of harm's way. Lonnie was too heavy and Pearl's tongue far too vicious for comfort. When all was clear, she waved them inside. Without so much as a sniff from Madam Buckingham, they managed to support their battered friend into the

Big House and up the spiralling staircase.

Lonnie's limp hand rested on a dark pad of velvet. He took in the sweet smells of rose petal and lavender. He reasoned with cool detachment that he must be inside a lined coffin. Dead as a doornail. At his own funeral. Mourners were tiptoeing past, unaware he was here with them in spirit as well as body. He was an echo, a whisper of his old self, but here nonetheless. It was a moving farewell which made him want to spill some tears of his own. He found his eyes blinking their way around a tiny dusty room hardly bigger than a closet. He wondered who had forgotten to put the coins on his eyelids. He looked in vain for the marbled columns of the crypt. If only his mind would keep a hold of things.

A voice too sick with remorse and sounding more like Carlo than a welcoming angel burst out, 'I've been a fool. I shoulda known Crick would settle the score. Not that he'd dirty his hands. More likely sent one of his bully boys.'

With a puzzled frown, Lonnie slowly came around to Pearl dabbing his face with a wet towel. She waved off Carlo's accusation. 'You don't know who attacked him so pipe down.' When she realised the patient himself was awake, she smiled down tenderly. 'So you're back with us in the land of the living. How're you feeling?'

'Thought I'd died and gone to heaven,' Lonnie managed to croak out.

Pearl plumped up the cushions and velvet coverlets that she'd brought in and bundled together as a mattress, quite frankly relishing her role as Florence Nightingale. Lonnie tried to force himself into a sitting position, unsuccessfully as it were, his shoulder and back stiff from the kicking and the chafes rubbing like nettles on his skin.

'Rest easy. You're out of harm's way.'

Having no choice but to be left to Pearl's fussing, Lonnie settled back down into his coffin. She took him through the full story about how she had discovered him left almost for dead. It was lucky she'd found him in time – Pearl deciding there was no need to give any glory to Ruby, the undeserving little tabby cat – because the rider had been intent on murder. He'd hightailed it when he'd heard the hullabaloo. 'If I hadn't come out when I did that madman would've kicked you into the next kingdom.'

'There's only one madman capable of it. And you want to know why I reckon it's all down to Crick?' said Carlo. 'Because Lonnie beat him in the horse race.'

Pearl raised an eyebrow. 'I could name a few other madmen around here. Hang on,' she said, giving him a look of astonishment as the penny dropped. 'Are you telling me he beat Crick? We won?'

Carlo was still going off half-cocked over Lonnie's beating. 'Go on, tell her I'm right. And when I find him I'll kick his bloody head in.'

'Stop pumping him for answers, yer chump. Can't you see he's groggy?' Pearl patted Lonnie's hand sympathetically. 'Don't go worrying over who done it.'

Lonnie was being coaxed back into a clammy fog of sleep, away from his pain. Pearl was speaking but her declaration was hushed. 'I wish us two could've been together, yer chump. But I can never be what you want me to be. Even with your bunged-up face, you're still far better looking than any lad has a right to be.' Murmurings half-heard, half-imagined. An out of kilter phonograph, fuzzily playing. For his ears only.

# HEAVY LEATHER BELT

## Item No. 4273

*Found in cesspit.*
*Heavy duty, working man's belt.*

A short time later, Lonnie stirred, more alert to his surroundings and the events that had brought him to the Big House. From the room below he heard a great crash. Thumps came in heavy succession. Bang. Bang. Bang. There was a roar of laughter and shrill squeals. Lonnie wondered if Mrs B had employed a vaudeville troupe from the Princess. After a raucous rendition of tar-rar-rar-bump-te-day, a voice like a parrot shouted, 'Parlee-a-mint is cawled, old chums! Moved tem-po-rare-re-lee down the road to this upper-tee establishment! Sit down, yer fat cow, before I deck you.' More laughter and applause followed.

All that popping of fine French wine and gin, the sporting and the entertainment, made Lonnie more miserable, especially when all he was fit for was to lie here and chalk up his injuries. He rubbed the grazes on his nose and chin. They stood out like volcanic lava. His lips were swollen. He opened his mouth, expecting teeth to tumble out and was mightily relieved when they didn't. His shoulder and leg ached. Red snake welts lay in wait on his stomach like ancient cave paintings. A vague image of an oak coffin appeared in the back of his mind, which he hastily tossed out. *Why am I feeling sorry for myself?* he thought. *I could have come out of this a lot worse. I could have not come out at all.*

The door creaked open. A dark-bearded gent tottered into the room, carrying along with him the unmistakeable and pleasant aroma of Havana cigars. He pulled in a curly-haired woman and lifted her dress to her thighs. Lonnie rolled his eyes at the sight of her bloomers.

'Not in here,' the woman objected, tugging down her dress and nudging the gent playfully with her knee.

'Poppycock,' he slurred. His breath was beery and he was having great difficulty unbuttoning the front of his trousers.

She protested again. 'This room's too dingy.'

Lonnie gave a deliberate cough, which startled the man and gave the girl a chance to run off giggling. Turning towards him, the man tried gallantly not to sway. 'Sorry, old chum, no idea someone was in here already.' With great formality he secured his front, apologised once more, and hastily vacated the room.

Lonnie shook his head. These toffs were a breed of their own. With the door closed and the room blackened again, he struggled into a more comfortable position. The night was going to be a long one. He listened to the merrymaking. It soon outlasted his efforts to stay awake.

When he opened his eyes again the house had fallen silent. By his side was a generous helping of currant cake and a jug of ginger ale. Some fattening up from Pearl, he guessed rightly. He managed to get some of the food past his lips and swilled it down with the warm, sharp-tasting drink.

It may only have been his mind, but the bite to eat made him feel a little stronger. He decided the cuts and grazes were only surface wounds, looking worse than they felt; although the same couldn't be said for his shoulder and leg, they hurt worse than they looked. That applied to his embarrassment as well. Since making a chump of himself with his misguided declarations to Pearl he figured he'd have to smooth things over face-to-face when next they met. No point in hanging around here then. Better to be home in his own bed.

He stood up slowly, straightening his legs. After testing them for broken bones, he opened the door a smidgeon and peeped out. There was a wide carpeted corridor with doors coming off to the left and right. At the far end an oak staircase curled its way downwards. One foot was out when he overheard the voice of Mrs B coming clear as day from the neighbouring room.

He ducked back into his hidey-hole. Mrs B was midway through an argument and he could make out every word.

'I'm sick of you asking. She knows nothing and she never will.'

'I'm not risking the law sniffing around.' The second voice was Burke's. 'It's my neck they'll be after.'

'That I won't forget. It was a hot-headed thing you did, getting into a fight and throwing him down the stairs. We both know I'm in as deeply as you. Look, I asked her the other day and I believe her. She's a godly girl. She doesn't remember a thing.'

'From now on, I'll be keeping an eye on that Daisy Cameron myself, see if I don't.'

'Don't you touch her unless I say. I mean it, Burke. If you interfere I'll send you packing. You know as well as I do the girl was only a snivelling child at the time. She's erased the night from her memory. I'm telling you once and for all, Daisy Cameron does not recall how her father died. Now get out of here and leave me to my business.'

Lonnie tried to sort out the story he'd just heard. So Daisy's missing pa had been killed in a fight with Burke. And Mrs B was involved, too. It was a shock to him. More so that Daisy had seen them do it. Only she didn't remember. It dawned on him what

Postlethwaite had said that day in the phrenological shop about fear and he fingered the back of his neck. At last it was all starting to make sense. Daisy couldn't remember by day because her memory of the murder was locked away at the base of her skull, only somehow it was forcing its way out at night in the form of a nightmare.

After Burke left, Madam Buckingham paused for a while by the window, looking out onto the lamp-lit street. She recalled the events of that night, when upon hearing a torrent of filthy abuse and heart-wrenching cries that even *she* found disturbing – and it took a lot to make her cringe – she and Burke had stormed up a flight of steep grey steps into the cesspit that Samuel Cameron called home.

'Stop yer thrashing, you cowardly sot.' Madam Buckingham remembered how the reeking, gut-wrenching, drunken excuse of a man had wobbled to his feet at the sound of her commanding voice and the sight of Burke's huge bulk beside her. From across his knee the bundle of rags that was his little girl fell to the ground. The thick leather belt was raised above his head, the momentum of the swing almost causing him to fall over backwards.

As the girl struggled to cover her bruised buttocks with her hands and pulled at her threadbare pinafore, her father's foot kicked out viciously and she rolled across the floor like a skittle ball. It was a sight enough to melt even Madam's own hardened heart.

The man wrapped the heavily buckled belt more tightly around his right fist. It was the same one he had been using on poor Daisy when the two interrupted him and he intended giving them some of the same. He staggered towards the two intruders, so drunk he could barely walk, let alone be of any real threat to the giant of a man facing him.

Sharp as ever, Madam Buckingham sized up all the danger signs and took a step to the side. At the same time Burke moved forward, grabbed the drunk by the shoulders and lifted him from his feet in a single movement, tossing him head first. Daisy's pa tumbled head over heels down the stone treads until he came to rest at the bottom of the stairwell with his skull well and truly caved in.

On Madam's orders Burke bundled the girl into his rough arms. They stepped over the rapidly spreading stain that was encircling her father's head, its colour the only relief to the drabness of the house. He carried the senseless child to the safety of the Leitrim, as gently as it was possible for a lumbering thug to do.

From that time until the other day, Daisy Cameron had asked no questions, simply accepted her home address as the Leitrim and her placement as seamstress, without so much as a murmur. Hadn't they, after all, done a good deed by ridding her once and for all of that wretched, gut-of-the-devil father of hers? Madam Buckingham remained convinced that the God-fearing sprat remembered nothing more about the events of that night. But if she did hear any different, she couldn't guarantee Burke would be as gentle with Missy Cameron the next time round.

# JAR LID

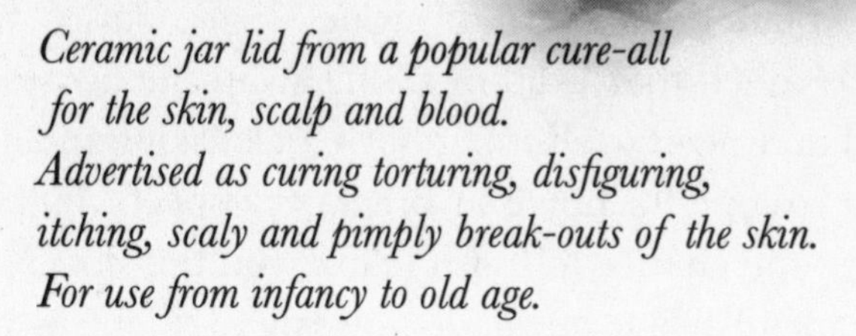

## Item No. 955

*Ceramic jar lid from a popular cure-all*
*for the skin, scalp and blood.*
*Advertised as curing torturing, disfiguring,*
*itching, scaly and pimply break-outs of the skin.*
*For use from infancy to old age.*

With the place to himself, Lonnie set up for a day of rest and recreation in his mam's armchair. Things were looking up. His grazes were already starting to scab over, thanks to the soothing lotion, and the swelling was subsiding.

It didn't take long for the first of his visitors to come knocking. Not that Carlo bothered to signal his arrival. He sauntered in without saying a word. He was hardly through the door before he pulled out the race purse he had been keeping safe, sprawled out on the rug and flung a fistful of the notes into the air, letting them fall like feathers on his head and face. 'How'd you pull up this morning?' he finally asked.

'Never felt better, mate,' Lonnie wisecracked.

'So fill me in. You're lassoed, dragged through the streets, kicked in the ribs, cut to smithereens. Anything else I missed?' Carlo gave him a sideways glance. 'You know, I felt sick on race night when I touched the scar and realised it was Trident you were riding. And there I was thinking you'd swapped them back.'

The blunt edge of the remark wasn't lost on Lonnie, who took a deep breath, knowing full well some explanations were overdue. 'See Carlo, it wasn't as much that I did or didn't swap the horses, only I didn't need to. Remember Crick asking me if I'd ever galloped a horse at breakneck speed, but I never got the chance to finish telling you the story?'

'You mean when he made you ride Trident as a pacemaker?'

Lonnie nodded. 'Crick didn't know I'd galloped him a few times before. It was always in the dark or when no one was around. One day we were going like the wind and I got a bit excited. I hit him with the whip, not hard mind you, just to keep his mind on the job, but he pulled up short and lost all interest. Hard as I tried I couldn't get him back into full stride again. This all ties into when I dropped my whip at the very start of the race.'

Carlo said, 'Yeah, when it slipped out of your hand, I tell you my heart sank a fathom or two.'

'It was no accident. I dropped the whip on purpose. Don't touch Trident and he'll ride like a champion, but you whip him and he'll stop trying. If Crick had half a brain he would've cottoned on. The only reason I never went past in track work was because I was holding him back. Crick would never've let me ride him again. The point is, Carlo, I could've won on whichever horse they gave me. I was always going to be on the winner. It's a good feeling to have outsmarted Thomas Crick.' He sat back. Sweet revenge, he called it. A crowd of onlookers to witness Crick's defeat, not to mention taking his money, too. Well worth waiting for.

'So what's going to stop Crick whipping Trident from now on?'

'Nothing if they still own him.' Lonnie hoped with all his heart the Glen had gone through with the sale.

Carlo wasn't as impressed as Lonnie had hoped he would be when he told him. 'You still shoulda told me which horse you were on.' With a sweep of his hand, he peevishly swiped up the money that lay scattered on the floor, straightened the ears of the notes, stacked up the coins and surveyed the amount in front of them. 'So how did you manage to win all this?'

'I put all I had on myself.'

Carlo's face registered surprise. 'And a bit more besides! Come on, you're not worth that much. Where did you find the extra dosh to wager?'

'Besides all the bets you put on me earlier, you mean? The truth is I put on a heap more later.' That was another detail he'd kept quiet about which he now explained. 'A few friends at the stable who knew I was mates with Bookie asked me to place some bets on Crick for them. And that night at the Eastern Market, Rose Payne gave me something to bet on us both. That sort of thing.'

'But Crick lost,' pestered Carlo. 'So how does that win us all this money?'

A brief flicker of guilt washed over Lonnie's face. 'I put it all on me to win.'

'All the bets? Even those you shoulda put on Crick?'

'I couldn't stand to lose all that money.'

'If Crick won and you didn't pay up, they would've been lining up to murder you.'

'But he didn't win.'

'You were nearly killed because you did! And there's me, thinking I had my own troubles.'

Lonnie could sense the friction in the air.

'You didn't let slip to Slasher that he should bet on Crick by any chance, did ya?'

This remark knocked Lonnie for six. He never even saw it coming. 'Why would you say that?'

'He's vanished with Annie's takings.'

Although Lonnie had fully expected to hear the news sooner or later, the knowledge that George had repaid the favour hung heavily on his conscience. He prayed the Push had done nothing more than scare him off.

'Are you going to let him get away with it?'

Carlo was pressing him but Lonnie couldn't seem to focus. 'Who?'

'Crick! He must have had you beat up. I'm up for a bit of payback if you are.'

What was Carlo asking? To wait in the shadows ready to beat the living daylight out of Crick? Slice his throat with a bit of broken bottle? Belt a knuckle duster into his face? Slip a knife into his heart? Lonnie had seen enough violence. He was through with it. All he knew was he had to see George as soon as possible and find out what was going on. 'Let it go, mate,' was all he could manage to say.

'Suits me fine, then.' Carlo replied, put out. He knew Lonnie was keeping something else from him. And he was dead right.

# BILLIARD BALL

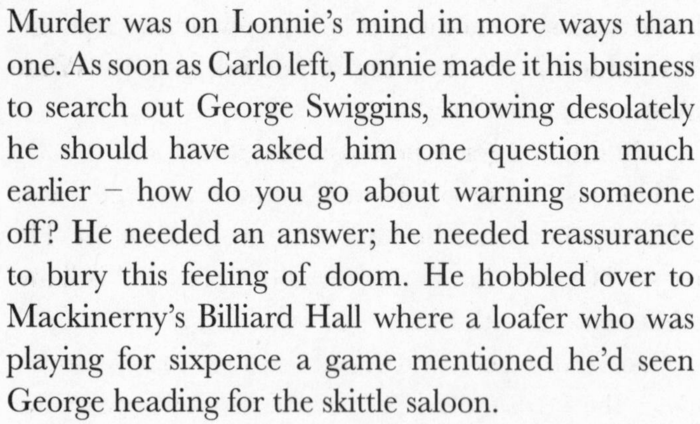

## Item No. 4169

*A well-used, chipped billiard ball.*

Murder was on Lonnie's mind in more ways than one. As soon as Carlo left, Lonnie made it his business to search out George Swiggins, knowing desolately he should have asked him one question much earlier – how do you go about warning someone off? He needed an answer; he needed reassurance to bury this feeling of doom. He hobbled over to Mackinerny's Billiard Hall where a loafer who was playing for sixpence a game mentioned he'd seen George heading for the skittle saloon.

'Hey, George,' Lonnie yelled, closing in on him, 'wait up.'

Making every effort to catch his breath, Lonnie faced the Push leader. 'What did you do to Slasher?'

George reached out to touch the healing scabs on Lonnie's face.

Shying away from the contact, Lonnie jerked his head back.

'Geez, me old pigeon, it's me who should be asking

what someone's done to *you*. Think you should really be joining us. There's safety in numbers. As for Jack, we sorted him.'

'How?'

George gave Lonnie an indifferent look then pulled him up close. Lonnie found himself staring at the scrapes and nicks from where George had been too rough with the razor that morning. 'I'm beginning to think you're my lucky charm,' the leader of the Push said cryptically. 'You seem to keep doing me favours. Easiest money I ever made without stealing.'

Lonnie looked at him in bewilderment. 'What money?'

'My little wager. Knew you had it in you.'

The last thing on Lonnie's mind was the race. This was not what he had come to hear about. He pressed George for an answer about Slasher. 'Tell me what you did with him!'

'Don't you go worrying about that mad vulture. Once the Push took over the business it weren't your concern anymore.' He flashed Lonnie a thin-lipped smile. Everything about his expression was stretched tight. 'Only Push know Push doings. If you want to know more, join us. Otherwise, shut it. We don't want no blabbering.' George flicked a spot of dust off his lapel as if he didn't have a care in the world. 'Ever seen a body wrapped and prepared for burial at sea?'

Lonnie felt a strong wave of revulsion. It was true

then. George had gone ahead and killed Slasher. Dumped him overboard in the bay without ceremony, leaving the devil to claim his lost and low soul as he sank, and George not even working up a sweat as he admitted to the deed. Here he was, without a hint of a worry, slipping Lonnie a purse, as if they were the best of friends and not accomplices in a murder. He tried to take in what else George was saying.

'Make sure Annie Walker receives this. Tell Pearl she's straight with her. Not a word about the Push, the glory's all yours. Between you and me it's a direct gift. Because I'm telling you, Jack was in no fit state to argue when we relieved him of it. Serves the mad bugger right.'

Lonnie's body gave an uncontrollable shudder at the vision of Jack's murder, his muscles and nerve ends seeming to expel the very last ounce of goodness in him. He'd got his answer all right. Slasher Jack was dead and he was to blame. He could already hear the hangman draw the bolt, the floor fall from beneath him and his neck snap.

It tickled George Swiggins to see him squirm. If McGuinness believed he was somehow to blame for Jack's disappearance, so much the better. Always wise to keep the upper hand. As for George, he had never experienced guilt over his own misdeeds. Supposing he ever had the misfortune to be afflicted by self blame, he would crush the emotion to pieces, ram his hard-knuckled fist into its cheekbone. All business settled as far as he was concerned, the leader of the Push idled off down the street, his hands in his pockets and whistling a tune.

# SMALL INGOT OF GOLD

## Item No. 3524

*Small ingot of gold with no hallmark.*
*All legal gold is hallmarked.*

'Pinch me if there isn't something beating in that hard shell of hers, after all.' Pearl could find no explanation for Annie's sudden change of heart. But there was no doubting her relief. She gave a splurt of laughter, her open mouth sending out a generous spray of half-chewed oyster over Lonnie. 'Oh and 'scuse my ill-bred manners,' she tittered, reaching for another.

A warm smell of the sea enriched the tiny front room of the McGuinness house. The bag of shellfish, hot and steaming, brought over to cheer up Lonnie and put him on the road to recovery, was empty.

'Got through those quick enough.' She eyed him wickedly. 'No wonder you love 'em so much, they do medicinal things for lads. Make your parts stronger, if you know what I mean.'

There was no denying that with Annie off her back Pearl was her old self again. She appeared to have completely struck out the memory of the past few months. If not for her teasing or the pride of his own manhood, Lonnie could have even believed she'd forgotten the night they spent together. Whatever the reason, her witty outbursts and high spirits were a fresh breeze, just what Lonnie needed to bring him out of the doldrums. And should he care to admit it, there was a great relief in never having to touch on the details of their love tryst ever again.

'I just can't get over how she marched up to me at the Governor and said clear as day, "You scums deserve each other". Meant the same thing, didn't it? That my debt's paid and I'm free of her and Slasher Jack.'

Lonnie knew only too well why Annie's change of mind had been swift, but he did not try to enlighten his friend. After all, what could he say? Tell how he had persuaded George to make Jack disappear? And now Jack was dead. That the money Annie received was her own in the first place? No, he couldn't come clean. Why, even now he was breaking out in a cold sweat that the law might be approaching his door anytime to arrest him for the murder. 'Sounds like you're off the hook,' was all the reply he could muster.

He fought to control his own low spirits. His forced smile was a weak front that, thankfully, Pearl didn't spot because she beamed right back at him. 'Too right.'

'Suppose you won't be needing this then?' Lonnie handed over her share of the winnings.

'That's plumb more than I've ever had in my whole life!' She shook her head wondrously. 'Is it all mine?'

'Odds went up just before the start,' he explained. 'Something to do with a large bet placed on a losing horse just before the off. Should be enough to set you up real decent somewhere.'

'As if I'd ever leave Little Lon!' Pearl would not hear of the idea, her dream of walking over the bridge and out of Melbourne gone of its own accord now she was free of danger.

Their conversation was interrupted by a knock at the door. Daisy arrived, loaded up with beef broth and plum duff on the same errand of mercy. 'I just called round to take a squiz at the new jockey. You know, the one everyone's talking about, the one from Little Lon, that McGuinness lad, the one Carlo said I should pick up my winnings from before he bets it on something else …'

Pearl put in her own twopence worth. 'Not the *good-looking* jockey who comes from …'

'… Casselden Place,' they chirped in unison.

'Stop taking the micky,' Lonnie said. 'And I only bet on sure things.'

'Same here,' the girls chorused and burst into a fit of giggles.

'Think I'll book you two in the circus as a double

act!' He handed Daisy a tidy sum.

'So much?' she queried, in astonishment.

'We won a bit more than expected. I've just finished telling Pearl.'

Daisy stared at the money, half expecting a strike of lightning to hit or hellfire to scorch the soles of her feet. 'I don't know how you ever convinced me to take part in this escapade, Lonnie. The devil himself must be taking me over.'

'Daisy Cameron having a small wager, tut-tut,' remarked Pearl. She was having none of this. 'Strike her down! If it'll make you feel any better, donate some to the Army and to Miss Selina. Then no one can say your heart isn't in the right place.'

'Well I don't suppose it will matter if I keep a small amount for buttons or thread.'

'Buy a sewing treadle,' corrected Pearl. 'You deserve a break. Make life easier.'

'Oh, I couldn't! Maybe not easier, but …' She seemed to be giving Pearl's idea some serious consideration. 'I could work faster, couldn't I? Earn more and donate it to the poor.'

'We're the poor, yer soft-hearted chump,' Pearl said fondly. When Daisy looked unnerved, she cheered her up with, 'Yes, you could do a lot of good for folks with a sewing treadle.'

Thankfully Daisy was reconciling herself to keeping the winnings. Lonnie saw a good opportunity to continue the spread of charity. 'Speaking of Miss

Selina,' he remarked, 'Pearl was just saying before you arrived that with her help she may leave the trade.'

'I never said such a thing, you're putting words into my mouth.' Pearl had better forms of entertainment going on in her head. 'With all this cash we could have a party like them pollies who were gallivanting around the Big House.' She gave a hearty snigger. 'Poor old Lonnie missed out on all the fun, slept through the whole thing.'

'What fun?' Daisy asked, although she preferred not to know what went on behind the closed doors of the Big House, or right in this very lane. She also felt the need to defend Lonnie, all cut up and bruised from that cruel attack. 'You can't blame him. He was all woozy.' She smiled radiantly at him, with reassuring loyalty.

Lonnie didn't see the point of Pearl's joke either as he recollected the boisterous goings-on below on the night he lay in the dark hideaway with too many aches and pains to settle in comfort. 'I heard them all right,' he said, 'and I met one of them gents as well. First I thought you'd sent a doctor, but he was only a drunken slob trying it on a girl.'

Daisy flinched. But not the devilish Pearl who, wanting one up on Lonnie, decided to elaborate on the events. 'You don't know the half of it. Every one of them pollies was as drunk as a brewery worker on a double shift. Should'a seen them, dressing up in our best feathers, the mace in tow. They were thumping on the parlour door while we had to act all la-di-dah; made us speak like we had pokers stuck up our arses.'

'Pearl!' Daisy reprimanded, shocked at her evil tongue. She stopped abruptly, her eyes incredulous. 'Wait a minute! You're not talking about the mace that went missing from Parliament House?' She looked at Lonnie's bewildered expression. 'Been all the talk since the theft. It's real gold!'

'That's the secret of it,' said Pearl, pleased as punch to be delivering this morsel of news to her astonished friends. 'Let's hope whoever sneaked it out has the brains to put it back where it belongs before the law gets wind of them.'

'I thought me winning the street race was the big news around here.'

'Old news,' Pearl replied with a cheeky grin.

'Life goes on,' Daisy added philosophically.

'Too fast from the sounds of it,' said Lonnie, miffed that his goodhearted handing out of the winnings had been gazumped by a golden mace. 'I got a story myself. It's about you, Daisy. I heard it while Pearl reckoned I was sleeping.'

'Me?' Daisy asked uncertainly.

Lonnie wondered if it was wise of him to mention it. With a little more caution, he replied, 'In a way I'm afraid to say. You may not want to know.'

'Is it important?' she said.

Lonnie knew Daisy had a right to make up her

own mind. Here goes, he thought, nodding. 'While I was waiting to sneak out of the Big House, I overheard Mrs B and Burke talking about the night your pa disappeared.'

At the mention of her pa, Daisy grabbed Pearl's hand and squeezed it tightly.

Lonnie recreated the events. 'Your pa must've been fighting with Burke and he fell down the stairs and hit his head. The fall killed him instantly.'

'Like in my nightmare,' Daisy agreed quietly.

'You were there, Daise. You saw it. Mrs B says you don't remember anything, but Burke thinks you do. If you ever breathe a word to anyone about this, you'll be in grave danger. I hate to admit it, but that shyster Postlethwaite was right all along. Your fear section here,' he tapped the nape of her neck, 'hid the memory and made you forget. Except you only put it out of your mind during the day, while you remembered bits and pieces in your sleep.'

'I know I should grieve for my pa,' Daisy said, filled with regret. 'God rest his soul, but my life up till then was horrible.'

'You don't have to tell us, Daise, we know. My mam was reduced to tears many a time knowing you were living in that squalor.'

'Your mam's beautiful. She's always been kind to me. In a strange sort of way Madam Buckingham's been kind too, setting me up in the room, arranging the work.'

'She's not a bit like Lonnie's mam,' cut in Pearl sharply. 'She's only been looking out for herself and Burke.'

'Don't be too hard on her,' replied Daisy. 'I like to think she cares for me, if only a little.' She looked at her two friends. 'What's done is done. It's the here and now we have to think about. I'll sleep better from now on. No misgivings. But this stays forever between the three of us. Pact?'

She turned her palm upwards and waited for Pearl and Lonnie to place their hands on top of hers. They were three children again, binding their secrets together like they used to do around the cesspit. She made them stand up, clasp hands and walk around in a circle. Soon they were chanting their childhood song:

*Around the rick, around the rick*
*And there I found my Uncle Dick*
*I screwed his neck*
*I sucked his blood*
*And left his body lying.*

'That's settled, then,' said Daisy.

'Anyone for an Uncle Dick?' Pearl offered, intent on brightening up their mood once more. So Uncle Dick was brought out of her basket in the shape of a bottle of French wine, Bordeaux, mixed in five parts, with the compliments of Madam Buckingham and the Big House pollies.

# WALL HANGING

## Item No. 727

*Home sewn tapestry bearing:*
*'Bless this house'.*

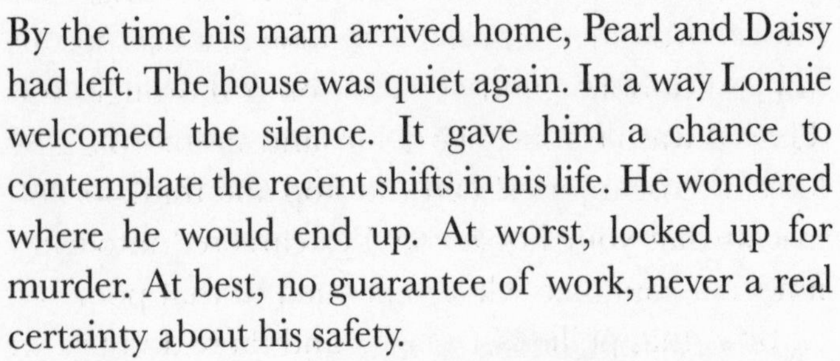

By the time his mam arrived home, Pearl and Daisy had left. The house was quiet again. In a way Lonnie welcomed the silence. It gave him a chance to contemplate the recent shifts in his life. He wondered where he would end up. At worst, locked up for murder. At best, no guarantee of work, never a real certainty about his safety.

'Lonnie, what in heaven's name have you been doing?' his mother exclaimed when she walked through the door and saw the state of his face.

'Some lunatic knocked me over with his horse. It's only a scratch or two.'

'You've been fighting?'

'No.'

'What makes me think you're not telling me everything?'

'Leave it alone, Mam.'

'And why should I do that, son?'

Lonnie braced himself for a lecture.

'You're never home these days, always out or coming in late at night. I wonder you ever come home at all, or if you're really helping Carlo all the time like you say. Surely his cart is working all right by now, the amount of hours you both spend fixing it.'

'You can't expect me to stay at home all the time.'

His mother's eyes searched his face in a baffled, sad sort of way. 'So tell me it's not true then. Tell me that everyone I've bumped into in Little Lon is lying. That it wasn't you flying through town on a horse? Not on any old dobbin mind you, but on a thoroughbred. That it wasn't you risking life and limb? My god, look at those injuries! Did you stop and think for one instant that your horse could've careered into some innocent soul, like what happened to that poor boy … or to that pollie last year. Stand there and tell me it's not true?'

'That pollie was drunk.'

His mother looked at him, at the empty glasses and bottle on the mantle. 'You dare talk to me about drinking.'

'But we were only celebrating 'cause I won. More money than we've ever seen in our lives.'

'Not only reckless, but a drunken gambler, too.'

His spirits dropped. 'Stop exaggerating, Mam. I've only been trying to fix things.' He wished she'd stop calling him a rogue. Whatever he'd done had been with others in mind. He added, 'The way Da did.'

'Decency, Lonnie. An honest day's work. Truth between family and friends. They were the important things in life to your father.' She pointed to the tapestry hanging on the wall. 'Well, may He bless this house! You could've been killed, or just as bad been responsible for someone else's death. What if you'd been arrested? Don't you take any notice of what's going on around here?'

'I've only ever done it the once.'

'It's not like you're still a little boy and think you can trick me. Remember that chicken walking down Bourke Street you picked up and brought home, the day I mentioned wanting a chicken for dinner and couldn't afford to buy one. Like the chicken just happened to be walking down Bourke Street! Or was I supposed to believe it'd just flown into our backyard when you changed your story? Lies aren't harmless when they affect other people. I don't even think you realise you're doing anything wrong.'

No use acting like a man when his mam was still thinking of him as a tacker. What did she expect? For him to stand back and let someone like Crick boast everyday how he was better than them? Day in, day out, being told he was no good. Was that how she wanted him to spend his life? There was no denying he'd been insulted by Crick. And if he was totally honest, he did want to get even. But he'd always tried to help his mam. He knew his own strengths and if he could make some money on the side what was the problem? As far as Lonnie was concerned his arguments could not be shot down. The world was changing. If his mam wanted to stay in the past then it was her bad luck. 'Seventy pounds, Mam, in prize money. Not really gambling,' he said sullenly, hiding the extent of the true amount.

'Can I expect any more shocks?' his mam asked wearily. Before he could reply she turned away, too upset to tell him off anymore.

In reality Lonnie knew there may well be one almighty shock still in store for her. The truth was if the law caught on they might charge him for Slasher Jack's murder, a wrongdoing he could not deny. At the end of the day it didn't matter about all the terror Slasher had cast over Pearl and many others. Lonnie knew deep down that there was no escaping some things – to knowingly send a man to his death was wrong.

# TROPHY

## Item No. 3769

*Miniature replica of the Melbourne Cup trophy celebrating the win of Glenloth.*

Over the next few days, Lonnie's grave fears were not reassured by the comings and goings in Little Lon. Mrs B's houses, together with Annie's, were raided by the law, for it was believed the mace had found its way to one of the brothels before being melted down and sold off. Parliament was in uproar, all eyes, as well as being pinned on each other, were watching the trade in gold. Two constables who obviously hadn't been briefed were caught short in the searches, found hiding in the water closet behind number four. However, no one out of the ordinary had as yet come knocking on Lonnie's door to march him off to gaol, and he was beginning to hope he had escaped detection.

After all the explosiveness in his own life of late everything else seemed mundane by comparison. He sometimes wondered if life meant to deliberately hand out disasters, which in his case seemed to come in lashings, so that good times would follow; as if the heavens needed to balance life's ups and downs.

Thankfully it had not taken long for him to fully recover from his injuries.

But his stroke of luck came when Ned gave him the word to start work at the Glen. He had settled in so well he could barely imagine having worked anywhere else. Golden Acres was a distant bad memory. Even his mam was going about these days with a smile, reassured her son had an honest, hard-working job – away from the Cricks – to keep him out of mischief, and hopeful he meant his promise never to street race again.

Lonnie's fears about Mr Alcock not buying Trident had been unfounded. It was incredible news to him when he heard how the Glen had sent Ned over to Golden Acres to buy the horse. Trident had been put out to pasture and given time to settle in before being put to work. He was now in full training.

In fact, life could not be more fortunate, if not for his guilt over Slasher Jack, which he still wore like a weighted saddle on his back. Nevertheless, Lonnie was determined to make the best of these go-ahead opportunities, which at this very moment meant pitching hay from a wagon, and he did it with the same enthusiasm he would have used digging for gold.

'Over here, lad.'

Ned's voice broke Lonnie out of his daydreams. 'Who, me?' he called.

'Of course you, Lonnie.' Ned waved him over. 'I've

just had our top jockey ride that horse you persuaded us to buy and I'm afraid it's not looking so good.'

'Trident?'

'Yes. If we keep him we'll be changing his name, something more fitting to the Glen.'

'If you keep him?' Lonnie knew how foolish he sounded to his new foreman, but he couldn't conquer the fear that something was wrong. 'You've got to let me check him, let me ride him, see if he's injured.'

'Steady on,' Ned replied. While he valued a passionate and testy spirit, he was far too busy today for an outburst. 'Pull your horns in a bit and listen to me, because you obviously didn't before. First, I do know horses and he's not injured. No question of that.'

Lonnie swallowed hard, forcing himself to stop the rambling. He took a step backwards to lean on the wagon. The last thing he wanted was to agitate his foreman. 'Sorry, sir, I'm not suggesting you don't know horses.' Lonnie was not questioning Ned's ability. He had seen enough to know Ned shared his own deep feelings for animals. Nor did he want him thinking he was a shirker, or worse, a fool.

'There you go, off and running again, shut up, lad, and let me speak.' Understanding the boy's discomfort, Ned softened his tone. 'Let me finish what I have to say then you can say your piece. Agreed?'

Lonnie nodded, even though he could hardly hold back what was on his tongue.

'Fine, let's say we agree the horse is not injured and that my very best jockey rode him. And, might I add, gave him every chance. And that I saw the trial with my own eyes. But Trident just didn't fire. Believe me, he seemed a very ordinary horse. Now you have your say and then get back to work.'

Lonnie was grateful to be allowed to speak his mind, although he realised there was no reason for Ned to give any credit to his opinion. 'I'm not so good with words, sir,' he started awkwardly. 'I can't win you over that way. But let me ride against your best horse and jockey, and I'll prove that Trident is no ordinary horse.'

The foreman shook his head, still unconvinced. 'It's a waste of time, my lad, and time's money. We're not paying you to play games.'

Lonnie knew if he let this chance slip by he may never have another opportunity to convince the Glen to hold on to Trident. He pressed on. 'Let me say one more thing, sir, and then I'll go back to work and make up for any lost time. For that you have my promise. But if you give me one chance to race Trident against your best horse and jockey, I'll prove he's fine. If I lose I won't argue any further and you won't have to pay me next week.'

Ned raised an eyebrow. 'Losing a week's pay will set you back hard. You really believe you're a better rider than my top jockey?'

'No, sir, but I do believe Trident will go so much

better for me. I don't know why, he just does.'

'Why I'm bothering I don't know, but okay, let's see you prove your point. Saddle up the horse. I'll arrange for a good jockey and horse to race you. Be at the six furlong post at eight sharp.'

Lonnie forgot his station in his excitement, saying, 'Thanks, Ned.' He quickly corrected himself. 'I mean thanks, sir. But Trident won't even get warmed up over the six furlongs. He's a stayer, can we make it further?'

'Don't try my patience, it's six or nothing. Besides, the rest of the track is under repair, you know that.' Ned shielded a sly smile. Here he was explaining himself for no good reason. He wholeheartedly agreed with Mr Alcock, this lad certainly had some pluck.

At two minutes to eight, Lonnie cantered Trident over to the track, then dismounted. Best to take his weight off the horse's back. He spoke in hushed tones, explaining to the horse the importance of doing its best on the track today. Even though Lonnie had faith in Trident, he waited anxiously for his competitor to turn up. When the Glen's top horse and rider drew alongside, Lonnie nervously remounted.

The jockey had no intention of being pleasant. 'Why I'm here in such a mismatch, I'll never know, but I'm going to enjoy thrashing you, if only for what you did to my mate, Thomas Crick.'

Lonnie gulped. *Here I go again*, he thought. *Just*

*when I'm about to ride in another race with such high stakes, I find myself up against a mate of Crick's.* He steadied Trident and whispered to the horse and to himself, 'We can do it.'

Ned leaned over the running rail and called, 'Are you two ready?' Both riders touched their caps in a salute of confirmation. 'Go!'

Down at the five furlong mark, Lonnie and Trident were three lengths behind. Lonnie chastised the horse. 'If only you didn't miss the start every time and get so far behind, you wouldn't have to work so hard later in the race.'

Trident stuck out his tongue the way horses often do when racing, but Lonnie could have sworn the horse was making a point.

'Come on,' he coaxed a few moments later, 'move up a little closer, we're approaching the two furlong mark. The race is nearly over.' Lonnie stood high in the stirrups, leaning forward to take the weight off the horse's back. 'Come on boy, come on.'

Trident understood all right. He went into top gear and finished off the race at a speed that Ned would later recall he had never seen before in any horse, stayer or sprinter.

On many a future first Tuesday in November, the Glen foreman would fondly recall this particular morning to anyone who cared to listen. How everyone knew him to be a tough bloke who, like all good Scotsmen, rarely showed his emotions, but the sight of that Little Lon lad and his horse riding so gracefully was one of those rare occasions that could break through his cast-iron mask. How it had made his face glow with anticipation. How he had shaken his head in disbelief and said, 'I swear that's not the same horse I saw earlier. What an unbelievable finishing burst!' How he had asked in amazement: 'Does he do that for you all the time?' How Lonnie had answered proudly: 'He does, sir. He does.' And how Ned knew, without a doubt, that one day Lonnie McGuinness would ride this horse in first place past the winning post in a major race. And there would be a trophy to prove it.

Ned was only too happy to give the lad his proper dues. 'Well, you'll get your pay next week, don't you worry! You never intended losing your wages, did you?' But he'd have to earn those dues from now on. 'I want you to ride Trident all the time. As your main job. You must ride him at all track work. You feed him, you groom him, you exercise him and you even sleep with him if he's sick. Agreed?'

At first Lonnie thought he was hearing things, that he had somehow got Ned's announcement muddled. But as the orders sank in he was in full agreement. 'Too right I will.'

Ned appeared to be as excited as Lonnie. 'Here's the deal then, lad. How'd you like to be signed up as an apprentice jockey? We'll get you riding at the races as soon as possible. Apart from a few minor refinements, I think you're up to it. You'll get a bit more money, of course. I suppose I should talk to the boss first. He's looking to see how you settle in, but I'll take the punt that he'll agree.' With a grin as broad as a beach at low tide, Ned reached out to shake Lonnie's hand.

Lost for words, Lonnie numbly returned the handshake.

'Move yourself, lad, don't just stand there like an imbecile, get that horse rubbed down.'

'Yes, sir, yes, sir,' Lonnie repeated, marvelling at his own luck.

Ned had one caution for him. A friendly word of warning for the future, he called it. 'A lot of names have been thrown around over a certain street race. Be very clear about one thing, don't ever enter one again or take any part whatsoever. You hear what I'm saying? Keep well away or you won't be working here for long.'

If Lonnie had ever felt undecided about his promise to his mam to never street race again, the prospect of doing so was forever erased. Ned's advice to go on the straight and narrow was the way it was going to be from now on. His future was at the Glen and he'd do his best to measure up. He vowed never to let this marvellous horse out of his sight. He wouldn't even go home that night. He'd sleep in the stable alongside Trident and dream up a new name for his favourite horse himself.

‘So Ned’s just found out what we’ve all known for ages. It took him long enough to realise,’ Daisy said, full of praise when Lonnie dropped by the next day to tell her his good news. ‘That you’re the best jockey around.’

# BRASS KNUCKLE

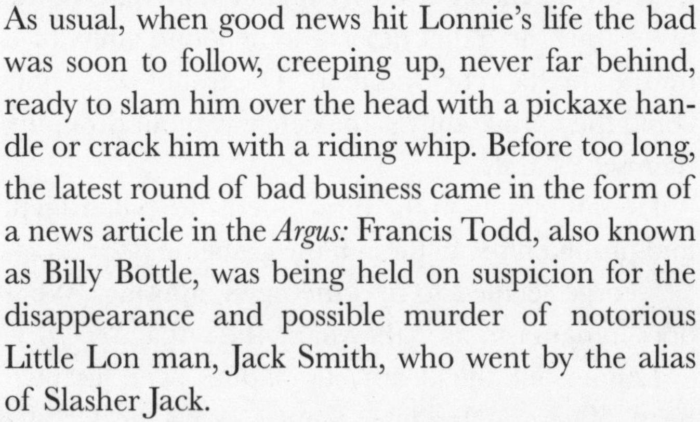

## Item No. 3965

*Common fighting weapon known to have been used by larrikins.*

As usual, when good news hit Lonnie's life the bad was soon to follow, creeping up, never far behind, ready to slam him over the head with a pickaxe handle or crack him with a riding whip. Before too long, the latest round of bad business came in the form of a news article in the *Argus:* Francis Todd, also known as Billy Bottle, was being held on suspicion for the disappearance and possible murder of notorious Little Lon man, Jack Smith, who went by the alias of Slasher Jack.

It seemed Billy had been arrested during a brawl at the Leitrim, charged with causing an affray and tossed into a cell. While being searched, he was found to be in possession of a range of weapons, including a brass knuckle and a certain knife, the latter turning out to be of great interest to the police for it belonged to the missing Smith who had recently disappeared in mysterious circumstances.

The report mentioned a diligent young constable, new to the job, who had noted a man hogtied in a wagon, accompanied by a band of larrikins believed to be the Glass and Bottle Gang. They were in the vicinity of the bay on the very same night Smith went missing. Caught red-handed with the knife, Billy had been locked up pending further investigation.

On hearing the news, Lonnie panicked. He had to let George know. The law may have got their facts wrong on the identity of the gang, but it would only be a matter of time before they cottoned on to their involvement. It didn't matter that Billy Bottle was a thug, he didn't deserve to be found guilty of a murder he hadn't committed. The trouble was, how could they prove Billy's innocence without dropping themselves in it?

He ran blindly in the direction of the billiard hall and pushed his way though the swinging doors.

George seemed to find the news amusing. 'What does it matter to us if they hang the ratbag?'

Lonnie felt the death cap sliding over his own head. The rough, itchy hemp on his neck. The twisting strangulation. 'We're the ones who damn well murdered him, so we're the ones they should be hanging.'

George laughed off his declaration of guilt. 'Speak for yourself. You may have killed Jack, me old pigeon, but I certainly had nothing to do with it.' His voice sank, low and threatening. 'If I were you I'd be very careful who you repeated that whopper to.'

'It's not a lie. We can't let Billy hang for our crime.'

George's sour breath hit Lonnie in the face. 'You're starting to annoy me, you little runt. I never killed anyone in my life, even if I did come close a few times. But if you keep calling me a murderer, I'll make you my first.'

'Jack's not dead?' It took Lonnie a few moments to realise he wasn't the only one who could keep a secret. 'But you told me you wrapped and weighted him for a burial at sea. That's what you told me.'

'Not my fault you got it all wrong,' snapped George. 'Thought you had a brain.' George had never come clean with Lonnie about what had really happened the night he'd lowered Slasher Jack over the side of the boat. His suggestion that Jack go to the Western Australian gold diggings and try his luck was a much more enticing choice than the other alternative on offer – of being dropped into the water fastened to a hundredweight of old iron. Jack cared little for his missing knife or money bag, and even less about leaving Annie Walker's employ. He was only too glad to escape across the desert with his life. And for the first time the boot was on the other foot. The aggressor now knew what it felt like to live in fear.

# IRON GRID

## Item No. 732

*A security grid for a small window, fitted with iron bars.*

Lonnie was cleared of murder in his own mind. Cuckoo mad though he may be, Slasher was still alive and kicking. The threat of swinging for anyone's murder had vanished and for this Lonnie was eternally grateful. The trouble was the law didn't know. Billy Bottle was still bailed up, which meant something else needed fixing before he could breathe easy again.

At last Lonnie felt it was safe to tell Carlo. There'd be no harm or implication for him. With this in mind, he hightailed it over to Cumberland Place and made his big announcement. 'Slasher's not dead!'

'Didn't you see the *Argus*? Billy's been charged with his murder.'

'Slasher's in Western Australia. Took off in a hurry to the goldfields without a word to anyone, not even Annie Walker.'

Carlo couldn't help but notice that Lonnie was looking a little too pleased and told him so.

'Only relieved, mate,' Lonnie said. 'He disappeared

in the first place because I set it up with the Push. Only to warn him off, mind, but I thought they'd gone and killed him.'

'You mean you've been walking around for ages thinking you're a murderer and you didn't even tell me?' Carlo was unable to hide his annoyance. 'What sort of mate are you?'

'I'm the sort of mate who thought he'd had a man killed. If it hadn't been for the police arresting Billy over Slasher's knife and me confronting George, I'd still be believing it. I couldn't involve you in a murder. You would've done the same and not told me.'

Carlo shook his head. 'Mate, you never fail to bamboozle me. But I reckon Pearl, for one, would've been much happier if George had broke Jack's stinking neck and tossed him in the gutter. So how does all this help Billy get out of gaol?'

'It doesn't.'

Carlo sighed. 'So what're we going to do about it?'

# RACING SILKS

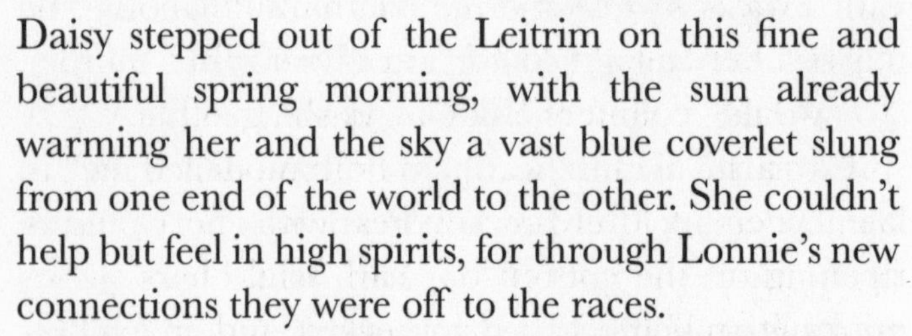

## Item No. 5127

*Square cut of silk,*
*possibly from a jockey's racing vest.*

Daisy stepped out of the Leitrim on this fine and beautiful spring morning, with the sun already warming her and the sky a vast blue coverlet slung from one end of the world to the other. She couldn't help but feel in high spirits, for through Lonnie's new connections they were off to the races.

When Lonnie had invited her she had given long and hard contemplation to the dangers, eventually winning herself over with a mission – guidance of a spiritual kind, should her friends be tempted to gamble too much.

No sooner had her foot touched the footpath than who should come swaggering down the street almost upon her, but Billy Bottle, lately out of gaol. He took a speedy step to the side, aiming a deliberate bump.

'Watch where you're going, Francis,' she scolded, brushing down her dress and pinning a stray hair back under her box hat. 'You nearly bowled me over.'

'Billy's the name,' he corrected in a hard-bitten voice. 'Look at you, dressed like a Sunday dinner.'

He gave her a smug lingering leer from top to toe.

It had been Daisy's plan to dress in her self-respecting Salvation Army suit, blue with the red trimmings. But Pearl had threatened if she turned up in her working clothes then she would as well. To prove the point she had slipped on a frivolously skittish gown with matching lace knickers and flapped around the floor doing a cancan. Told Daisy outright if she was going to hang around the spring carnival with a water hen then she would have no choice but to swish her feathers like a bird of paradise.

So Daisy countered this by dashing off a smart spring carnival outfit for them both modelled on the latest finery. A lovely cream dress with cherry prints ripening on the cotton for Pearl, while hers was a grey suit, much more high-necked and much less fanciful, apart from a peacock feather she couldn't resist pinning to the hat and which she prayed the good Lord would not think too flamboyant.

'Your larrikin stuff doesn't work on me, Francis Todd,' she said, ticking him off. 'I heard you were locked up.'

'Scum tried to pin a murder on me, but there's no gaol built can hold Billy Bottle.'

What a windbag! Daisy couldn't help but think if he puffed out his chest any more he'd look like a bloated frog. She tried hard not to laugh. 'Bet you're glad they let you go.'

'Shows you what mugs they are. Caught me with

Slasher's knife so they thought I killed him. Took 'em long enough to find out he's banged up in some Western Australian gaol.'

'But for the grace of God there go you.'

'Aw, I'm not that bad,' he said, placidly enough.

'Sometimes you make it hard for people to think so.'

'Reckon I give a toss?'

Daisy's Salvation Army training had taught her never to give up on anyone, so she pinned back her ears and let him mope through his whole hard luck story, wondering if there was any hope indeed for poor Francis Todd's misguided spirit.

The rhythm of Bella's clip-clopping along the street brought Daisy back to the day's purpose. She waved to her friends. Pearl was seated up front, pestering Carlo to let her hold the reins, while Lonnie sat amongst the golden hay in the back of the wagon.

Three sets of eyes descended on her at once. Daisy caught Carlo's questioning look at the same time as Billy swanked off down the street. He jumped in with the question they were all bursting to ask: 'What's he doing out?'

'It's quite a story,' replied Daisy, as Lonnie gave her a leg up onto the back board and she wriggled into a comfortable position. 'Seems Slasher isn't dead after all. Word came he'd been carted off to gaol in Western Australia. Lucky for Francis. He would've needed a miracle to escape a trial.'

'Woulda swung for it,' added Pearl, with a grotesque shudder, ''cause they found Slasher's knife on him.'

'He would've only had to prove he'd swiped it off some geezer,' said Lonnie, knowing any confession from Billy would have landed him and George Swiggins up to the neck in it. 'He never did come clean about who he'd been brawling with, did he?'

'Told them he was no dobber,' replied Daisy, none the wiser.

Billy Bottle over and done with, it was left to Pearl to put an end to the whole chilling episode. 'With a bit of luck they'll hang Slasher over in the west.'

Daisy decided now was a good time to make known she fully intended keeping an eye on their purses. 'Don't worry, I won't let you lose too much.' And by the time they arrived at Flemington, exactly how much they were willing to gamble on the day's racing had been wrung out of each and every one of them.

Daisy flatly refused to wager a penny. And she didn't have to fret about Lonnie who was prudently safeguarding his own future. 'This'll be the last time,' he said. 'Can't have a jockey riding one horse when his money's on another.'

Carlo, who was ever cautious with his money, fully agreed.

In a fit of irritation, Pearl came back with a cracker, all barrels directed at him alone. 'Stop being so stingy and enjoy yourself. It's not as if you belong to the Sally Army. Our one and only day out for the year, and you're such a tight-fister, Mr Scaredy-Dare, you plan to wreck it as well.'

'Why are you picking on me?' Carlo protested. 'What about them two?' He turned to Lonnie. 'What did I tell you, mate, she's trouble with a capital P!'

Daisy was in no mind to spoil anyone's outing. 'Maybe a tiny wager, then,' she relented. 'But if I win it's going straight to the Army.'

Nobody mooched for long and Daisy pretended not to notice the conspiring wink that passed between her three friends.

'So, lads,' said Pearl, as good-natured as ever. 'How do we girls scrub up?'

'You both look a treat.'

It was a relief to Daisy that Pearl had stuck to her part of the bargain and was wearing the dress she'd made. She'd added a few touches of her own, fresh cherries pinned to a ruffle on the bodice and a garland hat. Pearl looked every bit like a lovely, fruity pavlova.

'Yer can even have me for lunch,' she suggested, saucy as ever, picking off some cherries and offering them around.

# FRAMED NEWSPRINT CUTTING

## Item No. 1791

*From an old* Argus *newspaper.*
*Surprise win for Sinner's Repent at 200 to 1.*

Inside the grounds, scores of bookies and bagmen lined the rails under their gala flags and betting boards, trying their best to outdo each other as they shouted enticements. Lonnie had never been here for a major race day. Over the past few years, the spring carnival had become a society highlight, but it was a rare occasion when the likes of those from Little Lon were able to attend. It was only through Mr Alcock's kindness that Lonnie was able to come at all, a generosity of nature which he had secretly taken upon himself to extend to Carlo, Daisy and Pearl.

'Me and Mr Alcock are mates,' he reassured them confidently, as they gaped in fascination at the fine-cut suits and large sums being handed over for a simple scrap of paper that no one could read.

'Those betting slips must be coated in gold,' marvelled Carlo.

As the young friends settled on the lawn, a lively assortment of colour encircled them. The sun was bright. The sky expansive. The roses were in full bloom and they drank in their heady scent. Lonnie, who hadn't thought of his grandad in ages, could almost hear him singing up a ditty over the lush green grass, as green as any Irish meadow. Young women promenaded in rainbow colours. Here and there Daisy singled out a ribbon or feathers added to a dress by her own trusty hands.

'Anyways, lads, here's a few ring-ins you won't want to bet on!' Pearl chuckled, letting loose with her tongue as she larked about. 'Get a load of the bustle on that old slapstick. Ain't she a bit of mutton dressed as lamb with a sprig o' mint on top?' Her remarks were soon covering almost every creature on Noah's ark. 'Quick, a seal's escaped from the circus, catch the walloper!'

The sound of Daisy's shush-shushing, their happy laughter spilling over, mixed in with the bookmakers' calls of 'three to one the field'. Let anyone dare say his girls did not look as fine as any of these ladies in the members' stand, thought Lonnie, taking proud ownership.

The jockeys shone sharp in their bright silks as they assembled for the first race. 'I'm backing the red triangles,' said Pearl. 'Eight's my lucky number.'

Daisy decided to go with the yellow spots. Carlo slipped off to place a real bet on the indigo stripes. Lonnie stayed put to study form.

Since Mr Alcock had sent him here to watch and learn, he was keeping a keen eye on the trainers and owners who milled around the riders to talk strategy. Never had his life been better. The Glen was even paying him a day's wage to be here at the races, something he would gladly do for free. 'That's how Mr Alcock runs his business,' Ned had told him quite unblinkingly. The Glen had some new-fangled ideas, like a jockey should see racing from every angle before he took to the field.

Pearl scarpered off looking for Carlo, leaving Daisy alone with Lonnie while she stopped to take a sip of cool water. She followed his eyes up into the members' stand and saw Rose Payne, her father and Thomas Crick. 'We don't need the likes of them,' she said. 'We folks on Little Lon do well enough on our own.'

'That's a lesson I've well and truly learnt.'

Daisy pointed in a different direction. 'See that podium? You'll be there one day with a crowd of admiring racegoers and all your true friends around you. Guess what? You'll be the winning jockey.'

Lonnie gave her a sly grin. 'And Miss Daisy Cameron is a wise old owl who knows everything, does she? Tells the future.'

'Mark my words and see if you don't one day win

the Melbourne Cup, Lonnie McGuinness.' A wicked look entered her eye. 'You may be the bestest and cleverest jockey, but sometimes when you knock there appears to be no one home.'

Instantly, as if in the company of their own seven-year-old selves, they began poking fun at one another.

'Yeah and you may be wise all right. But sometimes your brain goes to your head.'

'Sticks and stones may break my bones but names'll never hurt me,' retorted Daisy. 'Anyway your face is so freckly you can't tell where one starts and the other one ends.'

'Well, I remember, Daisy Cameron, when you couldn't wait and wet your knickers!' It was all fun and games, matching wit against wit like they had played in the days before yesterday; all those childhood times before Daisy had joined the Sally Army and gone all prim and proper.

Lonnie continued the torment. 'What about your teeth? There's a gap as wide as –' He meant to rib her, but all he could think of when he looked at Daisy's mouth, generous with laughter and exposing that ever-so-appealing gap, was how she had grown up a beauty and her lips were a heart, a valentine and oh-so kissable.

Lonnie's thoughts turned to romance so swiftly it was like he was one of the young stallions tethered around the enclosures; his mind on a filly when it should be on the day's racing. He tried to shirk off the frisky feeling. 'I wish we were kids again.'

'Well, I for one don't,' Daisy replied. 'I like being grown up, the way we are now.'

'But we did have some good times, didn't we, Daise?'

'And a lot of trouble to go with them.' She swept off Lonnie's cap and playfully ruffled his hair. 'It's not over yet, you know. We've a lot more living to do.' She gave him an encouraging glance. 'Between us I reckon we can handle any trouble that's thrown our way and it looks like some's already here.' She drew his attention to Carlo and Pearl. 'Come on. We've left them alone for far too long and we both know how dangerous that can be.' She linked her arm through his.

Within earshot they heard Pearl snapping poor Carlo's head off. 'Don't be so stuffy, yer chump. Just because you're such a stick in the mud. Mr Know-It-All can never stop working to enjoy himself. I, for one, wanna relax and have some fun today.' She turned to Daisy for support. 'All he can think about is selling green ice-cream. You know he'd rather be walking around here with Bella and his beloved wagon than enjoying himself with us.'

'Time for our little flutter, you two,' Daisy said, coming to the rescue. 'I see that Sinner's Repent is running in the next race.'

## Author's Note

The author drew on the following sources of inspiration for *In Lonnie's Shadow*:

Heritage Victoria
Museum Victoria
State Library of Victoria
The *Argus* newspaper (c.1891)
The Melbourne streetscape and community (past and present)
*The Mystery of a Hansom Cab*, a novel by Fergus Hume (1886)
Traditional hymn 'Onward, Christian Soldiers', lyrics by Sabine Baring-Gould (1865)
Traditional nursery rhyme 'Around the Rick'